AS
LITTLE
AS
NOTHING

AS LITTLE AS NOTHING

A NOVEL

PAMELA MULLOY

Published by ECW Press
665 Gerrard Street East
Toronto, Ontario, Canada M4M 1Y2
416-694-3348 / info@ecwpress.com

Editor for the Press: Susan Renouf
Cover design: Caroline Suzuki

LIBRARY AND ARCHIVES CANADA CATALOGUING
IN PUBLICATION

Title: As little as nothing : a novel / Pamela Mulloy.

Names: Mulloy, Pamela, 1961- author.

Identifiers: Canadiana (print) 20220228000 |
Canadiana (ebook) 20220228019

ISBN 978-1-77041-636-9 (softcover)
ISBN 978-1-77852-008-2 (ePub)
ISBN 978-1-77852-009-9 (PDF)
ISBN 978-1-77852-010-5 (Kindle)

Classification: LCC PS8626.U465 A92 2022 |
DDC C813/.6—dc23

We acknowledge the support of the Canada Council for the Arts. Nous remercions le Conseil des arts du Canada
de son soutien. This book is funded in part by the Government of Canada. Ce livre est financé en partie par le
gouvernement du Canada. We acknowledge the support of the Ontario Arts Council (OAC), an agency of the
Government of Ontario, which last year funded 1,965 individual artists and 1,152 organizations in 197 communities
across Ontario for a total of $51.9 million. We also acknowledge the support of the Government of Ontario through
the Ontario Book Publishing Tax Credit, and through Ontario Creates.

ONTARIO
CREATES

ONTARIO ARTS COUNCIL
CONSEIL DES ARTS DE L'ONTARIO
an Ontario government agency
un organisme du gouvernement de l'Ontario

Canada Council   Conseil des arts
for the Arts   du Canada

Canadä

PRINTED AND BOUND IN CANADA   PRINTING: MARQUIS 5 4 3 2 1

For Darren and for Esme

In Memory of Terry Mulloy,
a passionate gardener, a remarkable man

Those who knew
what was going on here
must make way for
those who know little.
And less than little.
And finally as little as nothing.

—Wislawa Szymborska,
"The End and the Beginning"

Sometimes there are days, moments, that seem to fall out of the tight mesh of time and obligation, where we can live outside of our lives, slip the leash.

—Helen Humphreys, *The Ghost Orchard*

1 SEPTEMBER 1938

AWAKENING

Miriam knew she needed to fly when she lost her fifth baby. Those luminous nights, the pearl moon casting shadows across the village as she took flight, her arms spread, her body soaring, undulating through the air currents as she went higher. Higher so that she could no longer see the village; the space in which she existed seemed at once foreign and yet her own. This was her nightly journey, the one that might save her. For seven nights she existed in this liminal space, anchored to her bed, anchored to the idea that there was another Miriam who had overtaken her, one who existed in the bed of clouds that blindfolded the moon.

It was on the eighth morning that she heard the airplane she knew to be in trouble. Roused from a morning nap, she was startled by the sound, despite living so close to Hackley Aerodrome and Flying School. They'd become accustomed to the planes, but this sputtering was new, and it pulled her, still weak from the blood loss, from her bed. She grasped the heavy curtains that kept her room as night and squinted at the intruding light. She opened the window, surprised at the soft, balmy air, and looked skyward for the airplane that now seemed elusive. There it was; a choking sound that told her it was still up there somewhere.

She reached for a dress from the wardrobe and was soon clothed, the first time in over a week. She thought to take a cardigan, leave a note for Edmund, put an apple and two digestive biscuits in her bag. She barely knew where she was going as she stumbled down the stairs and outside to her bicycle. Her cardigan pulled on the metal sign on their gate, *Hawthorn Cottage*, as she passed through and she reached back to release it. There had been much discussion on the naming of their house; how important it was to Edmund, what with their own hawthorn tree in the back garden, while she'd wondered if it were too showy.

She was sore, and stiff, and in a weakened state, but the sun was out and this surprised her so much that it was enough to keep her moving, and soon she was out on the road, right onto Wycombe Street, then left on Guildford Road that took her out of town in the direction of the airfield. Out in the open she scoured the sky for any sight of the plane and spotted it ahead, teetering eastward. She pedalled toward it, trying to calculate where it might come down. She had gone nearly a mile when her heart, like a small animal yearning to break free, forced her to slow down. She had barely moved for seven days, in a delirium brought on by grief, by the stillbirth that had left her catatonic, her days and nights blended. Edmund nursing her, his own bewildered sadness set aside.

Miriam coasted to a stop, made adjustments to her position. The air filled with the pungent smell from the nearby dairy farm, giving life to her senses, an awakening that reminded her she was alive. A flap of paper caught her eye. A flyer on the signpost. The Ministry of Agriculture. A meeting in September. She knew what this was about. A grand plan. Her midwife muttering "these times, these times," and Miriam in her state, not knowing if she was referring to her or the events in Europe.

She peered at the flyer, which welcomed farmers and gardeners alike, anyone interested in the future of their country.

"It's coming," she'd told Edmund a month ago, when she was still able to take in the world around her. "What we hear is only a fraction of what they know." The chatter in the village like constant static.

"It won't come to that, love." Edmund so sure, as if he had a direct line to those in power.

"You think they have nothing better to do than prepare for a war that isn't coming." They were jittery at the Women's Voluntary Service meeting she'd attended, intense on the prospects of war.

Now this. The ministry telling them what to plant. It was hard to imagine Edmund giving up his dahlias in favour of potatoes. They were still flourishing, his dahlias, the arum lilies long gone, the hydrangeas muted, drying on the stems.

She stepped off the bicycle and walked until the beating in her chest slowed.

After five minutes, she spotted a stile where she sat after leaning her bicycle into the hedge. She rubbed her legs as if trying to keep awake the muscles she'd so abruptly activated. What would Edmund think of her, out roaming the countryside like this? A week of nursing her back to health only to lose her to a failing airplane.

She pulled the apple from her bag and ate it with her eyes closed, the world suddenly too much to take in. The deep crunch of each bite, the vexing wasp that had caught the scent of the sweet juice that dripped on her hand, a distant crow that seemed overly bothered about something, all sparks to remind her that life goes on. She concentrated on these sensations as she took long, slow breaths because she wasn't sure she could trust herself to remain conscious, her inclination so clearly driven to another state these days.

The airplane.

The quiet meant the engine was no longer running.

She stood, her mind alert with no thought now to return to her bed. She freed the bicycle from the bushes, hooked her shoe on the pedal, and pushed herself along until she could get her balance, thankful for the downward slope. There were things to be thankful for, even these days, even if it was a downward slope in the road.

1 SEPTEMBER 1938

IMBALANCE

The sky. The cerulean sky.

What sort of word was that—cerulean? How did it come to mind as he lay on the grass? Had he read it somewhere, this way of describing the sky? It was his aunt's influence, he knew. She, who would consider him a writer. Her confidence in him pushed him to comb through his vocabulary this morning, plucking words that might please her. He would soon see her, and that alone made him think this way, dredging up words usually reserved for the poets.

Frank was thinking too much, eyeing the sky, his mind in the clouds. That's what she would tell him, his mind always in the clouds. Anticipating the conversation he would have with her, knowing what she wanted of him. Happiness. Nothing more. He would finally tell her about his airplane that was in the shed, remind her that she was to join him at the air show in Croydon in two weeks. She would meet up with friends for lunch, she'd told him, they would have a lovely time.

Yes, the sky was quite stunning this morning. Cerulean.

He'd drifted off, allowing the sleep that had evaded him in the early morning hours to take him away, a hazy dreamworld that placed him in his shed, pasting the fabric onto the wing, only to have it fall off, drooping like drapery that weighed too heavily on the rod no matter how much glue he used. The frantic repasting, repeated over and again, was like a scene from the silent pictures he'd seen as a boy. She'd introduced them to him, his aunt Audrey, brutal comedies where the laughter was contingent on someone's failing. Even as a young boy he saw the imbalance of it.

An airplane. Awake now, but the sound of the engine further confused him. He'd never heard one fly over Brackley Wood before. He sat up, wiping his hands over his heat-flushed face, brushing a leaf from his hair, then closed his eyes, focussing on the sound of the engine he immediately knew to be faltering. Jumping to his feet he scanned the sky but saw nothing. He closed his eyes again, concentrating so he could determine the direction. East.

Abandoning the picnic basket under the tree where he'd left it to stay cool, he ran to the road, slipping on dew-stained grass as he went.

A flash in the sky at the top of the downs, the sun glinting off the frame as if the plane itself were sending messages. A biplane. Frank slowed his pace, made calculations on speed, trajectory, trying to determine where the plane would land, the engine coughing, wavering as it descended. He assumed the fear of the pilot, put himself in the cockpit, imagining the landscape before him, the need to determine a place to crash land increasingly urgent. There were too many trees, too many hedges. Frank was running now, past the flax field recently harvested, which appeared level but he knew was lined with irrigation troughs that might sink the plane. Past the grazing field, the land uneven there as well. He was nearly at the road that separated the two fields, the plane now dropping so that it appeared to barely miss the trees.

Frank flapped his arms and pointed to the road with no idea if the pilot could see him. He felt an exhilaration as if he really were both in the cockpit and on the ground. His body feeling large and commanding as he waved him in, knowing the road was narrow, a lane really, but also knowing the grade was solid, and as long as the pilot kept a cool head, he could lay it down between the hedges.

The plane swooped over him, propelling him forward with a whoosh of air so that he scrambled toward it as it touched earth, bumping along with great precision until it hit a pothole, which tousled its wings and tossed it into the ditch.

The propeller jammed, and the silence that remained brought Frank to a stop. Above, a crow flew by, squawking, as if to reclaim the airspace.

"Hello?" Frank called out as he walked to the plane. He feared what he would find in the cockpit. He looked for movement, for the gentle rise of shoulders or an intake of breath.

"Hello." His voice quieter this time. He held his hand out to the airplane to steady himself, the ache in his foot now noticeable, already beginning to shoot up his leg, and he was limping.

He looked in at the body slumped over the controls, and his mind flipped back to when he was a boy, out in the field alone, waiting for the return of his brother, who had taken one of the horses for a ride. His brother had sneaked out when the stable boy had gone to eat his midday meal, because he was a good rider, if a bit cocky, and yearned for some act of independence. Frank had trailed after him that day and saw him saddle the horse and disappear into the field. He knew that his brother's constant bravery would forever leave him behind. He'd walked as far as he could and waited until he could wait no longer, finally trudging across the field until he came upon the horse, riderless. Frank knew enough to get help before looking for his brother, knew there were rules of logic that he should follow, so even though he could not ride, he mounted the horse and returned home to fetch the stable boy. The search party found his brother face down in the bush near a stream, his body lifeless, or so it seemed to young Frank, whose own breathing caught in his throat, just as it did now as he looked for life in this pilot. The idea that accidents could happen, that they could kill you, hardly a thought that had entered his mind in those early years when his own deformed body seemed to define all conditions possible.

He stumbled around to the propeller that was nose-down in the ditch, trying to free it enough that he could get at the man, who was now enmeshed in the shrubbery that had fallen over on him in the open cockpit. But no part of the plane would budge, and Frank cursed it as though it were willfully stubborn, as though it were actively working against him. He heard a sound from down the road and looked to a woman approaching on bicycle.

"Is he alive?" she asked.

1 SEPTEMBER 1938

LANGUOR

How was it she was still here, Audrey wondered, at this place
by the river, the clear water bathing her feet, the warm balm
of sun directly overhead, not on her but around her as if draped
across the willow tree. She was reading the newspaper, waiting,
her eyes occasionally casting off to a branch floating downriver.

Chamberlain's Great Peace Plan: Striking Proposals for Hitler.
The headline everyone had been clamouring for. Chamberlain
would make it right, Audrey knew, the meeting with Hitler would
surely put an end to it all. The sun seemed to have gripped her,
brightening her mood on the riverbank as she reimagined
her life at just this moment, the news sanguine at last. This
was a changed outlook after days and days of hooded gloom.
A reprieve.

They were not new to this tussle of war, and perhaps that's
why she felt it so; scar tissue never healed. And now the giddi-
ness of its release. She could return to life, to her lectures, to the
campaign. She picked up her notes and pressed them against
her lap as a rogue breeze threatened to send them flapping off.

She willed herself to think of good things ahead with her work, the progress they could make on reproductive rights. And yet this was a funny thing, progress. How could they measure the changing of minds, determine a way forward when so many held views that marched in the opposite direction? It was not an adjustment of the dial that was needed, it was a complete turn-around of thought in this world she now occupied. There were stubborn minds that needed changing.

She pulled at her sleeve, smoothed the nap of her skirt.

Would Frank find her here, away from their meeting spot? A note left under a rock in case he showed up should direct him. But really, an hour was long enough. She'd waited this long only because she'd been preoccupied with next week's lecture, "Women and Peace," working through the argument in her head, testing phrases out loud as birds twittered in the background.

The wind was picking up and she knew she should go home, but the day was so giving with its sun, with the silky breeze that rolled over her, keeping her cool. Sweet serenity by the river, the quiet a sense unto itself.

It was not so earlier. In these past weeks she'd gotten used to the sound of airplanes, used to the fact of them but not so the disruption. They came as a swarm, the RAF moving about the country like confused and frantic insects. But this morning it was just one, a choking motor that eventually faded into the distance.

She pulled her handkerchief from her bag, wiped her brow, her neck, down her cleavage between her breasts. The heat would not last long, she should relish it. She'd learned to watch the rise and fall of the sun, chasing it for the warmth, for the light her body craved. The sun on her arms in the early morning radiating through her, then the need to shield herself from it in the after-noon as her skin became flushed in the heat.

Already the nights were getting cool. She must remember to get her flue cleaned. Frank might be right that she ought to get a gas heater, but she would hold off. It was the wireless she'd really wanted. She had just bought one, spending most of her earnings from the lectures she'd done this past month. It was not the news she craved. That was the purpose of newspapers. But the music she knew could fill the spaces when she was working, become a presence in her caravan. Music would connect her to the outside world without her actually having to be in it. She felt a kind of rousing in her in anticipation of long days on her own when her mind was too unsettled to work, especially with the days shortening and more time spent inside, when she would have something to keep her steady.

It was a long time since she'd been introduced to music, not just as background noise or something to liven a party, but as something stirring, something with texture, something one might absorb with their entire body. This had been Robert's gift, if she could consider it as such. Where was he now? she wondered. That column in the newspaper some weeks ago. Could that be the same Robert?

"What's this, a party?" Frank had come upon her dancing yesterday. The shame of being caught like this was fleeting. She felt intoxicated somehow, a release from the slow, long-reaching tendrils of war that had started to choke her. The afternoon sun had brought a shard of light through the curtains, an unexpected heat that made her feel as though she'd already had a sherry. The news that Chamberlain would go to Hitler, work things out so that war could be avoided, had affected her. Unaware how worried she'd been, she'd gripped the newspaper, scanning the latest update, and once she'd absorbed it, felt its potent effect, joy slipped in. The wireless that had only just arrived was soon whirring with music.

"A party? Yes. A party!"

She'd grabbed his hand, her body swaying to the rhythm of the jazz music, while he stood, allowing her to swing his arm as if they really were dancing. It was the West Indian Dance Orchestra, led by the Guyanese musician Ken "Snakehips" Johnson, who'd recently moved to Britain and formed a band with members summoned from the Caribbean on banana boats. She'd seen the band play at the Café de Paris in London. The music a direct link to evenings at the supper club all those years ago with Robert. She could close her eyes and imagine an oval dance floor, mirrors everywhere so that she would catch a glimpse of herself in the arms of someone like Robert. Someone like Robert, that's how she thought of him when looking back at that time, as though he were somehow not real.

"The occasion?"

"Chamberlain for peace." Audrey had grabbed her nephew's hands, the skin soft and cool. So delicate were these hands, so untried. He had no idea what this meant, this bid for peace. No idea.

"A picnic," he'd declared. "We'll celebrate our future tomorrow. I'll bring champagne. We'll meet at the bridge. Champagne for peace."

But there was no champagne because there was no Frank, and Audrey pressed down the feeling that something was off somehow. Frank would not have forgotten their arrangement.

1 SEPTEMBER 1938

ALIVE

"**Y**es, I don't know. I think so."

The crunch of her bicycle wheel as she approached him, the sudden mournful scrape of the airplane as it settled farther into the ditch, then silence again, the swift, hollow silence that shocked them still for a moment as if another catastrophe, possibly another plane, would descend upon them.

"His pulse, check his pulse." Miriam rushed to the plane after dropping her bicycle on the road. Frank remained still.

"A pulse?"

"Yes, his neck." She motioned with her two fingers on her neck, but by this time she was past him, reaching into the cockpit. She felt the cool, dry skin of the pilot, sliding her fingers across his neck, searching.

"Well?"

Hand held up to quieten him. "I've got it. He's alive." She felt giddy at this, as if they'd done their part.

"Can we get him out, do you think?"

Miriam looked at Frank as she stepped down. He was not a man of practical sense, she thought, noting the fine cloth of his suit. For a moment she thought to get on her bicycle and return home, as if the pilot was truly safe now. Her back ached, and her head felt light, woozy. She would not faint, she knew, but she was far off from having the strength to lift a man.

"Perhaps we can adjust the angle," she said, returning to the cockpit pulling at the branches that shielded him. "The pilot is pressed against the side. If we could arrange the plane so that he is sitting back, perhaps he could breathe better."

Frank took a few steps to the tail, glad for a task, then stopped. It was thrilling and terrifying, this adventure. What would they think of him? To have rescued a pilot. It was only later that he considered who he meant by "they." His family.

"Frank Wentworth." His hand thrust out to her.

"Miriam Thomas." She offered no hand but walked to the nose of the airplane, its propeller deeply embedded in brambles.

"One of us will need to climb up," she said. "We need weight to lever it out of the ditch."

Her eyes on his leg, he noticed, as he took a few tentative steps.

"I can . . ." She stepped forward.

"No, no. I'll climb on the back." He was already halfway onto the plane, one foot swinging up to the wing, the other reaching behind the cockpit. Then he was sitting backward, straddling the plane as if riding a horse.

"There. There I am." He slid farther back, and Miriam tried to rock the tail, running back to front to pull bushes away. This went on for some minutes until Frank lost his grip and slid off the airplane.

They were both panting, the need to get the pilot free suddenly urgent.

"We need help."

Just then, a groan from the cockpit. Miriam at his side, wiping the pilot's brow, telling him he would be fine, he'd had an accident, but he would be fine.

Words as a balm, words as a tonic. How did she know this? Then she was standing next to him.

"Go get help," she whispered. "My bicycle." She gestured.

Then shame; it followed him even now when he was being so brave. "I can't."

"Can't?"

"I don't know how."

"Never mind." She brushed past him.

He stumbled after her, told her where to go, where she could get help. Then she was gone, and he was left alone with the failing pilot. He might have conjured her. He might have believed her a mirage if she hadn't reappeared twenty minutes later. She'd met a farmer on horseback and sent him to Wentworth House to get a car.

"You have a car, haven't you?"

"Yes," and as if he were performing his own bit of magic, they heard the rattle of a vehicle. There was Michael, driving the car, and the farmer on horseback not far behind. There were ropes, and instructions, and Miriam back soothing the pilot, and Frank in the midst of it, his leg throbbing, his head, too, aching from the strain. The airplane pulled by a rope with the car. Frank disentangling the bushes, one clump at a time. Then, with a final jolt it was free, pulled from the ditch as a petal plucked, and Frank rushed to the cockpit, pushing Miriam aside, opening the door, and reaching so that the pilot could slump over his shoulder while Frank half carried, half dragged him out of the cockpit. The pilot's head lolling from side to side, like a drunkard's.

He managed to hold the pilot as he pivoted away, into the arms of Michael with the farmer behind to help.

No one noticed Frank as he disappeared to the other side of the airplane. Michael gave instructions to the farmer to have the bicycle taken back to the house. Miriam was in the back of the car with the pilot, a handkerchief from Michael to staunch the blood from a wound that had opened on his forehead. No one noticed Frank's unsteady hand reach out to the airplane, the other to his brow. No one heard him muttering . . . alive, alive.

1 SEPTEMBER 1938

ROSES

They were waiting for the doctor. Miriam by the bank of windows that overlooked the front drive, her eye on the rose bush that crouched below, the petals beginning to curl. Edmund should see this, she thought, the roses that were inferior to his, despite being grown by the house gardener. The satisfaction of those failed roses forced an inner smile, an odd distraction from the goings-on, but it *was* a distraction, one she needed after the excitement of the last few hours. Excitement, yes, that's what it was, she thought, her hand resting on the pane with no thought of the mark it would leave. It was thrilling. She had rescued the pilot as she knew she would. Frank had helped, but he'd been so ragged, overwhelmed by his effort by the time she'd arrived, his hair so ruffled by the brambles that it made her wonder if he'd been in the airplane.

She'd soon understood that the physics of the situation would require both of them. Leverage was needed. She'd instructed him to mount the back of the plane, then try to force a rocking motion until they'd untangled the propeller. Even then it would not break free, and in his frustration Frank had torn his jacket, and a fish-shaped grease stain had formed on his lapel. Then a bounce sent Frank sliding off the back end, and the jolt brought the pilot, she now knew as Peter, into a foggy consciousness. This she learned in the backseat of the car journey to Wentworth House, too short to enjoy the luxury of it, and in the confines, sickly warm, it was all she could do to keep a handkerchief pressed against the wound on his head.

Now Peter was stretched out on the sofa in the room that Miriam had at her back, while she remained distracted by the roses. The cook had finally given her a cup of tea after initially being distraught to find the injured pilot and the strange woman in the house as if they were wild rodents Frank had brought home. He was indulged, this man Frank, who lived alone in the house. They wanted to please him, the maid, and Michael, the driver whom Miriam had gone to fetch on her bicycle.

They were talking of airplanes, the two men, the pilot in repose, and Frank at a chair he'd pulled up close. She could hear Frank telling him about his own plane that he was rebuilding in the shed. She imagined telling her friend Mildred about it, about the airplane that crashed and the other one in the shed. That was what she was doing while waiting for the doctor, imagining being somewhere else, telling the story of her day. Telling Edmund about the roses, the airplane that crashed—a Gipsy Moth, the two-seater biplane, one of wooden construction with a plywood-covered fuselage and fabric-covered surfaces, that she knew was used to train pilots. She'd seen them at Hackley Aerodrome.

She'd tell Edmund about the rash urge she'd had to get out of her bed, out of the house, when she'd heard the sputtering engine, then of a force that compelled her to save the pilot as if it were a task she alone could do. She could see herself telling him the details. How she and Frank had agreed that she should take the bicycle to fetch Michael so that he could bring the car because Frank confessed he could not ride one. Then the drive in the motor car, the two men laying the pilot down in the back seat, and the journey back to this room that was lined with books, with curtains covering windows that looked out onto a glorious lawn that led to a glass-covered orangery.

She was trying to get a picture of herself as she saw these things, as she retold this story in her head, saw how simple it was to stand in this grand room, to hold her hand against the window, a thing only done by those who lived there. She saw herself as one who could demonstrate feats of strength that she'd kept in reserve, doled out sparingly, to handle the loss of her babies, one by one. As if she knew there was a finite supply of this strength, and that the tragedies would continue and there'd be no opportunity for replenishment. There were things she could do, she thought, besides waiting for a child. She could feel the pain in her chest, so sharp it drew her hand to it, and she worried this might be an attack of some sort. The babies had come, and then they had gone. It had been a taunting she'd known for years, had defined who she was, the childless woman at Hawthorn Cottage.

It was quiet in the room now, and she turned to see Frank looking up toward the window, then back to the pilot.

"I would like to take you flying in my airplane when it's complete," he said, and her mind was so hollowed out with loss that the day's events seemed to fill her with a different version of herself. And she heard this as an offer, even as a kind of rescue.

"Yes," she told him. "Yes, I'd like that very much." The brief bewilderment on Frank's face, his hand swiftly removed from the pilot's brow did not deter her. "I would like to fly," she said.

She felt an intense pressure on her lower abdomen, a sensation she could not determine as one of pain or merely discomfort, a sense of heat, as though all the blood in her body had gathered there.

"But now, I need to go home."

4 SEPTEMBER 1938

THE OBSERVER

THE TOUR OF THE YEAR

Venice, Dalmatian Coast, Julian Alps, Italian Lakes, Switzerland.

All these are included in one glorious, 26-day Motor Pullman Tour—by road through France and Northern Italy. Five days cruising down the Adriatic and home again through Yuga-Slavia, Italy, and Switzerland. Leaving London on September 16. See Europe from an Armchair!

TELEVISION IN THE HOME

10,000 New Television receivers will be installed before Christmas. Following a successful show at Olympia where the main objective was to show the real meaning and value of television as home entertainment, firms making television sets have sold out all they can turn out between now and mid-December. It has taken the London public two years to realize that it really is worth having television in the home and now the pressure is on the BBC to provide the entertainment.

CZECHS' LATEST OFFER:
WILL HERR HITLER ACCEPT?

Up to last night, no indication had reached official quarters in London about the result of the Hitler-Henlein consultation on Friday. So, as far as London is concerned, continued patience has to be exercised.

5 SEPTEMBER 1938

FRANK'S DIARY

The thing is I can't stop thinking about him. The pilot, I mean. Peter.

I should be asleep now, should have dismissed this as a good deed, but that moment when he came to, his hand reaching for me, touching my cheek as if to see if I were real. What am I to make of it?

That fleeting smile, then a whisper. "You saved me."

I wanted to reach out to him in that moment, tell him that he might very well have saved me. But—there must be a "but" here—we mustn't speak of such things. (Is this a line I've read before? Heard in a play?) At any rate, this is in my head, going round and round from evening until these early hours. We mustn't speak of such things. Three scotches, and I'm armed for the night. My bravery like that of a soldier. I am a soldier. Ha. What bravery. My war has its own hell.

I will go to him. The reason legitimate enough. Saving a life trumps all, I say. While there I will look him in the eye, I will hold his hand, no, lay my hand on his, and see if it is an angel he sees, or is it me alone, as I am.

Lay your sleeping head my love
Human on my faithless arm

It is Auden who is making sense to me tonight, the only thing making sense. Poetry. What else should make me feel the pain this way. It's true that it's pain I feel, as if my heart has already been broken. Why can't I have hope for this one? Why do I go directly to loss?

Did I kiss him?

I can barely admit it to myself, but it was as if I knew that I would lose him before I even had a chance. He was trying to tell me something. A murmured hallucination, and I leaned into him, our cheeks practically touching, I whispered, "I'm here, what do you need?" Then he was out again and my lips so close I could feel the rough edge of his whiskers, smell the musky oil of his hair. I turned, my lips brushed against his hair, then his skin. I wish I could say I regret it. It was wrong. Improper. But it's all I have now, and I'm afraid it will be all I have of him. I'm getting melancholic now. I'm drunk. Or maybe not drunk enough. I will go see Peter. With a clear head. I will get back to work on my airplane. At least he has given me that.

8 SEPTEMBER 1938

THE RIVER

The water stung her body. She shuddered as she slipped below the surface, her skin like goose flesh as the cold moved through her.

A flat, slow-moving river, still except for the ripple and splash of each stroke. She felt the cool wet-coarse cotton of her nightdress against her nipples as she dug deeper.

She thought of her mother and how much she hated, no, feared the water. A trip to the seaside a rare treat, the children kept close to the shore, allowed only to paddle along the edge of the water, the waves cresting mid-shin before Mother called them back. Audrey taunting her by dashing into the water, a quick glance back, watchful eyes willfully ignored, a few feet farther in the shallows, her bathing costume now wet, then the voice calling her back, reining her in.

Audrey pushed forward. Hard, strong strokes that took her upstream, her shoulders tensing from the exertion. Then, the river bend and she made for the willow tree that reached across the water. The tree blackened the river here, casting it always in shadow.

Her heart beat a pace that was a reminder she was no longer young.

Under the willow tree the water eddied, and the river was shallow enough that she could stand. She felt around for the flat rock, her toes curling against it for balance.

A rook swooped near, gave her a twitching glance as if admonishing her.

But this is my place, too, she tells him silently, the river is mine, too. I have claimed it.

A lifetime ago, just a child then. The sun like a giant sweet in the sky, the sea a shimmering turquoise. A seagull on a beach.

Her bathing costume was the colour of plums. A sandwich and a cake are wrapped in a basket, and the seagull senses the booty. But she does not know this, or even suspect it. It is the light and sparkle of everything, the sand, the quietly lapping sea, all there to bring her joy, nothing else. The seagull is part of it, too, this happiness, wildly soaring across the beach, veering out to sea then swooping back. Until half an hour later, when it plucks the cake from her hand.

Barely breathing, her hands held out in front of her, fingers still curled around cake that is no longer there. That instant, when the breeze seemed to still, the sea gone quiet, her body rigid from the shock of it, that this bird, so close, so large and looming, could come into her space, where it was just her and the cake and the sea. Then the whoosh of its wings, ruffling her hair, the movement swift, mean, treacherous.

Her body shaking, her hands flapping, her lungs emptying as she wailed; she struggled to catch her breath then released another wail that caught the attention of sunbathers. Her body vibrating with each gulping breath, the torment increasing as if the bird was still there, plucking the cake from her over and over again, she tried to stand up as if to chase her attacker but only toppled sideways. Her hands that had so recently been covered with icing now had a layer of sand on them, and she held them before her as if they were things to be rid of, her cries escalating so that her face was solidly red, tears streaming down, and her hands with their sticky, sandy coating, unable to wipe them.

The sunbathers looked uneasily at her, a few made as though to come to her, looking around for a parent or guardian as the child righted herself, still sobbing but less so, her emotions dwindling, wrapped up as a sour lozenge to drop into a rubbish bin later, knowing its taste would linger for years. This swift giving, then taking, a hard lesson, well-learned.

The river was narrow and she could have swum across it with three or four strong stokes, but it had a depth that surprised.

She did not mind the cold as she'd become acclimatized at the swimming pools at boarding school. That girl, Charlotte, in the changing room, Audrey tolerated her, yet she could barely speak to her. Audrey's body, like a sapling, a colt, all faint-kneed, strong but easily bent, her strength reserved for the water. Why did Charlotte intimidate her so? Sliding past Audrey, Charlotte's breasts, which had inconceivably blossomed in the past few months, brushed against Audrey's arm, and Audrey, not used to being touched, had recoiled in a way that had made Charlotte giggle in nervousness.

That girl of her youth long gone, Audrey understood her body now, fleshy, her skin changing.

Her nightdress chafed her breasts. She clutched a handful of material, pulled it away from her skin, and thought again of Charlotte and that encounter, how abashed Audrey was, to be touched like that.

At the far point of her upriver swim it was shallower. She flipped over to her back when she got there, dipping her hair deep so that it drifted like fronds around her, then she floated downstream, releasing herself to the river, her nightdress billowing around her. She saw the magpie she'd named Maudie high in the trees and worried for a moment that she'd left her pen outside on her lap desk, the silver one that might attract Maudie's attention. She didn't want to lose that pen, given to her by Frank.

The life of magpies: to collect shiny things. She closed her eyes and thought of Robert and his collection of shiny things, the young women he found irresistible. She'd been his shiny thing once, but that had been so long ago she'd hardly believed that version of herself had ever existed.

But she didn't want to think of that time anymore. History could reveal too much, she knew, especially the frail inadequacies of a younger self. Even now she suffered a pang of embarrassment when recalling that period, when their relationship broke down, the expected marriage proposal never materializing.

She brushed up against a tree branch that had fallen into the river and pushed herself away, turning over again in order to swim the last bit back to the caravan. Her mind like the willow tree, calm, lifting to the breezy thoughts that called her attention. She was reaching, it seemed, in all directions. Her arms and legs taut, a mild ache from the strain. She would relish her nap in the caravan later.

Her caravan. Her refuge. How many years has it been? Six now. That day she'd been out driving with Frank to a family luncheon and seen the caravan abandoned in the field, heard it call to her. She was not looking to shock when she told them she wanted to live in it, though her family would differ on this. She was always trying to shock they'd say. Those days in the war, what was she doing driving an ambulance, they prattled on at each dinner she attended, each wedding, funeral, Christmas, as if talking about it would undo the past. There was no way to tell them about the men, so badly burned, especially the pilots who, she learned, removed goggles and gloves in flight so they could see peripherally, so they could feel the machine gun button. This is what one had told her, a whispered voice that would be his last.

Her motorcycle. That, too, an affront. How she missed those days, roaming the countryside, getting cups of tea from roadside workmen when she was on the brink of freezing to death. Such a fine machine, a James. And that suit. A plug-in motorcycle suit that kept her warm. The war was over, so what else was she to do? That day she showed up to see her brother at university. He was mortified, though he was always mortified by her actions.

These days she only left her caravan to campaign. How did that spirit that allowed her to ride a motorcycle come to an end, how did she become the person she was now? A recluse, as her brother liked to call her. But he was only interested in the life of financiers and bankers. He struggled to label her: An activist? A woman who liked to think, to read, to be alone, to have a glass of sherry in the afternoon and an occasional whisky in the evening? Who swam in the river and wrote letters to Members of Parliament?

She kicked hard for a few strokes to prove to herself that she did have strength, that this was not beyond her, none of it, not the river, not the living alone in the caravan, nor the campaign that was losing ground as the threat of war increased. This thought rankled, and she tried to push it away. She was losing the battle for reproductive rights. People were shifting their focus, thinking about a war that kept lapping up on their doorsteps as if a spring flood, unwanted, unexpected. A ghost that lay in wait in all their lives.

Robert and his shiny things. The child. These memories would never leave her.

She was too old for love now, she thought, and this thought just formed, made her stop mid-stroke.

Is love what she needed? Wanted?

She was frightened of the coming war.

She swam harder now, pushing herself, her heart pounding, her legs fighting the stifling nightdress wrapping itself around her as she kicked, the weight of the material a force against her. She should have left it onshore, changed into her bathing costume. But she'd been too impatient. She gulped in air and took in water and was soon sputtering, coughing as the caravan came into view.

She felt the rush of water ballooning her nightdress, felt it fill and collapse around her, tugging against the natural flow of the river, as if a harness. She dived deep and flung her arms forward, releasing herself from the hindrance, letting the river take it. When she surfaced, it floated beside her, and the exhilaration of it, of swimming naked, caused her to swirl downstream, floating, drifting, her arms and legs loose, the nightdress following her like an obedient soul.

No, it was not love she needed. It was something more. Forgiveness.

She made her way crab-like to the launching place and lifted herself from the water her feet firm on the riverbed, her arms so spent from the swim she could hardly emerge. She grabbed a branch, swung one leg up to the shore, and stepped out of the water.

9 SEPTEMBER 1938

MIRIAM'S DIARY

My husband should have been a farmer.

He smells the earth, he lifts a handful to his nose and takes in the humus, filters the soil through his fingers as though he were a scientist. He plants each seed as if he were putting a child to bed, and tends so carefully to each seedling that you could almost see them grow. We had a terrible storm last year, and the fence blew down, snapping the dahlia stalks, and he was near tears when he tried to rescue them.

He inherited the store and post office but has no head for business.

He learned to cook after his mother fell ill when he was a boy. He feels at home in the kitchen, Yorkshire pudding his specialty.

He is impossible to argue with. He listens carefully, makes you feel as though your point has been heard, then in a confounding, quiet, regretful way he holds firm to his view. Just last night we were talking about Hitler's visit with

Mussolini in Italy in May. I saw this as a sure sign of being invaded. They had gone sightseeing in Florence. This, to me, signalled their bond against Britain. You don't go sightseeing with enemies. I pictured them slicing Britain in two, and I wondered which would be better, an Italian takeover or German. I could see that Edmund was mildly irritated, told me I was getting carried away as I tried to decide which country would better dominate us, but the thought of the two of them wandering Florence, going to museums, art galleries, as if they were ordinary tourists, ordinary men—it was galling. But Edmund sat nodding politely throughout my outburst then said it meant nothing at all, that it was all show for the newspapers. But I could not see it. I could not agree that the outcome of the meetings would lead to anything other than disaster for us. There are entire populations at risk here, I argued, it cannot be innocuous. Edmund told me I was too quick to jump to calamity. But I can't help it. I hear things in the village, the talk of war is more frequent lately, more hushed, as if Hitler himself is listening. I think Edmund sees his role as one who needs to keep a calm head, as if I might become hysterical over all this war business. I'm his wife. I was merely discussing the headlines. This was a conversation, not a deliberation on wartime tactics.

He keeps lists. Lists of flowers he grows, lists of books he's read, lists of tools he owns, a list of villagers who owe the shop money, and a subset list of those he will release from their debt even if unpaid. When he asked me to marry him, he gave me a list of five things he loved about me: the way I smile as if nothing is ever wrong, my adventurous spirit (I once led him across a field where a bull resided, on our way home from a picnic), the crooked finger on my left hand to prove the imperfections of being human, the way I see the world, that I don't cry easily. He keeps track of the weather, the goings-on in the village, the news headlines in a little notebook he keeps in his pocket. I don't know why he documents his life like that.

I know he doesn't like it when I wander off. But I need to walk. I traipse across fields and tell him I need air and he is offended, I think, as though by doing this I'm suggesting the air around him isn't good enough. He loves the outdoors, too, only he prefers it contained, the cloistered air of the pergola, the bank of flowers he's planted. The perfect rectangular shape of our back garden is all he needs. I tell him I'm not walking away from him, but I need to fill my lungs in a way I can't do in our little garden. I stride across a field, climb over one stile then the next, and, when I do that, I am marking out the boundaries, each field different than the one I've just walked through. It's a game for me, a puzzle, which way to go, which field will I explore next. He doesn't understand it and sometimes gets cross when I've been gone too long. He doesn't say as much, but he'll have put the kettle on, set the cups out, his way of telling me he couldn't wait any longer and had to start without me.

His parents died when he was young. First his mother when he was ten, and his father four years later, so he learned how to take care of himself early on.

He is an independent man in many ways, but then he is unexpectantly dependent on me. For attention, for reassurance, for comfort. Once he told me he didn't want me to forget him. I have no idea what he meant. Forget who he is, or who he was?

The business with the babies has worn both of us down. We've been preoccupied with it and yet try to forget it with other occupations—the garden, the shop . . . and now, for me, flying. I look to the skies every day waiting for Frank to take me up there.

He reads a great deal—Dickens, his favourite at the moment—and at times he will read to me passages, mostly about characters, descriptions of things they get up to. He reads them to me as if they were a letter from someone he knows, as if it's all a lot of gossip.

He would be a good father if given the chance. There is unexpected tenderness that surfaces from time to time, and it surprises me still. Sometimes I wonder if I have such capacity, to care so much about a bird whose wing has been broken, to be so moved by a villager's death. It's the fragility of life he sees. He seems to want to protect it.

I wonder what he understands of love, having lost his parents so young. I think it confuses him at times, the way it can enter and exit your life. I wonder if each time I leave the house he thinks a small part of love is leaving him.

10 SEPTEMBER 1938

RECUPERATION

"I felt like I was flying inside a tin can. The vertigo made me so ill I thought I was dying." Frank sat opposite Peter, their tea and biscuits on the table between them. "Mad youth," he continued. "Barely sixteen and wondering what all this flying business was about, so I crouched onto the floor of the back cockpit, then I popped up midflight. The pilot was a family friend. He thought I wanted to steal the airplane, but later forgave me. It's a wonder I ever flew after that."

He was talking too much. The sitting room dim, the air like the inside of a cupboard. Could he open a window? he wondered. Would that be rude? Instead, he kept talking, asking Peter questions: was he in any pain, would he be able to walk with his sprained ankle, could he get him anything.

"You must come to lunch. A celebration. A successful airplane crash." Frank not knowing how to pull back, how to just be.

"Is there such a thing?" Peter asked, shifting his leg from the ottoman, Frank jumping up to adjust the cushion. "A successful crash?"

"You're alive. And these days we must celebrate any small thing."

Peter looked at him as if assessing whether this might be a joke.

"Yes, I suppose we are more alive after having been up there." He looked skyward then reached for his tea, pushing Frank's cup toward him.

"Were you frightened?" Frank moved forward in his seat. "I should say I would be."

"I was focussed on not being frightened. That's what it is to fly, wouldn't you say?"

"Such control you have."

"You have not been tested in that way. You would have done the same, I'm sure."

"No, I suppose I haven't been tested."

To be tested. That is what Frank was still thinking about when he left Peter's room half an hour later. Because this is what he felt, tested, but not in the way Peter meant. They had talked not of the news of the day, not of family gossip, but of the beauty of flight, the privilege of seeing Earth at a distance, a separation that forced one to consider who they were in the world. The beauty, and the thrill, and the satisfaction, that's what they'd talked about, and how difficult it was to be on the ground. As if gravity held a greater force for those who flew, as if it were pulling all the component parts in their body into soil, claiming it for some unknown purpose.

"That woman. Miriam," Peter had said before Frank left. "You must take her flying."

"I meant to take you in my airplane when it's complete."

"I know. As does she. That's why you need to take her."

Frank felt the heat in his face.

"Take my airplane. She needs to be rewarded. Then when you finish your Gipsy Moth, I'll go flying with you."

An hour later he pulled open the hangar door at Hackley

Aerodrome and went to Peter's airplane. He began inspecting it, pushing it out from the hangar, its retractable wings tucked back against its body like a mechanical beetle, its tail appearing to drag along the grass. He went over every inch of it, feeling Peter's touch, the meticulous care. He made note of the sheathing on the wings, the plywood-covered fuselage, the resilient fabric that covered the surface. He checked the instruments and noted the placement of the compass, filled his notebook with diagrams and notes. He had rescued his airplane from conditions of neglect, so Peter's seemed excessively brilliant in its construction and care. Frank's airplane had come through a family friend who had known of someone who had had aspirations to fly. A single attempt barely saw the machine off the ground before it nosedived, enough to keep the man grounded. The entire folly of flying was abandoned, and so, too, the airplane. Five years it sat in the back of the shed. Weeds looking for a place to wander wove their way into seams and crevices, hip-high grasses sought to conceal the airplane until one day, after hearing of its deterioration, Frank offered to take it off his hands.

What had Frank learned of Peter since the crash? He was a Canadian, living nearby with his uncle, who'd invited him to stay and teach him to fly. He had a reputation as a good flyer, a stickler for checking his equipment before each flight, kept detailed log notes, and had flown through some challenging weather. To have crashed on a fine day due to a petrol leak might have been an embarrassment, although Frank had seen no evidence of it.

14 SEPTEMBER 1938

FLIGHT

The winds were in their favour. That's what Frank had told her when Miriam showed up at 8:00 a.m. as agreed. She'd hardly slept, was out of bed at 5:00 a.m., downstairs in the kitchen drinking tea, imagining she heard planes overhead. She and Edmund had breakfast together, a tense, terse conversation about the headlines, as if there wasn't drama enough being played out in their own kitchen.

"Ready?" he said, when she took her cardigan off the hook.

"I think I am." A peck on the cheek, a measured squeeze of her arms, and she slipped through the door. Then he sat down to put his shoes on, to get ready for his own day at work.

She clambered up into the cockpit of the Gipsy Moth, leveraged one leg on the wing while the other swung over into the hollow of the plane. The seat was frigid, the air still damp from the morning fog that clung to the low-lying areas.

"Contact," Peter called out, spinning the propeller.

"Contact," Frank responded, pulling the throttle forward.

Miriam braced against the roar of the engine, gripping the edge of the cockpit as the airplane rumbled forward. Frank guided it toward the grass runway, then they were gaining speed, the bounce a shock to her body until they were airborne, suddenly gliding, all resistance of land gone.

The steady roar of the engine rumbled in her body, a constant reminder that blood was thrumming through her veins. The uplift brought a lightness to her stomach, and for a fleeting moment she thought she'd be ill, but it was something else she felt, not pain or sorrow or fear, an impression so intense she thought she might faint. She held her head back against the cockpit, closed her eyes, and felt the brisk wind on her face. When she dared open her eyes, it was upward she looked; the fear of what she might see if she looked down left her paralyzed. She heard Frank's voice through the earpiece but couldn't understand what he was saying.

She closed her eyes again, but that made her dizzy so she pulled herself up tall in her seat, breathing in the battering air until she could steady herself. She was here, up in the same sky she'd viewed from her bedroom window. The airplane that called to her only two weeks ago had led her here.

One more breath. She dared look over the side and glimpsed the landscape, not as she imagined it as one great swath of green but more complex, lush, and segmented, the properties distinctly demarcated, the houses scarce and diminutive, the tonal range of fields prompting her to guess what was being grown in each plot.

Frank was speaking to her again, and this time she picked up the earpiece and held it to her ears.

"The village is to the left of us."

She looked out to the place where she'd been born, where she'd been schooled, where she'd met Edmund, who must now be scanning the skies, or holding an ear alert for the sound of an engine. She was surprised at how compact the village looked against the sprawl of countryside.

The plane banked as Frank circled for a better view, and Miriam gripped the sides, though she was getting used to the movement. They'd been flying into the sun, and now that they were turning, she felt the heat on her face, and that alone seemed a reason to be there, for that pure burning warmth. They were past Middleton, and she began making mental notes of the features below. She saw a thread of water that must be Walker River and the rise to the right of it would be Shipton Downs. She calculated the distance between the bridge and the downs, holding her hand to place thumb and finger as points four inches apart. She knew this distance to be six miles, and this began her lesson in scale and perspective. Her father had taught her to draw, assigning her landmarks to sketch. She would come to learn more of mapping, casting back to the Middle Ages when science was at its lowest ebb and the drawing of a map was determined by the artist's memory of other maps he had seen, or accounts of travellers, or facts of geography that everyone knew to be true. Sometimes it was the shape of the piece of skin or wood that was available for drawing on that determined maps. These were the factors she would think of when she began replicating what she saw from the air.

They were flying along the railway. Miriam looked ahead to see the plume of steam that announced the 9:30 train from London, and then they were upon it, flying over the train in an exhilarating rush of propulsion. The airplane swooped up, drew a circle, then headed back to the airfield. Miriam looked at the controls in her cockpit, imagined herself using them to fly the plane, hand on throttle, eyes on compass, the magnetic wand flickering as they traversed the sky.

"Heading back, now," Frank shouted.

She waved acknowledgement, then instantly felt sorrow as she became aware that in minutes they'd be on the ground. The county no longer seemed an abstraction to her, but land she could map out, mark the roads, rivers, churches, and farms that would make sense from the air. She made mental notes of all the landmarks she recognized. This was a world of looking down and seeing, so far away from the one of looking up and dreaming.

Her stomach floated as they made their descent, and already as they neared the earth she was wishing she was up in the air again. She felt the weight of tangibles, noticed the contours, shapes, and colours of buildings come into view as they skimmed across the air, just yards from the grass. Then a dip and they were jolted onto the runway, rambling to a stop.

Frank was already out of the airplane and coming to her, pulling the flap to her cockpit down so she could get out, but she was so dazed she was unable to move. She could hear Peter's voice in the distance, then the two men talking, and she sat fiddling with her gloves. When she finally stepped out, she could only thank Frank, unable to register the conversation between the men, and not wanting to leave where she had just been.

"I must go home now. I promised Edmund I'd be home for lunch." She was brusque in her departure, and hardly noticed the flush in Frank's cheeks.

18 SEPTEMBER 1938

CELEBRATION

Miriam knew she ought to have invited Edmund. Wondered why she didn't. But she'd decided that going to lunch was something she wanted to do on her own. She'd spent the morning choosing a dress, and in that time answered several casual and intermittent questions from Edmund, offering murmurs to his comments.

"I hope they don't serve watercress. You know how it makes you ill." She was nervous, felt her unsteady hand as she dabbed a bit of Pond's cream on her face. "Who exactly will be there? Why do need to meet them? Are you sure you're well enough?"

That question, at least, she could answer.

Once there, she'd made an excuse for his absence, and then felt guilty for the neglect. But it was hard to explain. Edmund didn't seem to understand that his grief was different from hers. That his was manifest as worry for her, while hers, a need to escape.

Now thinking back to her morning, the care with which she got ready while Edmund hovered, choosing from the dresses she had, and, in that moment, ashamed of all of them, she felt remorse. She cared little for clothes, but with Edmund fussing, she thought she ought to make an effort. At one point she put on the trousers she'd made when she thought it would be a more comfortable alternative on the bicycle or when helping in the garden.

"No, you mustn't." Edmund, horrified, walked away, knowing that nothing he said would influence her choice of dress.

In the end it was the blue dress she wore, and it was not lost on her as she stood in front of the curtains in Frank's home, the colour almost an exact match to her dress, that she could almost disappear in this room. She listened to Peter and Frank talk about gossip from the airfield, news of the upcoming launch of the *Queen Elizabeth*. Audrey spoke of a need for a break from her lectures. None of this seemed connected to Miriam. She could talk about the volunteer work she was doing for the war effort, how difficult it was to get supplies into the shop now with rationing on the horizon, but there was no point of entry for her. She listened to the wireless every night with Edmund and, of course, knew of the luxury liner, the largest ever built, but had no need of the gossip about strangers she didn't know. And the lectures that Audrey spoke of, what exactly were they?

Her hands behind her back, she rubbed the fabric of the drapery, felt its cool smoothness. And what about you, Miriam, she imagined them asking her, what exactly is your place in the world?

They were having a drink in the library, talk of war seeming to loosen the mood.

"Seven ships mobilized today," Peter announced.

"Mr Telford, over at the chemists', saw tanks with gun carriages clamber down the hill and assemble at Park Farm," said Audrey.

"I thought we'd no need of this," Frank muttered.

"Just in case," Audrey said. "Just in case."

The day was unseasonably warm, so the French doors were open though no one ventured past the threshold. Miriam could feel her face burning from the sherry she was sipping, and from the regret she now felt at leaving Edmund behind. The talk moved on to Peter's accident, with Frank telling his aunt Audrey about the airplane crash in a manner that was exaggerated, overdramatizing the incident; it had become a story to tell rather than an incident he'd experienced. This seemed a different Frank to the one from that day, and she had the feeling that he'd already told his aunt the story, privately, quietly, truthfully.

Peter, the pilot, was watching Frank, a look that Miriam read as slight embarrassment, and she wondered if this was because of the performance or the fact that it was his own traumatic experience being dragged out for all to see.

"Frank," Audrey said, moving to the door that opened to a view across the expanse of lawn. "The race, when did you say it was?"

Frank stopped mid-sentence and looked at his aunt as if she'd revealed something deeply personal.

Miriam watched the change in Frank's pause. The lowering of his eyes, a smile curling at one side of his mouth, like a child who discovered a puppy in the room and doesn't want anyone else to see it. He seemed less expansive now, an inward turn that made him appear preoccupied, unsure how to answer, more the man Miriam knew on that first day they'd met.

"Race? What race?" Peter spoke up, which had the effect of forcing Frank to step back, waving a hand before him as if smoke had entered his space.

"London to Manchester," Audrey replied.

"Next August." Frank looked at his aunt with a mock sternness that told her to hold the conversation there.

"Well, you've got almost a year to get your airplane ready. And to learn how to fly it." It sounded like an order, as if it were for her that he was to get the plane ready. And in some ways it was. It was apparent that Frank adored his aunt, and despite the appearance of merely enduring her odd ways, he'd spent much of his life ensuring he had her approval.

"I know how to fly." Frank, now scolding. "It's Miriam who needs to learn."

Eyes turned to Miriam, Frank's weak effort of deflecting now on her.

"Oh, yes. Now there's an idea. It seems everyone is learning to fly these days, and you will need a co-pilot for the race." Audrey's hand on his arm as if to direct him. She had a habit of moving a conversation ahead in leaps.

"What do you think, Miriam? It sounds as if my aunt is offering a challenge."

Miriam noticed that Frank's voice had gone soft, and she wasn't sure if he was trying to quell the idea that had been so rashly floated, or if he really was offering to have her race with him. There was a roar of machinery from outside, and they all turned to see Michael driving the lawnmower to the far end of the lawn.

"Now?" Frank muttered. "Must he?" .

Audrey had gone to put her glass on the table. Peter remained beside Frank, waiting for the decision about the race. The distraction of the lawnmower had stirred up the mood, the sound a reminder of the airfield.

"Go on, Miriam," Peter pressed. "This could be an opportunity of a lifetime."

She hung on that word, opportunity. Who could say no to an opportunity?

But this is not what she needed, she wanted to tell him, opportunities were what peddlers needed, a starlet on the West End, a land speculator. Opportunity felt cheap and flimsy, not connected to anything she desired, something given not earned. She also had the feeling they were taunting her, playing up her role as outsider, a kind of mocking.

It served her right for leaving Edmund behind. Left alone with these strangers.

She had let go of the curtain, and this feeling of being un-tethered was like a second entrance into the party, one where she might stride across the wool rug, her heels pressing into the pile with each step as she'd seen Audrey do just now, where she might accept the second sherry offered and stand next to Peter, looking out to the broad and verdant grounds, where her voice would be crisp, her sentences clipped with effect.

"I *would* like to learn how to fly," she said, pushing her hair from her face. "If my skills are proven, I'll co-pilot Frank's airplane."

Audrey flashed a look of surprise, and Annie, the cook, en-tered the room to say that lunch was served.

"And your Gipsy Moth?" Peter said to Frank as he set his drink down.

"A month, maybe two," Frank said, walking to his aunt to lead her into the dining room. "I should be happy to show you."

Later, they stood on the gravel verge outside the shed look-ing in on the airplane that sat dismembered. They were all a little drunk, a loose collective, each drifting in the yard, asserting their own vantage point.

"She will be a beauty when she's done," said Peter, and not for the first time did Miriam notice how eager he seemed to please, to reassure, to make sure everyone felt good about themselves. He'd already called Miriam a heroine for her part in the rescue.

Peter was asking questions about the construction, his inter-est now genuine, a tone of awe in his voice, as though restoring such a machine was far beyond his reach. He was thinking of joining the RAF, he told them, to which Frank responded with heavy blinking eyes. He'd come from Canada, was living with his uncle who had a Tiger Moth and was teaching him to fly it.

Their talk turned technical, and Miriam, feeling a slump after the luxurious lunch, stepped into the shade of the building. She now felt awkward, her status as rescuer diminished as they all moved beyond the talk of the crash. She was watching Audrey, the way she held herself, the layers of fine clothes, a stillness that could only come with having complete ease in this world. Her mind turned to Edmund. She pictured him alone in their kitchen, the morning paper folded in front of him so he could read it while eating his pie, drinking his tea. He'd told her the blue in her dress brought out the colour in her eyes. "You look smart, my love," he'd said, and there had been a fondness in his tone that made her want to cancel the luncheon.

"Miriam." She felt a hand on her arm and realized Audrey was beside her. "I wonder if you might come to my caravan for a visit sometime."

The caravan. She'd heard mention of it and thought it a holiday home, or perhaps a code name for her own grand estate.

"Yes, of course."

"Good." Audrey pressed her hand into Miriam's. "It's just down the hill on the east side." She was pointing off in a direction past the kitchen garden. "Next Thursday at four o'clock?"

Miriam nodded and excused herself, thanking Frank, then Peter for some reason, and rounded the corner toward home before anyone had a chance to talk her out of it.

20 SEPTEMBER 1938

EDMUND'S DAILY LIST

Newspaper headlines from *Hampshire Telegraph*:
Safe Blown Out: £250 Missing from Portsmouth Cinema

Doctor's Grave Warning: Your Stomach Needs Acid Says
Dr F.B. Scott

Cobb Breaks Land Speed Record: 350 mph on Utah Salt Flats

Through the Balkans on a Tandem: Emsworth Man's Trip

Missing Clothing: Alleged Theft from Isle of Wight Steamers

Fight in Portsmouth Prison: Convict Uses Razor Blade

Roadman's Wages Increase: Alton Farmers Are Indignant

Weather:
Cool with showers and bright intervals. Temperature 68°F

Birds observed:

Wood pigeons

Pheasant

Magpie

Green woodpecker

Fieldfares

Robin

Collared dove

Long-tailed tits

Blue tits

Blackbirds

Rooks

20 SEPTEMBER 1938

HALF NORMAL

"I was lucky it was just one foot, the doctor told me, at least I was half normal." Frank stepped away from the airplane, cleaned his hand on a rag. "The doctor, eager to impress, told me that both Lord Byron and Sir Walter Scott had had a club foot, as if he knew that one day I would read poetry."

They were in the hangar, Frank having invited Miriam to help with the maintenance of Peter's airplane, part of her flying education. She was wiping down the oil that had spotted the exterior of the plane and noticed that Frank's limp had worsened in the hour that they were working. What happened to your leg? she'd asked, remembering how he'd faltered the day of the crash.

"A deformity. That's what the doctor called it, as if the word itself, the fact of it being named, denoted an accomplishment."

She'd pressed him, asking, How long? Was there pain? Was there nothing to be done? He dropped his rag on the bench and sat at the stool, rubbing his leg that had tightened under the strain of too much standing. "I thought I was normal, my own kind of normal, until the doctor came."

"You were still a child then?"

"Five years old. I was in bed, foot bent inward, toes curled around as if napping. That's what I saw out of my squinting eye, my foot napping. I'd been sleeping, myself. Curled up like a whorl, the covers a protective shell, head tucked between my arms, all the while knowing that I was not safe, knowing that they'd be coming for me.

"*It's for your own good.* Even at five I knew it was nonsense. They were doing this for some reason that had nothing to do with me. For what? To fix me? The doctor wielding the Thomas Wrench, convinced that making the tiny adjustments would solve everything.

"I didn't care about my foot. Didn't bloody care. I wouldn't have said this out loud though. I knew how easy it was to bring on anger. My father especially. Who would see my bloody foot anyway? *At school.* That's what they kept whispering. They wanted it to be right when I went to school. Next year was not long away, and the manipulating with the wrench and the healing had better hurry up if I was to be right by then. I remember the doctor taking my foot, rubbing the rashed skin where the brace held it in place, forcing it to remain in that position, an infinitesimal adjustment that was supposed to take me ever closer to normal.

"The Thomas Wrench would do it, the doctor promised my mother, who was standing back, wringing her hands, my father away on business."

"How awful." Miriam leaned against the airplane.

"I remember my mother's hand on my shoulder. 'It's time, Frank,' she said. I can still hear the snap of the clasp on the doctor's bag. I can still see myself in that bed. My eyes shut tight, the soft tugging of my feet, my mother's hand trying to unfurl me."

Later. Barely fourteen when the Great War ended, soldiers stumbled home with their afflictions, and he could see his own as a kind of bravery. A day in the village with his mother, the war over but the tinge of it still in the air. Bunting sagged from the village hall, the smell of foreign cigarettes in the air, and soldiers out of any formation, limping and listless. One not yet twenty with a crutch under his arm marking him as a beacon and repository for so many sorrows. Everyone was tired, it seemed, tired of suffering, tired of just holding on, and though the war was well and truly over, they all wanted it to be gone for good, all traces concealed, gone from their sight, their daily lives. They wanted gone the need to ration, to wear dull clothes, to be mindful of petrol use. So, the young man shambled along, as a reminder of what had been, and in some ways still was, and Frank had felt a kind of equivalence with him; his own status as a cripple bolstered to match the beaten-down soldier's.

He'd offered Frank a cigarette, and this pleased him, knowing the soldier thought him more a man than he was. By this time the treatments were long past, the brace replaced by customized shoes that he'd worn to walk the corridors, balancing himself, straightening muscles, altering his body stance to minimize the limp.

An airplane had flown past as they stood in the street that day, the soldier pinching the cigarette to his lips and Frank gawking skyward, forgetting for the moment that he was not alone. He was a pilot, the soldier told Frank, his lame leg a result of a crash. This, an opening for Frank, who declared that he was to be a pilot one day, would have his own airplane, inventing his own life story as he went along, as if he were a character in one of the books he'd read.

"Good man," the soldier said to him, and these words sealed Frank's fate, his declaration now a vow he could not break. Frank stretched his spine, raising his height by a good inch, a constant readjustment of his body normal for him, and cast a glance at the soldier's uniform, looking for the wings that marked him as an RAF man. He saw none. He looked at the soldier, who had reached the end of the cigarette and was now looking across the village as if suddenly remembering where he needed to be. He tossed the butt, cocked his head up to Frank, wished him luck, and wandered down the road.

"Frank?" Miriam at his side, a bottle of solvent in her hand that she was capping. "It's late. Time to go home."

"Yes, it's late, isn't it. Time to go."

22 SEPTEMBER 1938

THE CARAVAN

A udrey watched Miriam walk down the hill toward her caravan, arms held close to her sides as though she expected to slip, each step carefully placed. Her dress was a similar cut to the one she'd worn at Frank's, this one fox brown, which suited her. Audrey liked that Miriam kept her clothes simple, it said something of her character.

Miriam kept glancing up as she approached, and Audrey saw that mixture of trepidation and awe that she'd seen in others who had come to visit. Not that there'd been many.

Audrey went out to greet her, took her to the river, where they stood admiring it, the trickle of the water lapping the bank, the sun hitting the surface with a flickering shimmer.

"I swim here. Almost daily," Audrey said.

"Really?"

"We are water creatures, you know. Apart from the proboscis monkey, we are the only primate that plays in the water for the sheer joy of it. And whose offspring take naturally to it from birth. We are also alone in having subcutaneous fat, like whale's blubber, for buoyancy and warmth." Audrey took in a deep breath as if the river air itself had special properties. "Come, let's have tea."

Inside, the plate of scones she'd had Annie make for her sat on the table, and the kettle was on the two-burner gas stove and grill she'd bought in the spring. The luxury of it, a small indulgence.

They sat adjacent to each other, Miriam on the bench by the window, next to her a bookshelf built into the wall of the cupboard, and Audrey on the wooden chair, their knees nearly touching. Miriam pushed herself to the back of the bench and swung her knees to the side, her hands on her lap like resting kittens. Audrey placed the diminutive table off to the side and poured them each tea from a set placed on it.

"I'm sorry I haven't any jam," Audrey said. She was making too much of it, she knew, this lack of jam. She'd already explained about having Frank's cook, Annie, make the scones and her forgetting to ask for jam, and that seemed to occupy Audrey to the point where it was difficult to jump off to the other more serious topics she wanted to talk about. This was an opportunity to speak to someone of some standing from the village, someone who might be interested in what she had to say. It was a hard subject to raise, she knew. She'd seen women squirm at the mere mention of abortion, avoid all eye contact, sometimes turn and walk away. It would be hard for Miriam to walk away, Audrey knew, though she felt no guilt in bringing her here.

"It's quite all right," Miriam murmured. "I don't have a sweet tooth."

There had been discussions about setting up a clinic in Godalming. What would a woman like Miriam think of such an initiative, Audrey wondered when she'd thought of inviting her to the caravan. Then, exactly what was a woman like Miriam like?

She'd seen Miriam as bright, one who thought beyond the world of the village. She wanted to fly, of all things. They owned the village shop, she'd learned; they were respected, people might listen to their views. If she could convince her to help with the campaign, they might have the ear of the villagers, even of the county women. That's what the movement needed: local leaders.

The sun broke through at that moment, and the lace curtain painted intricate designs across their hands.

"Ah, glorious sun," Audrey boomed, her arms raised upwards as a gesture of hallelujah, which made Miriam smile, this spontaneous physical reaction, so much more boisterous in the tight space. Audrey reached for a bottle from the top shelf over the books and for the two sherry glasses beside it. She poured a measure and passed one to Miriam, who suppressed a cough when she sipped the drink that turned out to be whisky and not sherry.

"My apologies. I should have warned you. A gift from Frank. He worries that I'll freeze to death. This is his solution. He is one of the few who don't see my domestic decision as a spectacular display of stubbornness."

"He is good to watch over you. You *could* freeze to death out here," Miriam said, looking around. "I nearly froze to death from stubbornness once." She took another sip of whisky. "I was a teenager—stroppy, mule-headed, angry at my mother. One night I decided to sleep under the stars."

There was a boy at the heart of this argument, one that Miriam liked, but he was older, worked in the pub in the next village, not one for a mother's approval. Miriam stomped off, but her idealized notion of sleeping under a starry sky was akilter to what the night actually offered. It was October, much too late for such stunts, but once she got something in her head, her judgment, like the sky on that night, clouded everything. A cold front from Scotland rolled in and painted the landscape with milky hoarfrost, and there was Miriam in a makeshift tent of canvas and boughs, a mile from home. She'd lasted a few hours before she abandoned it, the point having been made. But she became disoriented and walked for over an hour, cold, lost, and in despair that she'd ever be found. Fear, she told Audrey, came later. After a farmer came across her, bundled her up on the horse he was riding when checking on a cow gone loose, and took her back to her house. Her mother, waiting, a kettle of hot soup on the boil.

"The strange thing about fear," Audrey said, "is that it creeps up in anticipation of something, and again in the aftermath, but lets us alone when we need to cope."

"'The only thing we have to fear is fear itself.'" Miriam's deep-voiced recitation surprised even her. "Roosevelt," she said, feeling the heat go up her neck. "My husband heard him on the wireless once—he's taken to quoting him."

Audrey laughed, sat back, her look one Miriam mistook to be judgment.

"That's good . . . very good." Audrey shook her head. "When we find wisdom in our politicians, is that a good sign or not?"

In these close quarters, Audrey was able to catch the scent of the other woman; rosewater, she guessed. There was an intimacy brought on by the whisky, and their proximity made the meeting feel conspiratorial. Miriam's guard was down, Audrey could see, at first so formal and now she was quoting American presidents. Her instincts had been right. This was a woman to know.

"I'm campaigning for a clinic," Audrey said, each word enunciated fully.

"A clinic?"

"We need to raise funds so that women, all women, including those from this village, have the knowledge about the functions of their body."

Miriam blushed.

Audrey talked about abortion activist Stella Browne, and the advancements she'd made, gave Miriam a pamphlet that was used in other clinics. "Browne was one of the founders of the Abortion Law Reform Association in 1936. Its membership is almost four hundred, many of them from the working classes. You should hear her speak. She advocates for the right of women to have a sexually active life, with access to birth control and abortion."

"I know the functions of my body," Miriam said when Audrey finished. It was not the blush of embarrassment, Audrey now saw, but one of anger.

"Yes, but there are many women who don't. And we need your help."

"Help? What can *I* do?"

"Women who know can help women who don't know. Knowledge is strength."

Miriam remained quiet.

"Will you come? The meeting is next week. Stella Browne will be speaking."

The caravan sunk into half-light with the shuttering of the sun, and Miriam's face blanched so quickly that Audrey thought she might be ill. Miriam looked outside and then at her watch and saw that it was after five o'clock.

"I have to go." She knocked the table when standing, then steadying it, reached for her coat. "Thank you." Her voice formal again.

Audrey stood, too, flustered by the sudden shift in the room. "Of course, it's late." She stepped aside to let Miriam pass through to the door. Audrey offered to walk her to the house, have Michael drive her home, but Miriam told her she'd left her bicycle by the road and that she would outrun the darkness.

Outside on the landing they said their goodbyes, and Audrey saw the colour return to the other woman's face. Whatever had come over her had passed, and she now seemed hesitant to leave.

"Next Tuesday at the Guild Hall," Audrey called after her.

26 SEPTEMBER 1938

WORKING TO SCALE

In the days after her first flight with Frank, whenever Miriam closed her eyes, she saw the fields marked with arboreal borders from the air. She saw colours: gold, umber, mustard, the greens of emeralds, seas, ferns. Trees verging the fields in clumps and rows. Order and chaos in the design that spread as far as she could see. The villages from the air were like an embankment of grey boulders where nothing thrived. Sometimes, she'd see movement across a field, a cow or horse, but mostly the view was static. This is what appealed to her, that nothing seemed to move, or change, that it was laid out for her pleasure. The idea of pleasure, not as a novelty but as a way of living, appealed to her. Up in the air, with no concerns about lost babies or impending war, she stepped through a magic barrier, one that she wanted to break through again and again.

The windmill, too, appeared in these visions. She'd spotted it that day, on the crest of the downs, its arms waving like someone in distress. They'd banked and flew closer, circling to get a better look. Its arms, like a giant's, seemed more urgent up close, a signal sent across the land to all who would take notice. And this frantic waving was like a warning flag, her heart suddenly stuttering, the emotion it elicited a reminder that the alarms of war were creeping ever closer. Miriam had wanted the windmill to stop, to forego calling attention to itself, the whole presentation too showy somehow. It would be impossible for the villagers to hide with that on the edge of their homes. A signal to the Germans that people lived nearby.

The sea, the briny air a fresh sting against her face as they'd followed the railway tracks to Portsmouth. She'd never seen the sea, and from the air it frightened her, the infinite water and the ever-receding horizon. It jarred her to be frightened like this. A new boundary, the sea. To live so near it and to never have seen it. This shocked her now, seeing how close she was. That's what flying did. It closed the space between things, as if a string pulling a purse together, the seaside now shouldering her village.

A landing field. That's what she needed. If she found one near the shore, she could be paddling in an hour. How far by land? she wondered. A day? It had never crossed her mind to go there.

The train tracks that marred the landscape seemed like escape routes, a way out to other places she'd only read about. The books Edmund read to her, Dickens, spoke of a London from the past, yet she had not even been there. She thought of following the tracks. She could do that, follow them, see what other life lay beyond.

The day after her flight she'd sketched the scenes, recalling a time when a pencil and sketchbook were her way to give shape to her world. She placed railroads, rivers, and churches in relation to each other, and then shaded the fields around them. The ash-coloured stone of St Peter's Anglican church, its slate-tiled roof crusted with moss, the cemetery that spread out from the back of the church to the field, housing villagers from several centuries. The hedgerows that nearly concealed the road in parts, Mr Stevens's apple orchard from which he made his prized cider, Mr Matheson, the cooper, whose shop was on the edge of the forest that supplied the wood for his barrels. As she filled in the landscape, other landmarks came to mind—the train station, the Carter farm, Frank's home—and the scale soon became a problem, with one place bumping up against another, so she began drawing each location the same size and cutting them out to be placed on a larger canvas. Once she started to work to a scale, she had a clearer picture of the land as she'd actually seen it.

The images were so complete in her mind that she was shocked to see them on paper, as if the pictures had been stolen from her. She couldn't shake the views from the sky now etched in her mind, and after days of looking at the ones she'd recreated, she'd given them to Frank, as a gift, or advance payment for the flying lessons he'd promised, so when she went to Hackley Aerodrome to meet him for her first lesson she was surprised to see her sketches on the wall inside, those personal renderings now so publicly displayed.

27 SEPTEMBER 1938

THE MEETING

"**W**hy is it that you live in a caravan?" The impertinence. But Miriam didn't care, she felt she needed to know why this woman lived in a painted caravan. They were early for the meeting, time enough to walk along the river.

The silence a rebuke. But no, it appeared that Audrey was just gathering her thoughts.

"From the moment I saw it, I knew I would. It really was so beautiful, the wild spray of greens and reds, the intricacies of the markings. It was as though I'd fallen in love again, the stirring in my heart, the flush in my cheeks, that's what love was . . . what love is, isn't it?"

Audrey stopped then, as if surprised by her own words. Miriam stopped, too, waiting, wondering if Audrey was really expecting an answer to her question. Why was she speaking of love? How had Audrey gone from the lure of her caravan to the first blush of love? Miriam looked at her sideways, waiting for her to speak.

"Listen to me, talking of such things." Audrey pulled the brim on her hat and took a few steps farther down the riverbank.

"But whatever you think of me, I can tell you I was once like you. Young, a touch of the reckless, eager to step out of my life."

Miriam was fretting, a quick glance back toward the meeting hall, a nervous fingering of her collar. What did Audrey know of her life? What could she possibly know? Just then a swan stomped out of the river, all elegance gone as it approached them.

"She doesn't want us around," Audrey said, grabbing Miriam's arm and leading her away.

They were soon at the hall. Stella Browne had arrived, so there was a feeling of suppressed energy, everyone thrilled to be in her presence, but still they talked in whispers. The walk had taken longer than expected, and they now worried about being stuck at the back.

Audrey led Miriam to the side door and made it to the second row. They stared at the stage, just as the gathering audience did, without speaking. There was a mood of conspiracy. A conspiracy of silence. What did they have to hide, these women? Miriam wondered. They seemed confident in their right to be there, but these were women used to surreptitious activity, many of them at it for decades. Theirs was not a popular cause.

When a woman walked along the row in front of them to her seat, she saw Audrey and gave a fleeting smile in acknowledgement, a look of indifference to Miriam. It was the first time Miriam questioned her right to be with Audrey. There were things Audrey wanted in her, she knew, but there were things Miriam could gain, too. Were they just using each other? In some ways, yes, she supposed, but now Miriam considered how they could possibly balance each other. It was hard to be an equal with someone like Audrey.

The audience erupted as Stella Browne came onstage. Her appearance was as eccentric as later reported, "rather untidy, careless about her looks and appearance," wearing "aggressively unfashionable clothes" with "wisps of hair floating from her untidy coiffure." She told the audience that there were two groups of women concerned in the discussion on abortion. "There are those who wanted to have children but for the serious disadvantages in which they found themselves. In many cases they simply couldn't afford to have another child to feed. The second group were those women who did not want to have children, even though we have been told again and again that there are no such women."

"It is," she said, "a crime against humanity to force them to become a mother. Let them choose, for what is this ban on abortion? It is a sexual taboo, it is the terror that women should not experience. They should experiment and enjoy freely, without punishment." She leaned into the microphone. "Will you help, so that this terror shall be lifted from women, from love and from sex, which should be beautiful and inspiring but cannot be when two people have this ghastly shadow of undesired conception at the back of their minds the whole time? Will you help to make the world more fit to live in, and humanity better worth life and love?"

"Well?" Audrey was threading their way through the groups that had clustered after the lecture. "What did you think?"

"I'm not sure what I think. I didn't expect her to be . . . so free."

"To talk about desire, you mean?"

Miriam slowed her step, looked at Audrey. "Have you known love, Audrey?" They were out on the pavement now, Audrey guiding Miriam by the elbow to a tea shop.

"Desire," she said, opening the door. "I've known desire."

They sat at a corner table, with windows looking out at clouds that promised a downpour.

"I was young, barely twenty-one. There was a party. A garden party, and then Robert arrived. The memory of it is like photographs in someone else's album." She paused, glanced at someone coming into the tea shop. "Yes, there I was. Sitting with my family, my dress pinching on the side, and, oh, I was restless, unable to take it any longer, so I stood up to adjust it, but that movement, like all my movements those days, was awkward, and my skirt caught in the chair leg and the next thing I was tilting over. Then there was a hand at my back, another reaching for my arm. The teacups rattled on the table. Utter chaos. I can still hear my mother's voice. 'Oh Audrey, do sit down.' Robert, still standing behind me, invited to the garden party by a cousin.

"I taught him how to play croquet. I remember the wind ruffling the lace at my neck, felt his eyes drawn to it. My face flushed, and then a tingling in my forehead." She looked down at the menu that lay on the table before her.

They looked up at the waitress and gave their order, scones and tea.

"He was not one much for games. But, anything to get away from the table. I remember his smile, slanted as he lit a cigarette. I breathed in his exhaled smoke and felt intoxicated. I started babbling on about croquet being one of the first sports that women played in the Olympics. It was in Paris. The 1900 games. I showed him how to hold the mallet, my hands damp as I placed his hands on the handle, showing him how one hand needs to be lower. I had never been this close to a man outside my family before. I felt the heat of him next to me. I felt the burrowing of his attention. This had never happened before.

"His eyes were grey, like washed pebbles, and I sensed the intensity of them, as though he wanted to say something to me. It was forceful and flattering. Then the hard crack of the mallet broke the spell, and he became childlike when he saw where his ball had gone, blocking the entrance to the first hoop. I remember his scent, light, floral, soapy. A grown-up smell. Then came the rain, sudden and furious. He took my arm, and we raced to the gazebo where the party had gathered.

"Wild abandon. That's the only way to describe that moment." Audrey looked at Miriam. "I ran across the slick grass alongside Robert's long, confident strides, strands of hair smeared across my face, I kept telling myself, Don't fall, don't fall. We made it to the gazebo before the rain turned to sheets. We stepped inside, his hand at my elbow as if we were together. Then, I saw that others had gathered in the gazebo. I had no idea where they had come from. Who they were. And then there was a woman next to Robert, as if she were with him."

"A woman?" Miriam leaned in.

But Audrey was looking past Miriam, as if the woman of that day had reappeared with the telling of the story. "It's funny what you remember. I'd forgotten about teaching him to play croquet."

Scones and tea were placed in front of them. The voice of the waitress, the jangle of the door brought Audrey back. One of the women from the lecture had entered the tearoom and seen Audrey, so they were obliged to invite her over. There was no further mention of Robert.

28 SEPTEMBER 1938

THE MECHANICS OF FLIGHT

"First of all, I'm going to teach you how to fly straight and level." Frank was standing next to her by the airplane, one hand in his pocket while the other gestured, floating airily over the cockpit.

"You need to fully understand the use of the controlling surfaces. The rudder, the elevator, and the aileron."

Miriam was concentrating, repeating each word internally so that it registered.

She rolled the words around in her mouth and watched as he walked to the end of the wings, his hand touching the bottom one. Frank seemed to have regained himself from the day of the lunch, more the man she knew at the accident. His speech, clear and earnest, even the way he held himself, his body looser, told her that here is where he could breathe with ease.

"Now these are the ailerons," he said, pointing. "There's one on each bottom wing. Would you mind reaching into the cockpit and moving the control column to the right?"

"Like this?" Miriam gripped the instrument and moved it as instructed.

"You see, that causes the right aileron to go up and the left to go down, which causes the airplane to bank."

He told her about the airstream that would be caught in the incline of the right aileron, thus pushing that wing down while the force of air on the underside of the left wing would be pushed up, and as he spoke she was imagining the feeling of sitting in the cockpit, the airplane tilting while soaring through the air. This sensation made her stomach lurch. Nerves, she thought.

"Birds have known this forever," she said, but her voice was too soft, and the wind carried her words off in another direction. She thought of the simple magic of flying, and what it might be like to control this machine that seemed fragile, even ominous propped on the ground like this. Frank leaned down on the wing to demonstrate the banking possibilities, then moved to the tail of the airplane, reaching out to the horizontal wings on either side.

"The elevator is also operated by the control lever."

Miriam could see that he wanted to make her understand, not just how the controls worked but the way in which the airplane responded to small adjustments, the impact of air currents, and how to manoeuvre the controls to take advantage of other forces. It was the mechanics of flight that he wanted her to understand, but also to feel.

"For the elevator, the controls move frontward and backward. Go on. Try it."

Miriam pushed the control column forward, and the elevator dipped down.

"When I push the column forward and the elevator goes down, it's trapping the air, which forces the tail up." She was starting to understand the air stream and the effect of the pressure it exerted on the inclined surfaces.

"Exactly. And the nose down."

Then the final component, the rudder. He told her that the rudder of the airplane, controlled by the foot pedal, operated like that of a boat, in that it forced the turning of the machine. He stopped then and took a few steps away. He had been assured, precise in his presentation, and now there was something quiet, youthful in his stance. His body dipped slightly to one side, and he seemed uncertain how to proceed. It was only three weeks since Peter's crash, since she had met him, and in their enthusiasm at having rescued him, the lesson had been a rash offering. Her impulsive acceptance felt as though she were overstepping. But she knew if she hadn't accepted, the offer would slip; she'd be forced to come to her senses, to be reminded that she was still recovering.

She pulled on the aviator cap and stepped up into the cockpit. This catapulted Frank into action as he rushed over to give the last instruction on the shuttle lever that she would operate when taxiing for takeoff.

"I need to impress upon you to keep the controls absolutely steady," Frank said, his tone returning to that of a lecturer. "They are very responsive to the slightest movement you make." He connected her to the cockpit radio and showed her the mouthpiece where she should speak clearly if she needed to ask him something.

Inside the cockpit Miriam felt as though she had entered a womb, one with hard surfaces, room to breathe, and she settled in, her fingertips grazing the instruments as she recited the instructions.

Aileron, elevator, rudder.

Frank was behind her, speaking into the mouthpiece, asking if she was ready. This question hung there for a moment, her mind still on the instruments which she now held in each hand, the shuttle lever in her left, the control column in her right. She moved her feet so that each foot could press the pedal that controlled the rudder.

It was impossible to understand why she had faith in this machine, its responsiveness to the adjustment that would command lift-off, allow it to turn, circle around. The physics of it were a great comfort to her.

Later, when she walked home, her head still fizzy with the thrill of it, she thought about Edmund and how he had spent his day. She'd asked him to come, to see her first flight, but he claimed he could not close the store. They'd had words, sharp words that were meant to hurt.

"I don't have time for that today."

"*That* being my first flight. Oh, come, Edmund, it will just be a few hours. Put a sign up to say you have an appointment, or that you're ill. No one will mind."

"But I'm not ill. I don't have an appointment."

"Your appointment would be to see my first flight."

"But that would be dishonest."

"Dishonest, but faithful."

"I have always been faithful."

On it went until it was time for Miriam to leave, and Edmund, overheated by emotion, had gone to the bedroom for no reason other than to escape the conversation.

"I'm off," she shouted through the door.

"Be careful." His words weak, barely heard.

She glanced back when she went through the gate and saw him standing by the side of the bedroom window, watching her leave. She wanted to wave, but she also did not want to acknowledge that she'd seen him.

The day had been spent on small adjustments, a constant fine tuning to take into effect wind, height, speed. She could see that she and Edmund had their own series of adjustments. The small gestures that could alter a mood, make someone happy. It seemed she and Edmund were on a particular track, careful to avoid a state where they would be weighted by the other's disappointment. He had told her to go flying, a tone that suggested that he knew she needed to get it out of her system, while he kept an eye on the situation in Europe.

When Neville Chamberlain had gone to Germany to meet with Hitler a few weeks ago, it was the first time he'd flown in an airplane. The state of mind he must have been in, Miriam thought, to be introduced to flight and Hitler on the same day. Such intensity; it was impossible to think where his emotions might have landed.

It was a battle of the mind to lean into war, then accept that it would not come. This, their constant torment. What exactly was the situation in Europe? This, the question no one could answer. But efforts were being made to keep peace on the agenda. Edmund was talking about joining the air raid wardens, so even as they turned away from the glare of war, they were forced to keep their grip on the fringes of it.

For now she would hold on to the knowledge of this flight, having seen the village from the air again, and she would go home to Edmund and describe it to him. She would explain what she'd learned about airplane flight. She would demonstrate with pieces of card how the aileron trapped the air when turned up or down, and though he may already be aware of these fundamentals, he would nod his head and offer "marvellous" when she was done. They had talked about getting a motor car once, but Edmund didn't see the need when they could walk everywhere they went, and she didn't have any compelling argument for pushing the decision, so it floundered, neither a yes nor a no. It could have been that moving forward was hard for both of them; it may have been that Edmund was overwhelmed by it, not fully understanding the way the car operated, or perhaps he saw a burden in it, this machine that would propel them into the future.

He would be pleased for her, somewhat bemused by her passion for flying, then when she finished, he would turn the wireless on, and they would listen to the news.

"Sitting comfortably," she shouted into the mouthpiece.

1 OCTOBER 1938

MIRIAM'S DIARY

She was like a bird on the riverbank that day, listening as if the river were speaking to her.

I could see that, despite her reclusive ways, Audrey was quite aware of everything around her, everything and everyone. She talked of phases of the moon, the stationmaster's son who'd been called up, the cook's new recipe for Victoria sponge, Hitler's advances.

She was queenly, spine rod-straight, but she was not looking down on me, that I knew, she was looking outward, always outward.

She told me the story of how she'd acquired the caravan.

Stella Browne's speech frightened me at first. Why were these women all so angry? That woman, so unkempt, her voice squeaky, how could they take her seriously? This has nothing to do with me, I thought. At first. But everyone around me was glued to her words, and so I listened. The air, dusty and still damp from an earlier rain, and me trying to imagine what it would be like to be pregnant and not want the child. Destitute, poor, violated. I had no idea. Then, freedom, pleasure, control. These words tossed out at us like gold coins.

That day in the caravan. "You mustn't give in," she'd said, "You must hold firm."

Sometimes it was hard to know what she was talking about. I think Audrey was someone used to being heard, and she was not always aware that others struggled to follow her thinking.

"The pilots. You've got the right to be one of them."

Ah, yes. The pilots. I just wanted to fly planes, and Audrey was petitioning for my right to be there at all. She wants me to go to a march, take the train to Godalming.

I don't think she's ever married. But intimacy, that she has known. I must know more of this Robert.

That day in the caravan. The air so close I thought I would faint. Audrey smelled of lavender, the immediacy of her toilette in the caravan laid out on the table next to us: eau de cologne, an engraved brush-and-mirror set, a jar of cream. Everything on display for me to see with Audrey not in the least bit worried or embarrassed by what it might reveal.

It was her smile that put me at ease. That and the way she would rest the edge of her fingers on my arm to draw me in, as if to say it's all right for you to be here, for me to be here. We are together in this world, in this moment.

No one has ever looked at me like Audrey does. Those sage green eyes, I could not escape their watchfulness. Not even Edmund has looked at me like that, his tendency to look at the air around me. Not that he doesn't see me.

We'd agreed to meet by the river, have a walk before the meeting. I was not surprised she was late. Flowers call her attention, as do trees, a fresh bud, the soft plush of moss, a perfectly rounded stone. Where I see the expanse of the landscape, Audrey sees the particulars.

The particulars. That's what she called them. Those things that most people think undeserving of attention, the very idea of interrupting our conversation to listen to the rat-a-tat-tat of a woodpecker. Nonsense. That's what most would say.

I could see that sadness is part of Audrey, too. Like a dropped veil it emerges, sudden, leaving her almost trance-like. She would drift into someone else. For all her love of her home in the caravan, the happiness in the way she touches the few possessions she has, with care as if it is all a private museum, and the way she smiles at me with a kind of joy I'm not accustomed to, even that cannot fully conceal the part of her that is dark inside. She works hard at being happy, yet I've seen something slip in her, like the world has suddenly fallen in shadow.

When I think of her as a bird, I think of the strength of her, but I also think of something soft, vulnerable, fragile.

There are moments I want to protect her. But from what? Herself? Is that possible?

2 OCTOBER 1938

THE OBSERVER

PEACE IN EUROPE

So the Browns, and the Joneses and the Smiths
and the Robinsons
Can again enjoy motoring abroad with
autocheques.
What about winter sports, the Riviera,
or North Africa.
Ask for a special booklet.

THE DAYS OF TENSION
How London Faced the Situation
Preparing for War but Hoping for Peace

Nobody is likely to forget the sight of London
preparing for war during the days of tension that

ended with the good news on Friday morning and Mr Chamberlain's triumphant return.

Preparations made the week unforgettable. Trench-digging began immediately. At one point the lawns of Hyde Park were normal and untroubled and the next it was as if a thousand furious moles had got to work.

PLANS TO HONOUR MR CHAMBERLAIN
Nobel Peace Prize Suggested Streets Named after Him Nations' Tributes

Suggestions to honour Mr Chamberlain in some tangible form for his great services to peace continue to be made in many parts of Europe. The French nation is now concentrating on how best to repay the 'first artisan of peace'.

3 OCTOBER 1938

THE TOUR

Audrey barely made her connection to Leicester at St Pancras station. A cloud of steam drifted over her carriage as it pulled away from the station, and she sat back, her breathing heavy from the run to make it. The smoke masked the smell of oil, tobacco, and the faint damp whiff from a nearby factory. The morning train had been delayed, and she'd had to dash through the crowds to make the noon train. Past men in black suits, each clutching an umbrella, a newspaper under one arm, and women moving as though wading through water, their appointments less urgent. Past the third-class carriage where two passengers were hanging out windows smoking, while arguing about something that rightfully belonged to "our William." Audrey scanned the station for an abortionist, as she'd heard they often set up in St Pancras or Paddington stations to serve women who came in from rural areas.

She'd lost her footing as she stepped on the train and bumped into the man in front of her, who turned and tipped his hat to apologize. She picked up the paper he'd dropped and handed it to him just as the whistle blew.

They were in the first-class carriage, with its worn leather chairs, wood-panelled walls, and attendants ready to offer a cigar or a cup of tea—a far cry from the third-class carriage she'd taken that morning. A group of gentlemen sat at one end of the carriage, their armchairs angled to form a circle, and one man was blustering through a commentary on Chamberlain's activities as he read his newspaper.

"That's it then," he said, bringing the newspaper into a fold, his eyes grazing over the men, then darting up to the carriage to rest on Audrey for the briefest moment. She smoothed her skirt and turned her attention to the view outside. He was so loud, so demanding of attention, so needing to be heard.

Having settled into her seat, Audrey felt the coarse rub of her woollen coat against her neck, like an abrasive, so she undid the top button, rubbed her skin.

Her right shoe was pinching, and she longed to pull her shoe off, but the man she'd bumped into was sitting across the aisle, and though his chair, like hers, was set facing the window, she could not see a way of discreetly removing her shoes. She leaned back against the cool leather and closed her eyes. She had to review her notes for the speech, but for now she needed to catch her breath, claim this space. The gentleman across the aisle lit his pipe and snapped open his newspaper.

She, too, had been anxious to read the newspaper. She'd seen the headline in the *Daily Mail*. "Millions Bow in Thanks for Peace." Audrey had planned to go to Leicester the day before, but the train had been delayed by the rain and the crowds at church. She'd gone as far as Guildford, had seen throngs, like a demonstration forming, making their way to the cathedral at the top of the hill. She saw one family huddled under an umbrella, a little girl in a red coat crying as rain blew into her face. She should not be affected by this war, Audrey thought, and here she was dragged into giving thanks that they'd narrowly missed it.

A national sigh of relief. The Munich Agreement. Signed with Hitler, giving the Sudetenland to him in exchange for peace. She felt the relief of this, the second time in a month that war had been averted, but whereas the first time she'd felt a kind of euphoric rescue, this time the sacrifice of one region of Czechoslovakia to aid the rest of Europe felt like stealing someone's silver to have a party.

But it truly was a great reversal. They'd come so close. Nine thousand children were to be sent to Sussex, Northease barn already turned into a hospital, sixty children laid out on mattresses in the gallery, notices posted giving instructions on which Tube stops to take for evacuation in London, noting that people were to be taken up to fifty miles outside the city for free, all manner of organization recited on the BBC two nights ago. Now, instead of bombs on London, she could continue to travel freely. What a close shave.

"The A.R.P. men continued distributing gas masks at the Sunday Schools at those same churches," she heard the man at the back of the carriage bellow. "I guess they hadn't heard about the end of war." Laughter.

Frank had taken her to tea after her aborted trip, told her that he'd heard on the wireless that people up and down the country had gone to church to give thanks for peace.

They had planned to go to lunch the day before, and he wanted to apologize for cancelling at the last minute, but he'd been out flying with Peter and wanted to get further advice on where this flying might take him, professionally speaking, now that war had been averted. It was not like Frank to collect strays like that, Audrey knew. Once, in anger, his father had called him a misanthrope. When Audrey asked him what exactly his plans were, professionally speaking, he waved her off, told her he had much to consider.

Audrey picked up her newspaper and read of the hundreds who had queued for an hour in the rain to enter the City Temple in London where the Reverend Weatherhead led nearly three thousand people in a service of thanksgiving. Westminster Abbey had been more crowded than on the day of the coronation. The rain, like a monsoon sent to challenge them, was no match for the millions who decided they needed to go to church, to thank God, the vicar, and anyone else who would take credit for it.

Last week the prime minister's statement in the Saturday *Times* had signalled this outcome. "How horrible, fantastic, incredible it is that we should be digging trenches and trying on gas masks here because of a quarrel in a faraway country between people of whom we know nothing."

At St Paul's Cathedral, the dean, Dr Matthews, had reminded the congregation that the universal feeling of joy and relief in England was not the case in another nation. "I mean Czechoslovakia, whose people are suffering from a sense of bitterness and loss. We should be selfish indeed if we omitted to remember them in our prayers."

Audrey folded her newspaper, fanned herself against the pipe smoke of her neighbour. She should have gone third-class, the only other option since they'd done away with second. There she could be invisible amongst the other women, the couples, the people who had little to prove. Here she was on display, the lone woman who was there to form an audience, to be impressed. What if she joined them? she thought. What if she walked down the aisle, sat down, and gave her own opinion of the war, or better yet, gave a tutorial on abortion rights. She glanced over once more. Some minds could not be changed.

She thought of the women she would be meeting in Leicester and how she might divert their attention from the celebration of peace back to the "Individuality of Women," the topic of her speech tomorrow. But how could they focus on the individual needs of women after such a collective experience they'd been through? The sand-bagging, the trench digging, planting gardens. There was no joy in war, but she understood that it offered something. Community? A sense of purpose? No, that was whitewashing it. It was about survival. Nothing more. She would be addressing the Women's Alliance of the Labour Party, channelling the ideas of Stella Browne.

The prevailing idea that abortion causes mental and emotional injuries is a red herring in an effort to have us stop the discussion. The idea that a woman might have a choice, that aside from any reasons around sexual abuse, financial constraint, or social attitude, a woman might find maternity repugnant in itself is one we dare not speak of.

This would lift them out of their torpor, Audrey thought, making a few adjustments in her speech.

I knew a woman, someone of independent financial means, good health, with an intellectually and sexually active life, who has had three terminations and not suffered septicaemia or melancholia as had been the predicted outcomes.

This statement had drawn a few gasps at the meeting, for most assumed Stella was speaking of her own experience. Rumours were that she'd had at least one abortion, and that she was flaunting it seemed both daring and dangerous.

Audrey made further notes, but her mind kept darting back to the newspaper. That fragment of relief when she'd heard the news that Chamberlain had reached an agreement was now clouded with a relentless unease. The sacrifice of the Sudetenland. What had they done?

Laughter erupted at the back of the carriage, jolting her back to the train.

The attendant appeared, and she was offered tea, which she gratefully accepted, steadying the rattle of cup on saucer as they hit a bump on the rails. The voice of the man at the end of the carriage had quieted somewhat. "Shame on you," she muttered. "Shame on us all."

The train was coming to a stop, and the pipe-smoking man on the other side of the aisle caught her eye. His look was purposeful, searching through Audrey's window as they came to a stop. He leaned forward, still looking, smiled more broadly, then marched out to the platform. Audrey watched him, thinking that there was something of him that reminded her of Robert, the quick glance at his reflection in the window barely noticed. He was at the W.H. Smith & Son book stall, already paying for his purchase.

Back on the train, the man nodded to Audrey as he settled back in and, gesturing with his book to the newspaper that lay folded on the arm of his chair, a photo of Chamberlain barely noticeable above the crease, said, "He's done it."

Audrey, so deep in her lecture notes, wondered who "he" was, thinking immediately of the universal man, the one who might object to her lecture. Whom would she be speaking to, she wondered, the believers or those who needed to be convinced? She looked to her neighbour. What was he talking about?

The war. Chamberlain.

"Yes," she said, finally. "I suppose he has."

20 OCTOBER 1938

STAINS

F rank felt the sliver from the frame enter the skin of his middle finger, not as pain but as an irritant, the piece of wood embedded more deeply than he initially thought, drawing blood that would stain the fabric he was handling.

"Bloody hell," he muttered. He'd wanted to get the wings wrapped today, the painting done a few days after that. Time had suddenly become a precious commodity, one constantly working against him. He had spent the past few years doing little more than thinking, though to the outer world he was managing his father's country estate. This thinking itself seemed to have a purpose, and he felt he was getting closer to realizing a direction. Where others might have done the Grand Tour, his was internal, through reading, conversations with friends, writing some poetry. Some felt he was hiding, that he had fashioned himself a recluse. But he saw this time as a necessary preparation. He had a vague sense of why he was drawn to the dilapidated airplane, but only recently understood the need on a more primal level.

He pinched at the sliver of wood, blood oozing until at last he was able to draw it out with his fingernails. He pulled his handkerchief from his pocket and wound it around his finger, wiping the blood off as he did so. That's when his brother, Charles, walked in.

Frank looked at his younger brother standing in the doorway. He should wipe his hands, he knew, and shake that of his brother. But disappointment held him back, disappointment at failing to finish wrapping the wing, at having been stymied by a bloody splinter, and now having to deal with Charles, this sudden arrival like a clear and precise deliverance of an omen.

"Charles," he said, his smile broad. "What has brought you here? It's good to see you."

Charles held his expression, then walked around the garage, stepping over parts, the heels of his shoes clicking as he went. His eyes flicked between Frank and the airplane, but he could not bring himself to ask the question that was surely on his mind.

"I've come to see you. To talk."

Frank looked up at him.

"At father's suggestion."

"Ah, I see."

Frank wiped his hands and thought how predictably the conversation would unfold: the repetition of concerns, the suggested change of situations, the view that Frank ought to engage somehow, and he felt sorry for his younger brother.

"What do you think?" Frank gestured to the airplane. "I expect it will be ready in a fortnight."

"Well, that is grand," Charles said, indulging his brother. Then he changed tack, moving swiftly to the subject of the house, their father's plans, the thought that he might sell it. Charles was next to the airplane now and reached out to touch it, gently, as if it were something to be patted. "But we're also looking at other opportunities."

"Opportunities?"

Frank observed the wing that was still exposed, the linen like an oversized bandage hanging loose down the side of it.

"What are you hearing of Hitler in London?" Frank asked. Charles looked up, startled. Was this a trick of some kind?

"I know as much as you do," he replied. "Chamberlain has given us peace, but Hitler has a roaming eye. We live in hope."

"Hope is dangerous in these times. It speaks to a kind of helplessness. And this is not the time to feel helpless, is it?"

But Charles did look helpless at that moment, and bewildered.

Frank could not remember the point at which Charles had aligned himself with their father. In their younger days Charles had a constant hand at Frank's shoulder. This had given way to a state of neutrality, where Charles could neither defend nor protect one from the other. Now, it seemed, he always appeared as an emissary for their father, their views fused together so that there was no doubt, no debate.

"Help me with this, will you." Frank bent to pick up the fallen linen, holding the end out to his brother. "Here, cut along this line," he instructed, holding the fabric taut for him. He picked up the glue brush and slathered it then pressed the material into the wing, smoothing out the wrinkles and bumps with his hand and the back of a knife.

"Just two more pieces and I'm done," he said, motioning to Charles to stretch the cloth over another part.

Frank could see that Charles was getting agitated, his mission hijacked by airplane repairs, so he asked his brother to tell him about the opportunity he had in mind and, through Charles's presentation, learned about the National Trust scheme to preserve the nation's country houses, those with architectural merit that represented a more illustrious period in England's history, a scheme that would help those who were struggling to maintain what for many was a burdensome inheritance.

"Father's idea is to donate it to the National Trust, thus avoiding the death tax that, frankly, we can't afford. We remain in the house as tenants on the condition that we open it up for visitors on the weekend, free of charge. However, my idea is that we keep the house, but open it up to the public with a charge for admission, that way the house stays in the family and we derive an income from it."

"I remember Lord Lothian gave up Blicking Hall in Norfolk in this manner."

"He saved it, is a more accurate description."

Frank was trying to imagine the villagers lining up, paying . . . what . . . what exactly would they pay to see the inside of their house? And where would he be? Reading a book in the library, drinking scotch, pretending he wasn't being observed like some animal in a zoo. What if Peter was visiting, or Aunt Audrey was over for lunch, would they carry on as if nothing were out of the ordinary? He'd felt so long a captive in the house, it seemed his own private prison to conceal him, to protect him from outside forces. He did not want to think of money, of property. That's what men like Charles and his father were for. They knew the cult of greed, little else.

"I am to be evicted then."

Charles stepped forward, about to object, but Frank waved him away, as if he were a branch obstructing his way on the path.

"I've been told that if war comes many of the country houses will be given over to use as hospitals, or to house evacuated children." Frank looked at Charles.

"Impossible. There will be no war." This sudden assertion, so much like his brother.

22 OCTOBER 1938

MIRIAM READS HER BODY
LIKE THE WEATHER

There was a dull ache in her breast, a tingling in her nipples. The occasional cramping she'd felt in her abdomen these past weeks was more a nuisance than a hindrance, which is why she'd agreed to make the trip with Frank. He had seen so much in her, saw her future in flying spread out before her in a way that she had not put thought to. It was hard to say no to him, but still she knew her body was sending coded messages, ones she was trying to interpret. Was this her body's way of finally relinquishing her last baby?

Frank wanted to fly to London to see the balloons. They needed the practice and could go via Croydon to familiarize themselves with various routes.

It was the best thing for her, she knew, to be up there at four thousand feet. It gave perspective. It took her away from a body that seemed unwilling to give up the signs of pregnancy. Almost two months now, she calculated, and there were days when she imagined she was conjuring symptoms, a way of not letting go, a constant and gentle reminder of failure. She was tired, too, and that made her question everything: Edmund's brisk cheeriness, Frank's unwavering support, her own ability to navigate to Croydon. She'd worked on the map for the past week. How had she come to see the Earth like this? How had she felt this need to place herself in the landscape? She'd taken the map of Hampshire, four miles to an inch, then plotted the landscape details and redrew the entire thing, highlighting their route with rail lines, identifying towns and villages as she'd seen them from the air, a church steeple, a windmill, the curve of the high street, the green roof of a country manor. She used a colour-coded system to memorize the routes: churches—red; rail lines—black; rivers—blue. She'd questioned pilots on what they'd seen and pieced it together, and now at four thousand feet, she was mentally ticking off each landmark.

The barrage balloons had her worried though. It seemed a ludicrous effort, as if they were still playing at war despite the peace agreement. The city had decided to do a demonstration of them, a run-through to make sure they worked, to make sure the barrage operators knew how to raise and lower them effectively. Her friend Mildred had told her about them.

"Have you seen pictures of them?" Miriam asked Frank before they took off. "Elephants, they call them. Three times the size of a cricket pitch. Four hundred and fifty of them over London."

"A flimsy bit of nylon to stop those German bombers. Is there a kind of genius in that?"

"What do you mean?"

"A simple solution. Fill the balloon with hydrogen, suspend them with heavy cables, and no German pilot wants to get near enough to drop his bombs. We'll win the bloody war with puppets!"

"But there is no war, and it seems a waste. Everything seems a waste these days. Why are we still pretending? And these balloons will be a threat to our pilots, too. I heard them talking at the airfield. That means they're increasing risk, not lessening it."

"Well, I hope we get close enough to see them. A remarkably simple bit of engineering."

In that moment she saw him as he might have been as a boy, the wonder of discovering engineering feats, the awe that would come at a moment when he saw an invention that would all but overwhelm him.

"What happened to your leg," she'd asked him not long after they'd met. She'd known about the Wentworth family. Rumours adrift, in and out of the village like morning fog. She'd probably seen him once or twice; she knew he was a cripple, probably even knew he'd been born with the affliction, yet she asked, because she wanted to hear the story from him.

"What happened to your leg?"

Part of her wanted to hurt him that day in the hangar, to embarrass him. The luncheon had left her feeling scorched, their kindness like a weapon readily released. She was no longer a hero; she was a visitor. Each role had its own mantle. That's why she'd grabbed at the offer of flight. Snatched it from Peter's hand. Knowing she would never get the chance again and wanting somehow to even out their places in the world.

She'd felt a cramp in her abdomen just then, as if her body were convening with his in some way.

His story told her that he'd suffered, the braces, the horrid wrench; she had forgiven him everything then—his class, his money, his misdirected invitation. Suffering, the unexpected equalizer.

They couldn't fly directly over London, Miriam told him before they left. They would need to see the balloons at a distance.

His disappointment worn like his own deflated balloon, so that she understood this meant more to him than just a spectacle. We'll get close enough, she told him.

And they did, following the perimeter of London.

"They're better viewed at a distance," she shouted into the mouthpiece. She knew about perspective, angles, scale. At that height, not a thousand feet above the balloons, the angle narrowed the distance between them so they appeared almost touching. It was true they were a sight, the bloated oval shapes in shimmering steel grey nylon held in place by cables that anchored each to the ground.

"Magnificent," he mouthed when she banked the airplane.

Later they would talk about this sight, which at once displayed engineering boldness, and yet they were ominous, as though an alien presence, unidentifiable, almost monstrous.

"Time to head back," she said into the mouthpiece.

Thirty minutes into the return, the weather turned. She readjusted in the seat to ease the strain in her back and kept her eye on a horizon that was getting lower with each mile. Rain forecast, they'd been told at Hackley, but they'd be home in time.

There were dark streaks of rain ahead, as if lead were melting from the sky, and she felt the pressure change in her head. She took one hand off the controls and held her arm against her breasts as if they needed protection, but it was her entire body she wanted to protect, not from the weather, or even any kind of war that might erupt, but from itself, an existence that had her enslaved to its hormonal shifts, the constant monitoring and nurturing that had left her weak in spirit. She should not feel this way, up here in the clouds, her place of refuge. She shifted her attention to the airplane—throttle, flaps, airspeed—touching the instruments as she did when doing a pre-flight routine, muttering the fundamentals of flight, re-engaging with the machine that would deliver them home.

"Weather ahead," Frank's voice bellowed.

Miriam saw that the ceiling had lowered even more, rain falling in sheets now less than two miles away. Her mind on her map and the landscape on either side of the path she'd chosen. She needed to drop into the valley ahead, keeping to one side in order to give herself room to manoeuvre should she need to escape.

"Diverting west," she shouted, as she banked the plane. She gripped the controls as the plane swooped, suddenly feeling birdlike, a hawk patrolling its territory. Do birds see boundaries in the air? she wondered. How do they know when to leave one place for another?

Miriam had no appetite for competition, no juice in her blood that would help make the King's Cup Race a success. Flying was a personal quest. Each flight a discovery of landscape, the reading of the wind, the rush of propulsion, the exhilaration of a landmark detected. She focussed on the technical aspects when she was flying but remained dreamlike on the impression it had on her. The visual sensation summoned a new language. The verdant pastures, the cobalt rivers, the demarcations that put sheep in one field, cattle in another. Stone and brick brought structure to the landscape, a signifier. Industry, innovation, patience. This is what she saw when she was flying. Not the finish line.

But they'd agreed. A race from London to Manchester. And the trial run, under the pretense of seeing the elephant balloons, was really an opportunity to test their mettle. The bad weather was perfect. Ready-made to challenge their strength, her fortitude, her knowledge of how to dodge a storm cloud.

This an unspoken arrangement for Frank, who was unable to express his desire to win when he'd asked her to co-pilot the race. But he'd showed her in so many ways how much it meant to him. In his casual but direct comments that resided in a question—your landings are improving, you might want to ease up on the aileron when banking, have you noticed how the elevator sticks a bit when taking off?—an opportunity to seek an opening as they made their plans. He could hardly contain himself, she saw, the will to win so strong he kept himself harnessed from the strain of it.

She checked her map, not wanting to rely entirely on her instincts that told her there was a dip in the landscape ahead, not quite a valley but a rising to the west that they could snug into, a hope for some protection from the rain and the wind.

"I'm taking it to twenty-five hundred feet," she said, pushing in the throttle.

Frank was calculating their time, she knew, comparing it to that of the trip he'd made with Peter—the rain would skew things, of course, but they'd have to adjust if it rained on race day.

She pushed hard, her concentration so intense she forgot about her body, the race, the barrage balloons that would save them from Hitler's planes, and focussed on the airplane and the rain that was thrashing around them. The ceiling so low she felt she could reach out and touch treetops. The wind buffeted them, the turbulence staying with them for a few miles, then they were in the valley, outwitting the elements.

She scanned the sky and saw a break ahead, saw her chance to get them back by going farther west, over the downs and to the north of Ashleigh. Another gust lifted her from her seat, but she was gripping the instruments so hard she barely felt it. The rain was letting up, her face washed in the constant stream, cooled in the wind that came in from the west. She would be there soon, she knew, this test a decent one. She had got them through the worst of it, had held her own map in her head as she'd guided the plane to where it needed to be. The race seemed possible now, even a challenge she might enjoy.

25 OCTOBER 1938

A RESPONSIBLE MAN

E dmund was not what one would call a joiner. The sociability that was required as shopkeeper and postmaster far exceeded his inclinations, so although most would call him "a good sort of fellow," this was often followed by "a bit of a loner," which to many was regretful, a cause for suspicion. That he had Miriam in his life was an unacknowledged but accepted blessing by those in the village, for she, too, was often described as one who kept to herself but was more connected, more likely to stop and go through the exercise of asking after one's family. They were friendly, mildly inquisitive, knowledgeable, and on the periphery of the village goings-on; they did not lean into gossip, or make a regular night at the pub, or sit on committees to plan the village fête or cricket derby with a neighbouring village.

A Responsible Job for a Responsible Man. The sign in the village hall drew him in. The Ministry had posted them around to attract more air raid wardens, keeping the recruitment drive on as a precaution. News of the chaos in Bristol, where it was reported that half the gas masks distributed didn't fit properly, and in Birmingham, where arrangements had been made to evacuate 300,000 citizens but with no arrangements made to cater to them, was the talk at the recruitment office.

Many were surprised when Edmund signed up, could not envisage him walking the village, reporting on blackout misdemeanors, training youngsters and old widows on how to wear a gas mask. But if anything, it was Edmund who was most surprised, and though he had mentioned it in passing to Miriam, even he couldn't fully fathom what had pulled him across the threshold of the village hall.

When he was orphaned at fourteen, he worked at the shop he would eventually inherit, under the supervision of his uncle, who had reluctantly stepped in to take over. Theirs was a tidy life—regimented meals, silent evenings spent reading, going for a walk, catching up on house repairs. His only interaction with others was at the shop, and his uncle would press upon him that there was a steady but modest affluence that separated them from the villagers, and so he learned not to look down upon them but to respect the difference in their status. It was as though his uncle had created a class for them on his own, which Edmund understood and kept on. The separation of class could have been his uncle's method of protecting them from requests for credit, or it may have been his attempt to shove them closer to gentry. But this separation remained throughout Edmund's life so that he didn't have friends as such, but a series of interactions at the shop that he interpreted as a good substitute for friendship. Still, at times it didn't seem quite enough.

Bloody fool, what have you got yourself in for? he muttered on the way home, clutching pamphlets, a steel helmet, and a gas mask that smelled of old tires. Already it seemed like too much responsibility.

He didn't believe in the war, didn't believe that all the fuss would ever amount to much, but he'd been reading about the preparations in London, not just the distribution of gas masks, but the digging of trenches, the building of bomb shelters, and there seemed to be an accelerated energy around these activities, an added vibrancy that he saw he could be part of. He had been caught up in the moment, he now realized. They were forming a "report and control room" for the district, to be based at the police station. They would need air raid wardens to advise people on precautions and enforce the use of blackout curtains so that no artificial lights were visible from the air. They would work with other personnel—firefighters, rescue and first aid, a plotter, a runner. He'd seen the ordnance map of the district that filled one wall so that they would be able to place pins where activity took place.

He had thought it might be good for him. To talk to people outside the shop. To be out in the village with a purpose, to see and be seen in a new light. He could feel himself getting easily agitated these days, what with Miriam taking up flying. He needed something that would direct his attention elsewhere.

That man Thompson who'd come into the shop to post a letter the other day.

"How's Mrs Thomas?" he'd asked, an easy smile that unsettled Edmund. What was he getting at exactly? "Saw her at the airfield last week," the man pressed.

"She's learning to fly." Edmund dropped the change into the man's hand.

"She'll be in the RAF soon enough." Again that smile.

Edmund had decided it was a game they were playing. That's what he sometimes did when he couldn't follow the intent or direction of a conversation; it somehow took the pressure off.

"Pity they won't have her."

"Well, she may have her own ideas. The war's off for the moment, but it's hard to let go these days."

Edmund had watched the man leave and rushed to the door, locked it, and put the *closed* sign up. Was Miriam planning for war? Is this what this was all about? The race? The flying? It was all so far away. Germany. Poland. Czechoslovakia. They'd already had their war. It didn't make sense to do it again. He went to the cupboard and opened a pack of cigarettes he kept there along with a flask of whisky and stood at the back door, looking up at the sky. He took a swig from the flask, coughed as he drew from the cigarette.

He was committed now. A warden. He had to hope he was right and the war would not materialize. As he approached his home, he saw that the lights weren't on and remembered that Miriam was at a meeting with Audrey. He went inside, hung his steel helmet and gas mask on a coat hook, and put the kettle on.

26 OCTOBER 1938

PROPAGANDA

The message: how to get it right? It was this challenge that kept Audrey in her dressing gown at ten in the morning. Condoms, IUDs, stem pessaries, cervical caps, spermicide pessaries. To list them was to educate. That was her thinking as she lined the words up on the notepad. Instructions, yes, that's what a woman would want, would need, in fact. Surely, clarity counted for something.

Instead, everything was shrouded in euphemism: feminine hygiene or marriage hygiene. *Douching with Lysol, the perfect antiseptic for marriage hygiene.* Disinfecting daily, the advertisements promised, would save your marriage. Why was it always the woman? Audrey wondered. Why were they responsible for saving the marriage?

She slid the notebook onto the bed and stood to dress. Miriam would arrive soon. She would have perspective. She would know what women wanted to know.

What would the younger version of herself have wanted to know? Audrey wondered. Robert, again. Creeping into her thoughts. That conversation with Miriam, she'd revealed more than she intended. Yet it had felt good to tell Miriam, someone who knew nothing of her past, had no investment in her unsound judgments. There was more to tell, of course, and who knew, perhaps she would. Miriam had asked about desire, but Audrey could tell her more about doubt.

The problem began with the pewter dress. Audrey had been to London to see her friend Evelyn, and they'd seen it, clear lines, an unfussy finish, a good dress for the times. But it didn't quite fit right, two darts would pull it in nicely, and she could pick it up in three hours. So there it was: sold.

They would have lunch at the 19 Club, Evelyn told her, a gathering place Audrey had heard of but not yet been to. Corner table, near the window with a view to both the park outside and the expanse of the crescent-shaped restaurant.

The dress seemed a silly indulgence, but Evelyn insisted, and their entire day was navigated around it. A museum would have been a treat, but they still needed to return to the shop, and then she would have to rush to her train. These little pellets of thought were firing in her mind, triggering a growing agitation as she watched platters of food move like a ballet across the floor, waiters bowing, directing, serving, amidst discreet whispers, a bellowing laugh, a woman who spoke too loudly of her neighbour's affair. The day was dull, which made the glass ornamental lights glisten as if they were candlelight. Evelyn was waving to someone, talking to Audrey from the side of her mouth, saying something which she didn't catch but gathered was gossip, Evelyn's currency. It was hot, too hot for the cardigan she was wearing, and when she removed it, turning to fold it away, she caught sight of Robert at a table tucked at the back near the waiters' stand. He was with another man and two women, and they were leaning into each other, absorbed in their conversation. She could see that they were enjoying each other's company with comfortable familiarity, friends perhaps.

He caught sight of her in that moment. His expression slackened; a question crossed his face before an exuberant smile pulled him from his seat and he strode across the floor to her. There were the usual introductions, explanations, announcement of plans for the rest of the day. And the fact that there was no awkwardness at this unlikely meeting struck Audrey as odd because it seemed they were all out of place in this restaurant. Audrey had told Robert about coming to London, but he'd said he had appointments. Did this count as an appointment? The two women, cousins of his friend, it turned out, looked as if they might create a party right there in the restaurant. Their laughter, haughty and intense, signalled that they were well on their way, the two of them at the centre of it. And Audrey, getting irritated by a day that was dismantling on all fronts, wishing only to be at the portrait gallery alone rather than here in the silly restaurant pretending to care about the chatter around her. It was the contrivance that got to her, a wasting of time, and the elaborate and delicate conversation they had to get through before returning to their respective tables with promises of future meetings, that made her want to escape.

She felt that she'd caught up to Robert that day, in experience, in sophistication. They had been seeing each other for several months now, and, up to that point, she was fearful that she would always lag behind. Robert glanced over at her once or twice during the meal, and Audrey couldn't tell if it was to assure himself that she was still there or to check if she'd gone.

She would eventually learn that it was hard to close the door of mistrust once it had been opened. Patterns repeat. That was inherent in the design. That, too, she learned.

This she would realize years later, after she'd been to war, seen honest men who understood something of life die in devastating conditions. By then she would understand how her privilege had unbalanced her in those unquestioning days. In her world, social convention trumped social welfare. It was a revelation when she realized that.

But it took time for these thoughts to form. She would understand it as a kind of maturing, a grace and knowledge she could never have had at twenty-one. She also understood that one can believe what one wants to believe at any time of life.

For some months she forgot about his face that day at the restaurant. The transformation, subtle, barely perceptible, would only become clear to her later. The way one expression vaporized into the next, as if practised, was something she would learn to see as a deficit. This was the beginning of her alternative education, on the day of the pewter dress.

The lamb stew that day was the best she'd tasted, but the dress she endured for two outings, then relegated it to the back of the cupboard.

A sharp rap on her door.

"Come, Miriam, help me with these buttons," Audrey said, pulling the dress back over her shoulders.

"Am I early?" Miriam set her bag on a chair, before hooking the four buttons at the back of Audrey's dress.

"Not at all." Audrey swung around. "I was thinking of the pamphlet I'd like to do."

31 OCTOBER 1938

COUNTER BEATS

The sound a constant backdrop. His off-steps. The clip of one foot then the soft thud of the other, a counter beat down the main hall, the tiled floors providing the percussion that announced his arrival. Clip, thud, clip, thud. It was the steady off-kilter beat that he'd known since he was a child. The sound always elevated when others were around. Alone, he did not hear it. As if it were akin to the sound of his own breath, a nightingale by his window, the rustle of the leaves, nothing to hold his attention.

He once thought it made him special. He had imagined himself as one chosen for this gift of an improper foot. Shy, considered backward because he did not speak until he was five, he was glad that it was his misshapen foot that people were drawn to. He was barely a person, just someone who wore this affliction, so he'd learned to observe with downcast eyes, to be looked at but not seen, to be considered an idiot because of his physical deformity. It was a beautiful hiding place.

Even his mother would come to him with a swift pat or a whispered kiss on the forehead before fussing with his orthopaedic shoe, realigning its position as she asked him about his lessons. It was his father who introduced him to shame: Frank, ever observant, noticed how he marched ahead when they went out. The message—unworthy—was clear. The looming figure of his father leading the way, never a hand reached back, never even a look to be sure he was keeping up. A recollection carved into his bank of childhood memories.

And now, clip, thud, clip, thud, resurrecting that memory, a hot blush coloured his cheeks as he felt Peter at his side while they walked down the corridor. It was the curse of hard surfaces—tile, wood, stone—that revealed his secret. His limp long mended, he could thank his father for that. The shame an impetus to hours spent walking up and down the corridor, a mirror at each end so he could adjust his body movements to compensate for his foot. If his father had noticed the improvement, it would have made the effort all the more rewarding.

This shame like a disease that made it impossible for him to relax in Peter's presence.

He'd misjudged things, thrown by Peter's sudden arrival at the door, prompting a rushed and flustered invitation for a drink on the terrace that had them walking through the house, the steady off-time rhythm like a metronome. He could barely utter a word.

Fumbling at the drinks tray, the stopper of the scotch carafe slipped from his damp fingers, rattling as it wobbled across the tray. What was Peter doing here?

"Scotch?" he mumbled, turning to Peter, who stood closer than he was expecting.

"I'm dying for one."

Frank plunged the scoop into the ice that Annie had quickly brought in and dropped the cubes into his glass, then Peter's. Golden scotch. Everything would be fine now. Frank sipped too quickly, listening to Peter talk of the news from the airfield, a new flying schedule introduced, and an influx of pilots eager to train.

But really it was an ancient scar on Peter's face that was holding his attention, shaped like an arrow across the underside of his chin. How had he been so marked? Frank wondered. What childhood prank or adult foolishness had left him branded? Peter's cheek was now brushed pink from the alcohol, the flat vowels of his speech seemed exaggerated, the hand perched on his shoulder holding Frank in his place. What was Peter telling him?

A new service. Flying letters, parcels around the country. A communications network set up for war because trust in Hitler's commitment to peace was waning.

"You'd be perfect for it," Peter was saying, and Frank topped up their scotch and walked away because this was too much to take in. He couldn't figure out if Peter was mocking him. A flying postman? Is that what he was suggesting? Peter would sign on with the RAF while Frank flew around delivering mail.

"The Air Transport Auxiliary," Peter continued. "There was a man at the airfield talking about it today. If war comes and telephone lines, mail service, all communications break down, they will need pilots to fly from one end of the country to the next delivering messages, parcels, supplies, even delivering airplanes to the RAF."

Delivering airplanes to people like him, that's what Peter was trying to say. This was the best that could be expected from men like Frank. His afflicted foot that he'd once thought made him special was now so carefully concealed. Who was he kidding? Everyone knew the RAF wasn't an option for him. This would be as good as it gets. How could he ever feel an equal to Peter?

As if reading his mind Peter turned to Frank, tilting his glass at him. "I wish I had your knack for engineering. You'd be an asset for the ATA, I'd say. It won't be enough to just fly planes if war comes. I can fly an airplane, but what if I were to go down again? I've already crashed once. What if you hadn't come along? What if I'd gone down in enemy territory? What skills do I have that would save me?"

The scotch was affecting him, his voice louder with each sentence.

"I suppose we'll all need to be bigger than ourselves."

"Yes, yes, that's it. It's not enough to be who we are. We have to be better than we are. But how can we know what that means? How can we be sure that we'll be up to it if we are not tested in times of war?"

An ice cube settled in Peter's glass, and he swirled his scotch.

"Are you making a case for war, Peter, as a way of self-improvement? Or perhaps self-fulfillment?"

That laugh, an eruption that changed the mood of the room. It took Frank a moment to adjust, to be sure that the laughter wasn't directed at him. Later, once he knew Peter better, he would recognize this as a nervous gesture.

"I'm talking about being tested." Peter was strolling the room, as if taking it in for the first time.

Did Frank need to be tested?

It seemed the wrong reason to be part of the war, but Frank knew that he would join the ATA, knew that he wasn't looking to be tested so much as to be part of something outside his life in this house.

"I know you are. We will all be tested in our own way."

3 NOVEMBER 1938

SECRETS

"**Y**ou've come too late for me, but give me some pamphlets for my girls. I don't want them to have the life I had." The woman gripped her handbag as if afraid Audrey might snatch it.

The grim, grey walls gave the room the air of a bunker, and it felt as though they were hiding, the four of them: Audrey, Miriam, Gloria, who managed the clinic, and this woman—Betty, she called herself, but who could say if this was her real name.

"What do I know of a French letter?" she was nearly whispering now. "I thought it was one of those fancy papers. Who would I write to in France? I thought to myself? But I knew more than some. My friend Louise, she had no idea how the baby got in there, and had no idea how it was going to come out."

It was Audrey's idea to visit the clinic. They would go and listen, she said. Miriam considered it spying at first and thought it both thrilling and shameful under the current circumstances in which they lived. Recorded lives, watchful neighbours.

But Audrey had explained that they would be helping the women, too, giving them "access to knowledge"—a phrase she was using a lot these days. She said it as if together they were an oracle, a well of authority from which these women could draw information they so desperately needed. This is what she liked about Audrey, the way she would speak to her, and of her, as if Miriam had this "knowledge," too. It made her surer of herself, and sharper. Sometimes in their conversation Audrey would speak to Miriam as if she were an audience, and she knew this was part of why she was valued, someone on whom Audrey could try out arguments.

There were other things Audrey valued in her, she knew.

"You have a certain bravery," she'd said.

But this made Miriam feel like it was something she had stolen. Bravery belonged to soldiers, with their headlong rush into death, and so she denied it, told Audrey that she was not at all brave.

"But you are," Audrey argued. "You have endured losses most women won't know of, and now you are learning to fly. That's bravery of a different sort."

"I have no choice," Miriam told her. Grief was a trait she had mastered; it felt nothing like bravery. Nothing seemed a matter of choice. "I have to exist in the world. We all do."

The clinic was in Farnham, some twenty miles away, and Audrey had driven Frank's car to it. They were told it was around the corner from the fishmonger's, a location that was discreet but accessible.

When they came upon it, the clinic appeared shuttered, though the door was unlocked. Inside, the quiet of the waiting room allowed only the brisk scrape of a chair leg, the gentle clearing of a throat. Betty had been waiting in a chair in the corner of the room. One hand kept brushing down her skirt, the other adjusting the brim of her hat, and when Gloria entered from the back room, she started, half rising before settling back, waiting to be told what to do. They were led into a small room that had a large window overlooking the back alley. From outside Miriam heard the steady beating of someone cleaning a rug, but otherwise there was a stillness as they settled into their chairs, Gloria telling the woman that Audrey was a famous campaigner on birth control. She didn't explain Miriam's presence.

Later, when they had time to talk before the next visitor, Gloria's tone had been apologetic.

"The doctor refuses to send them here," she told them. "He thinks those vending machines in pubs, the ones with condoms, is all that's needed. And women won't come here on their own. They might be seen as promiscuous, or disloyal to their husbands. Sexual intercourse is not something to be discussed. In their view, ignorance protects them, naïveté is a way of preserving their innocence. So, few women know we're here, and those who come arrive like fugitives, afraid their husbands will find out."

Tea was made, and Gloria told them about women, married women, who were left floundering when they were told to "take the kettle off before it boils," with no idea what this meant.

"Those that do get pregnant come to ask about herbal remedies, or a gin bath, wondering how much gin to take, and how long to sit in a hot bath. One woman claimed her aunt used a leech to help bring on the miscarriage."

Miriam looked to the door, willing someone to come in so she didn't have to hear more.

"Five hundred pamphlets, we distributed." Gloria's voice, normally high-pitched, had reached another octave. "We're like a secret society." She went on with more stories of the women in the village, but Miriam had stopped listening. She was thinking about secrets, the way this room seemed like a repository of concealed lives, and whether the keeping of knowledge was the same as keeping a secret. A secret, like currency, to be saved, or to be traded. The women who came to the clinic gained this currency, passed on the information, informers all, careful who heard them, often shutting out those with whom they shared a bed. What secrets had she held from Edmund? What did he keep from her? Could she hide such a thing as contraception from him? Could she acquire these pessaries Gloria was speaking of and use them without Edmund's knowledge?

At breakfast Edmund had told her about the "spyclists" that he'd read about in the *Daily Herald*. The article was based on a translation from a German cycling magazine offering advice to Hitler Youth groups travelling abroad. They were asked to take photographs, especially of industry, and to get lists of names of all those taking part in anti-German movements. They were told to record "in their head" landmarks like steeples and towers and bridges in such a way that they could recognize them at night. Edmund had been so enraged by this article, the pretense, the subterfuge, so galling. That these youth would be welcomed as tourists, perhaps given directions, offered a cup of tea, in some cases celebrated at a local hall, only to betray their hosts in this way. It was the moral degradation that upset him, that people would do such a thing without conscience, rather than the fact that they were instruments in the preparation for war.

This is what she felt like now, a spy, gathering information covertly, the purpose of which was questionable. She would tell Audrey that later, that she'd felt like an intruder, that she didn't feel she had a right to this information because surely she'd have been told about it by now.

"Too many babies," Betty had said. "What do I want with so many?"

They heard the click of the outer door, but not the footsteps that would take the woman to the chair, so careful she was. They'd finished talking to Betty, who was folding the pamphlet into her purse, her head low as if she might be looking deeper for something inside it. Audrey wondered if she was stalling, not wanting to walk past whoever was in the other room. News of these visits could get around, not always for the judgment of it, but for the assurance. They were not alone. Not a one of them.

Gloria knew what she was up against, knew that only desperate ones come, and knew there was a limit to how much they would expose of themselves.

"Come, Betty," she said, leading her by the elbow. "It will be quicker to go out this way." The exit led to the alley, yet Gloria presented it as if it were the main entrance, door swinging wide, head held high.

The woman from the waiting room called herself Elspeth, and despite her pallor there was a haughtiness about her. She'd come for a friend, of course. Two months along. No husband, little money, but Elspeth would help her, she was quick to add.

"Does the father know?" Audrey wasn't sure if she should be asking such a question. Elspeth blinked, nodded in a swift, twitching manner.

"Is she well? Healthy?"

A quick nod.

"Family?"

"No."

"On her own then." Gloria sighed.

Audrey examined the woman because there was something familiar about her. The voice, too. A Northern accent.

"Working?"

"Yes, but the Carringtons left a week ago, so it's not so bad." Her hand flew to her mouth.

That's it, Audrey thought, leaning forward. Elspeth was head maid there. That dinner four months ago, she'd taken Audrey's coat, helped her with the earring that got stuck in the collar.

Elspeth recognized her, too, though only her widening pupils gave her away.

"She wants rid of it." A harsh whisper.

Gloria placed her clasped hands on the table before her, dropped her eyelids as if concentrating to compose what she would say next.

"There are herbs she can take."

"She tried them."

Shooting a glance at Audrey.

"I've heard of doctors ..."

At her lecture a week ago Audrey was asked what happens when it fails, when women can't get the birth control they need, or when the birth control doesn't work, what was left for these women who did not want the baby. Audrey had told them about the Abortion Law Reform Association that had recently been established to campaign for the legalization of abortion. This had been genuine progress, she'd told the women.

"What does that do for me now?" the woman had asked Audrey. "I've had four babies in the past six years. My husband will beat the life out of me when he finds out I'm to have another one."

This knocked the campaigner out of Audrey, leaving her as a woman who could feel the deep personal anguish of another. What does this do for me now?

"Perhaps the father—"

"This was not done by a husband ... or boyfriend."

Audrey felt her breath catch, tried to keep a steady eye on Elspeth as she thought of something to say. She had been violated.

That would not make a difference, she knew. The law was the law. Just months ago, in June, Dr Aleck Bourne was arrested after performing a termination at St Mary's Hospital in London on a fourteen-year-old girl who'd been sexually assaulted by five off-duty British soldiers from the Royal Horse Guards. She had initially gone to St Thomas Hospital but was sent away on the grounds that she might be carrying a future prime minister. The only justification for abortions in the Infant Life (Preservation)

Act of 1929 was when the mother's life was in danger. Dr Bourne's argument that she was suicidal won him an acquittal.

"There's nothing to be done, I'm afraid," said Gloria, leading Elspeth to the back door. She gave her a pamphlet and a few notes on a slip of paper and walked her out.

The glare of the sun blinded Miriam and Audrey as they walked away from the clinic minutes later, so they didn't see Elspeth until she stepped in front of them. There was no accusation, no challenge in her look, yet the directness of it shifted responsibility over to Audrey. There were women Audrey knew who'd had an abortion. No one talked openly about it, or even acknowledged it if suspected, but she'd heard of women who'd found doctors willing to risk their practice to help. Help some women, that is.

"I can make the inquiries," Audrey said.

Elspeth nodded once, whispered thank you, and turned away.

"Does she know who did this?" Audrey called after her.

"Yes." The answer firm this time.

The Carringtons' son. So the rumours were true.

Later with Audrey at the wheel, the intensity of the day allowed them to be looser, more vulnerable in their talk.

"There is much we don't think about," Audrey said. "Stella Browne considers the bearing of children as a voluntary rather than involuntary condition. She is adamant on that point."

Miriam looked out the window and saw a motorcyclist by the side of the road having a cup of tea.

"I had not thought of it in that way," she said after a moment.

"We should not have to pay such a heavy price. Especially if what we want is to love and be loved."

Miriam glanced at Audrey, felt her face go hot. She twirled the button on her coat, grabbed the handle of the car when Audrey hit a pothole, her speed too fast for the road. Then

Audrey slowed suddenly, she was saying that if she'd had a choice she would not have become pregnant, that if she'd had a choice she would not have given up her baby. In that moment Miriam understood what knowledge meant, the power of it.

"We know what we have experienced," Miriam said to her. "Choice never seems to be an option."

Audrey's hands were steady at the wheel as she accelerated. "That's what I'm talking about. That's what we need to talk about. Choices."

7 NOVEMBER 1938

THE CHAIN HOME

The peastick had survived the storm. Edmund was examining the structure that stood five feet tall and ten feet wide along the fence that, during the summer, when the dahlias were in full bloom, shielded them from their neighbour Mr Stokes, who, of an evening, would stand out smoking his pipe in the back-yard. On those nights, the smoke would drift through the dahlia leaves, and Edmund would look over in expectation of having to acknowledge Mr Stokes in some way, but his neighbour was often far off in some universe that didn't allow him to take note of anyone around him, conducting a kind of vague surveillance of his own garden, which Edmund knew to be a patch of grass with a few geraniums along the fence. He had not lived there long, having moved in after his mother died and he, being an only child, inherited the house. Edmund didn't know him well, heard he was an engineer, not married. It was hard to get the balance of being friendly while not interfering.

The peastick had survived but now it stood as though in shock, stripped clean of the growth it had so faithfully supported all those months. Edmund picked at a few strands that hung loose and tested the overall sturdiness. He'd need to replace it next year.

The sun broke through and the instant light brought the garden alive with reflected brilliance. The rain had been harsh, heavy, constant, and had been whipped around by a wind like they hadn't seen in years. Neither he nor Miriam had slept well, what with the thrashing the house had been taking. Now that he stood amidst the debris, he wished she were there with him to help clean up.

She was out with Audrey again, to a meeting that Miriam seemed to know little about. Reproductive rights, she'd said with a flick of her hand. Why was she so drawn to Audrey and her world of lectures? And the flying she'd taken up. He hardly knew her these days. It was on his mind to talk to her about these interests, not to stop her, but just to ensure this was what she wanted. He'd always known her to be a reaching-out sort of woman, with a steady yearning he'd considered a curiosity in the early days. It was what drew him to her, he knew, so this sense of unease seemed wrong-footed.

"Quite a storm," Mr Stokes called from across the fence. Edmund realized he'd been looking over toward his neighbour, his mind drifting all over the place.

"I haven't seen anything like it in years." Edmund took the few steps over to the fence, uncertain whether he'd been invited into a conversation. Mr Stokes was holding up what at first looked like a broadsheet but was in fact an architectural draw-ing of some sort of tower. Perhaps the Chain Home, Edmund thought, a ring of early warning radar stations spread along the southern and eastern coasts. He'd seen sketches, like cut-out dolls holding hands, standing sturdy along the coast to protect them from the German air force. They were remarkable in what they could do, detecting enemy aircraft while they were still in France. If he knew Mr Stokes better, he would ask him about them, whether he had any knowledge of how they worked, whether he thought they'd survived this storm.

"We expect Germany to be our undoing, but here is nature marching in, destroying everything in its path," Edmund ventured. He knew his neighbour was a clever man, cleverer than he was, though the weather was a topic in which Edmund was well versed.

"There's still time for Germany to get a hand in."

"Yes, I daresay there is."

Edmund raked the foliage from under the peastick structure with his hand, his fingers stiff with cold, his spirits low. The plants would survive, he knew; it was the perennial regrowth, the magic of something hidden, dormant, coming into being again that bonded him to his garden. Its predictability, its steadfastness.

"It's the bloody chaos of it all," he muttered, more to himself than to Mr Stokes, who was back looking at his drawings.

Why couldn't things just settle down? Why couldn't they go back to the way they were before? Though, if pressed, he would not be able to define what he meant by before. His garden made him nostalgic.

For the next hour he worked at stabilizing the peasticks, with Mr Stokes still in his garden, now smoking his pipe. He wished he could ask his neighbour about his line of work, what the drawings were that held his attention so. He was curious, yes, but also cautious. What if there was something untoward going on next door? How would he recognize it? Moreover, what exactly could he do about it?

In three days Edmund would read about the events in Germany that would become known as Kristallnacht, the Night of Broken Glass, the destruction and looting of Jewish businesses in cities throughout Germany, a series of pogroms against the Jewish population, and he would think of his garden and the chaos that had brought on a lingering sadness he could not explain, and could certainly not have shared with Miriam. He was not one for fanciful thinking, but the events in Germany that had hordes of attackers smashing homes, businesses, synagogues, anything belonging to the Jewish population, made him think of the maelstrom in his garden, and he wondered if the storm they'd had might be a kind of omen of what was to come.

20 NOVEMBER 1938

THE ABORTIONIST

The gate was swarming with dried brambles; a blackberry bush crept along the fence unfettered, ignored, so that its prickly branches formed a barrier to the cottage garden. Miriam reached out, pinched a stem, and pulled it back so that Audrey could go through the arbour gate, ducking as she did so.

"This is taking discretion a bit far, I'd say," said Miriam as she followed her in. They'd entered a wild garden, faded sprays of blues, pinks, the brown-tinged petals of red geraniums left to die on the stem, feathery tufts and leggy plants—leeks, sweet William, fennel—gnarly clumps of greenery, one species crouching into the next, and a broad bed of parsley that seemed intent on bringing a sense of order to the garden. Farther down a pathway there was a table on which stood a teapot, two cups, two plates, empty save for some crumbs. There were blankets draped around two chairs, the late season heat bringing everyone outdoors.

"Hello?" Miriam called out, but her voice was timid, as if there was something untoward in the scene. "We should go knock on the door," she said, turning to Audrey, but at that moment a woman appeared with a tray.

"Oh," she uttered, now holding the tray like a shield.

"We're here for Dr Whittaker." Audrey stepped forward.

The woman eyed Miriam and Audrey, the tray lowered to her side.

"He's not available at the moment," she said. "He's ill."

"I'm sorry to hear that. We'll come again another day."

The slow whine of the door opening drew their attention, and a man walked out to them, his step slow and deliberate, his eyes sweeping the ground before him.

"What is it, Alfred?" The woman went to him, held her hand out to his.

"I've come for my tea," he said, then sighting the two strangers, smiled. "We have guests."

"You should be resting now." Her hand firmer on his, the other against his back as she guided him inside.

Audrey and Miriam exchanged glances, both now aware that their trip had been a waste.

"The autumn joy are beautiful." Miriam walked farther along the path, reaching out to the plants along the way. She went to the end of the garden, to the rose bush that climbed the trellis. She leaned into one, sniffed deeply, and turned back to Audrey.

"No scent," she said. "It's such a disappointment, one expects it always, then nothing with these new breeds."

They'd come to see Dr Whittaker unannounced because they'd heard he'd retired, and they'd had hope of convincing him to perform one more abortion. There was no reason to expect that he would agree to it, even if he wasn't incapacitated as he obviously was, but they could do nothing but try.

It was gossip they were going on, gossip about the abortionist outside Farnham. Audrey had seized on this lead, one that would put into practice what she preached, and they'd made inquiries. Miriam had asked Mildred, who near laughed in her face, her arm sweeping across the room where two of her children were in a battle over a toy, the other hand resting on the mound of her stomach. What would she know of such a thing? she said. But she did know someone who might know something. Within a few days they had directions to Dr Whittaker's.

"We can't help you, I'm afraid." The woman reappeared, speaking to Audrey while Miriam was still down farther in the garden. "How far along?" she gestured.

The sun was low in the sky, the light intense in the garden so that the woman held a hand out to block the glare.

"I'm Audrey Wentworth and that is Miriam Thomas. We're here for someone else."

"Edith Whittaker." She placed the dirty dishes on the tray and motioned for the two women to sit. She told them that the last procedure he'd done was two years ago, the decline rapid and startling since. Hardly anyone came around anymore. She figured news like this, of the doctor's downfall, spread like influenza. Gossip. The rot of it. The way people cling to it as if it connected them somehow, like the mesh of spider silk, loose and awkward. "I thought no one came around anymore because they knew not to," she said without rancour.

She'd been his nurse as well as his wife. Loneliness spanned her days now, she admitted. She missed the patients, the feeling of usefulness.

"It's a servant." Miriam's tone abrupt, rude. Audrey looked at her sharply, but there was no response to the rebuke. "She was assaulted. She's quite desperate. We told her we would try to help. Dr Whittaker was her last chance."

Edith scooped crumbs from the table, flung them into the flowers, her eyes flicking toward Miriam, then over to Audrey.

"I am sorry," she said, finally, looking toward the house. "For him, for me, for the young servant woman." She paused as she heard a motor car passing by. "I can't get used to them yet," she said. "The noise startles him—the airplanes, too."

"How did you know?" Audrey asked. "How did you notice his mind was going?"

"Incidents like this. We'd have tea, then ten minutes later he'd ask when it would be ready. At first it was hardly noticeable, a forgetfulness we all expect. Then names forgotten, a look he'd get as if stranded in the forest. In the examining room he rallied. The routine of everything saved him. Though the last one I had to take over." Her eyes lowered, then she got up and crouched in a nearby bed of herbs and pulled out a handful of leaves.

"Pennyroyal," she told Audrey as she handed them to her after wrapping them in a cloth. "Tea infusion thrice daily for the next week. This garden looks a mess, but it's our pharmacy. Groundsel for menstrual cramps, feverfew for fevers, migraine headaches, and problems with menstruation and labour. Shepherd's purse for headaches and bladder infections, and burdock for colds, rheumatism, and stomach ailments." She was pointing and pulling at the plants as she identified them.

"Come back for more if you need it," she said. "It doesn't work for everyone."

Audrey was clutching the pennyroyal as they left. Edith walked them to the gate, absently picking at stray weeds and deadheading the flowers. The afternoon had dissolved into a mood of melancholy, the regrets almost too abstract for them to speak of.

"Come back again," she repeated. "I have other remedies if this one fails. Parsley. Cotton root bark, blue cohosh, mugwort."

Miriam stepped through the gate and paused, a thought forming. She turned to the doctor's wife to speak to her, but she was already stepping back into her garden.

26 NOVEMBER 1938

LONDON FOG

I t was hard not to think of the past now. For years the lectures had kept Audrey firmly in the present, and even with hope, the future. Now everything was speeding up; the past and the future a constant pendulum from which she was trying to free herself. The war, the abortionist, that pregnant woman she was trying to help, and the question of desire that lingered even now. What had Miriam released in asking about it? What power it had, desire. The power to change her life.

The river, an antidote. Up and down she swam, daily, to shake this thing that had got hold of her. Her past.

She'd woken in the night, sweat quickly turned to a chill that had her shivering under her covers until dawn. It occurred to her that she needed to confess, she needed someone to bear witness, to hear her speak of that time in her life when all innocence had seeped away without notice. It was Miriam who'd got her started. Now she knew she must tell her more, things her family didn't know, things she was not sure she herself knew. That's what was needed. A release from all the things she had come to know.

When Miriam arrived, she told her as much, this need to tell her things about her past.

"Perhaps a priest—"

"No, not a priest. I want you to listen, that's all."

They had arranged to meet for tea, but Audrey was too agitated to sit so they walked instead. "Feel this," Audrey ordered removing her glove and holding her hand out to the sun's warmth. "This heat is like a gift this time of year." She slid her glove back on and tramped along the river's edge.

"I was to have lunch with Robert," she began after they'd walked up the riverbank. "I had arrived in London on a series of lies. The first was I had told Robert I was free that day so we could meet. I wasn't free, exactly, since my cousin Margaret and her husband, Benedict, were arriving from Somerset, and I was expected to be there. The second lie was to my parents: First my mother, whom I told that I'd arranged to have lunch in London with a school friend who was leaving for America. Then to my father, to whom I embellished the story with a visit to the doctor, knowing he would not accept a lunch date as an excuse to miss family obligations but would not question a medical appointment. That was far too personal a topic for him to pursue. The last lie had been to the taxi driver who took me to the restaurant to meet 'my husband.' I told him that for no other reason than to hear the sound of it. The unacknowledged lies, of course, where those that sat deep inside me, buried to protect me from the reality of how uncomfortable I was making this trip, pretending to be someone who might dash up on the train to London for lunch, who might be in love with a man I knew so little about.

"I barely noticed the fog at first, but the train that took me into London began to slow, and soon all my imaginings of the day, my rehearsal of the moment we would meet, the details of the conversation I would initiate, receded, and I saw that the landscape was becoming shrouded. By the time we reached the station we were at a snail's pace, and I became angry, frustrated, anxious that I would be late for my meeting with Robert.

"I should have anticipated the fog that was then so frequent, though in fact I'd experienced it only a few times. Three or four times a month it descended like a ghost to hold London captive. Trains stalling, cars crawling through streets, walking treacherous, breathing itself taunting death. It's London's location in the Thames estuary that makes it prone to mist, but combine it with the coal smoke and it creates the pea-souper and makes living in the city a health hazard.

"But Robert was there waiting for me, and he, too, seemed timid, pleased to see me, as if I mightn't have come. And there was champagne, oysters, and a friendly chap who stopped by our table to say hello to Robert, suggesting Sussex at the weekend as if it were an event and not just a place, and the time passed as if neither of us had anyplace to be, no further appointments to make, or trains to catch, so when we stepped outside, into the sulfurous yellow mist that stubbornly blocked our way, we hardly knew what to do.

"A taxi to the train station. But the driver said it was no use. No trains running, he told us. But Robert was adamant. *Just go, man,* he told him. *We'll see to it.*

"But the taxi driver was right. No trains running. So we began our charade as Mr and Mrs Robert Fuller and took out a room at the train hotel. We did this with so few words—*I mustn't. There is no other option. Well, of course*—that we were in the room before we'd even imagined what it would be like to be there. It was difficult to be the lesser one, to not know entirely what to do, especially when we were finally alone, the heavy door clunking shut. Alone, we had no purpose, and the silence made us both awkward, so I wandered the room, touching furniture or curtains as if I were considering making a purchase."

Audrey paused as the sound of an engine ripped in the distance, her head cocked as she glanced up. "A tractor," she said. "I have become attuned to all manner of noises these days."

"Come," said Miriam, leading her away. "There's a pathway to the forest along here." They walked through the field from the river and soon they were in the enclosure of the forest, on a pathway just wide enough for the two of them.

"I had a heightened sense of curiosity that extended to sex," Audrey continued.

"My experience was so limited I felt not so much desire, but a series of questions, of what a man looked like under his clothes, what one was to do, where one put one's hands, should I lean in or step back from a kiss? I had been educated on the mechanics; it was the nuances that left me adrift.

"At any rate, a message was sent home. I would stay in London with my friend, I told them, the one who was to go to America. 'Boston,' I told my mother the next day when I returned home. 'Sarah will be visiting her aunt in Boston.' The lie slid off my tongue so effortlessly I barely blinked. I had become a sophisticate in the last twenty-four hours. 'How dreadful,' my mother consoled, 'to be trapped in London with that relentless fog.'

"But it wasn't dreadful. Not at all. Robert was sweet. He ordered tea, more champagne, spoke of his plans to go to France in the summer, and I imagined this was setting me up for an invitation. I had so little knowledge of life outside of my family that my constant emotion was one of yearning.

"Such a different time. You asked me about desire, and it's true that's what guided me, but it seemed in line with the mood before the Great War. Yearning was everything. This was the era of optimism, hope, innovation. My parents had taken me to the Paris Exposition in 1900; I'd been on a moving sidewalk, seen talking films, an escalator, and everyone's favourite, the Palace of Electricity. So many lights—five thousand multicoloured incandescent lamps. The extravagance!

"That day in London with Robert, the posh restaurant, the luxurious hotel, it had symbolized something of that time in

Paris, and those lights, which, to my child eyes, seemed like they would forever lead me to my own brilliant future.

"But in London that night it was gas lamps that lit the hotel, and somehow the room where we spent the night took me back to Paris, and I held on to the mood after I'd gotten up, unable to sleep, and sat by the window, in the shadows from the one lamp I'd left on. I rode the tide of this gaiety all the way home the next day and the day after that, feeling intoxicated.

"It took me nearly two months to acknowledge that I was pregnant, a full month after Robert had left for France. It wasn't as though he'd ignored me during this period, it was the fact that his attention, so warm and companionable, was altogether less frequent than I'd expected. I saw us as lovers, he seemed to think of me more as someone to take to a party. One of Robert's lovelies."

Audrey walked over to a tree that had died still standing, though one large branch had split away and lay across the forest floor, moss and decay creeping over it. Miriam went over and perched on it.

"Have I told you too much?" Audrey asked, joining her.

"Probably," said Miriam. "But there is no untelling, is there?"

"There's more. But not for today."

The engine that had gone quiet started up again, and Audrey jumped up. "Bloody noise. Is there nowhere to have peace? Even here. Is there nowhere to hide?"

28 NOVEMBER 1938

THE LONG COLD NIGHT
INTO WINTER

I t was the houseboy from Carrington House that went to Frank's looking for Audrey. Frank sent Michael to get his aunt and bring her to speak to the young man who looked quite frantic. It was Elspeth. She was not doing well, very poorly in fact.

It had been a week since Audrey had seen her, two days after she'd been to the abortionist. They were still searching, she'd told her. Though in fact Dr Whittaker was their only lead. They'd met at the fence on the edge of the Carrington property. Elspeth, flushed from the run, eyes watery, her body keening with the news that they'd had no luck. They'd find someone, they would send a note, Audrey promised. She had networks, people in the cause who might know.

When she arrived at the Carringtons', Audrey could see that Elspeth was nearly delirious with fever, her face ruddy, glistening with sweat. She ordered linens and a basin of cool water. She leaned into the young woman, wiping her face with a damp flannel, assuring her that the doctor would be there soon. Elspeth was frightened, her face a grimace as she tried to lift her head.

"I did it," she whispered. "I did it." Audrey sat back and dipped her fingers into the water, brushing the young woman's forehead, her face, her neck, until she was able to consider what she needed to do. When her mind was settled, she left the room to find Michael, who she instructed to take a note to Dr Whittaker's wife.

Everything seemed urgent and frantic now that she knew the circumstances, the need to get the specific kind of help that would be used in these situations. She wished Miriam were here; they'd come to rely on each other. They should not be friends, the two of them, too many barriers forbid it, the difference in age, in class. And she hardly knew what it meant to have a friend.

But to rely on someone, did that constitute a friendship?

Audrey rushed back to Elspeth. "He mustn't know," she muttered, over and again in her delirium. There was a young man she wanted to marry, Audrey learned, but even in the flush of illness she would not reveal his name. Audrey wondered about the young man who'd fetched her and now stood out in the hall looking as though he'd seen a ghost. Was he Elspeth's betrothed?

Edith Whittaker arrived within the hour with a medical kit that included herbal tinctures. She had brought her husband, fearful of leaving him alone, and had asked for tea and biscuits for him. With just her and Audrey in Elspeth's room, she lifted the covers and saw that Elspeth had lost a lot of blood. She hauled the bloody linens away and lay new ones as best as she could. Audrey fought nausea as she gingerly pulled the sheets from one side when Edith ordered her to do so. At least the war had prepared her for some things.

The heat from Elspeth's body filled the room, and Audrey longed to step out into the hallway. When a maid swept in after giving tea to the doctor, Audrey told her to get rid of the soiled sheets that lay in the corner and followed her out the door as if ensuring that she do so. But in fact, it was the cool air of the hallway she needed. This was not the time to faint.

"How long has she been ill?" Edith asked when Audrey came back after a moment.

"The houseboy said she fell ill yesterday," Audrey replied.

The two women kept vigil through the night, an unspoken responsibility to this woman whom they each felt they had let down. When she died at dawn, they left the house, instructing the maid to inform the Carringtons as soon as they returned later that morning. Audrey would come back the next day and let them know the full story, the one that put their son at the centre of this mess.

Winter crept in with Elspeth's death. As they neared Christmas, bitterly cold winds brought heavy snow to parts of southern and eastern England. Audrey cancelled her lectures, kept her stove running, and invited Miriam over from time to time. If Miriam had any thoughts of being Audrey's project, she quickly quelled them, bringing maps she'd drawn as if she could lure Audrey from her isolated outpost with them.

Frank came, too, ensuring that Audrey was eating well, puzzled by her sudden reclusiveness. He had come to rely on Miriam. Her natural flying ability gave him confidence that they could win the race. This he boasted to Audrey, who saw that he was not himself, yet she could not determine who he had become.

"You mustn't be so much alone," he scolded her in those days after Christmas, when hoar frost kept everything glistening.

"Why? Why mustn't I be alone?" she asked him, knowing that he, too, had the habits of a hermit.

"It's too much. To be alone, just listening to the wireless, reading the news in the newspaper. We'll all go mad if we don't escape it."

The real news of these winter months was the campaign of terror against the Jews in Germany, many of whom were beginning to leave this country of torment.

That Hitler had managed to mesmerize the Germans with parades, brightly tinted flags, and operatic staging, the rituals restoring colour to their lives, presented a phenomenon that was difficult to understand and harder for Audrey and Frank to connect with as they sat drinking tea by the fire in a caravan by a river several hundred miles away. But the link was there: they would be affected, they had already been affected.

2 DECEMBER 1938

MANCHESTER GUARDIAN

GERMAN REFUGEE CHILDREN TO
OCCUPY HOLIDAY CAMP

More than 200 refugee children from Germany who are due to arrive at Dovercourt Bay Holiday Camp, near Harwich, to-day will sleep in little chalets with electric light, carpeted floors, and cozy beds. Some of the chalets will be converted into classrooms, where a staff of German teachers will continue their education. A number of volunteers have arrived and stocks of clothing are being graded. A full medical examination will be carried out on disembarkation at Harwich.

The government has rejected the idea of a compulsory national register and compulsory service in peace time. In this it is indisputably wise. Any attempt to apply compulsion before we are in war or under its direct menace would set up enormous social friction. It would also consort oddly with Mr Chamberlain's optimism about the friendly intentions of the dictators and of his 'go-getting for peace.'

BOOK OF THE DAY
D.H. Lawrence by Hugh Kingsmill

Mr Hugh Kingsmill's life of D.H. Lawrence has at least two negative virtues: it is not written by a woman, and it is not written by a devotee. He has given the fullest account of Lawrence's life that has yet appeared, with a number of details I have not seen in print before, but refuses to be tempted into criticism. Yet Lawrence was an artist and unless one comes to terms with him there is much to be missed.

4 DECEMBER 1938

SMALL TENTATIVE GESTURES

"The children have arrived in Harwich. Almost two hundred from a Jewish orphanage in Berlin that was destroyed during riots." Edmund held the newspaper before him, reading to Miriam.

Perhaps because this had been so much on their minds—children, that is—this particular story brought the possibility of war to them, a reminder of the superb and cruel irony that life could present. Miriam fixed eggs on toast for them both before leaving to go on her flight with Frank.

"But they'll be placed in homes . . . good homes," she'd told him.

"Good homes!" His look incredulous. "Who will determine what good homes these children should go to? The wounds have penetrated. The scars are for life."

She'd never heard him speak so harshly, the paper snapping with each turn. Was he angry at Hitler? The authorities at the orphanage? The people who had taken them in? There were so many ways to see why this moved him so. The loss of his parents when he was not quite a man, the loss of his own unborn children. But there was no way to take this further, to move from this distressing situation that was sending so many signals about war, about humanity, about how divisive they could be in their own kitchen, with their own private fears, disappointments. They were operating as islands at the moment, visiting each other through careful words, small tentative gestures.

She went to him, put her hand on his shoulder, and yearned to pull him into her arms, but he was too worked up, too detached from her in this moment.

"They need food, shelter." This would only rile him.

"They need so much more than we can give them."

Miriam wondered if he wanted to take one in, provide a home, at least for the time being. This thought frightened her, the responsibility of it. Already she was moving toward some other service if war came. She rubbed her hand along the side of his cheek. "You're getting yourself worked up, Edmund."

And later, during that flight when clusters of cumulous clouds splashed ominous shadows across the landscape, making her mapping more guesswork than precise scenes, she could not get these children out of her mind, nor the conversation with Edmund, who said that they were being moved around like cattle, that they would never get over this displacement. They had already suffered having to leave their childhoods, their mothers, their fathers, and now they were sent to a holding pen in another country.

These worries, she thought, as she banked to return to the airfield, why did they chase her here in the sky, her one safe place?

The landing had been one of her best, and when she and Frank jumped from the cockpit and folded the wings back to take the plane to the hanger, he told her so.

"You'll be ready for the King's Cup," Frank said, but he had turned to Peter, who had come to help take the airplane inside, and whose wry smile made Miriam wonder if there was a joke being played at her expense. She left quickly to change from her flying suit and realized that she'd forgotten her maps in the airplane. The doors remained open and she could hear no voices so she thought they'd left, but when she rounded the corner she sighted them, Frank's hand at the back of Peter's head, their cheeks resting against each other as Peter held him in a half embrace.

The wind blew up, sending debris skittering across the floor, but the two of them seemed oblivious to the wind, the leaves, the quick intake of Miriam's breath. She knew she ought to step back, knew that with the slightest turn of a head she would be caught, but she was so immediately absorbed in the scene, shocked by the daring, the brutal truth of what she was seeing, but also by the tenderness, the shy expression of adoration that comes from fresh love.

She took a step back, turned, and took long, brisk strides away and waited a full ten minutes before returning to the empty hangar.

13 JANUARY 1939

SABOTAGE

"The Wilkes's boy was knocked off his bicycle by John Fisher driving his motor car during one of the blackout trials," Edmund said, while still on his hands and knees before the wireless. "'Black as tar, the night,' the driver said. No moon, the road barely visible. I don't know how the ministry expects drivers to see with no lights. There was the Wilkes's boy right in his path." He sat back on his heels. "Nothing seems to be working as it should."

They'd become attached to their wireless, a Marconiphone, newly purchased, and a way of staying connected now that the national network had been established. Their nightly ritual, listening to the 6:00 p.m. news. They tried to glean something that would tell them whether war would soon be with them.

But Edmund was having a steady battle with the new wireless, erratic interruptions, crackling, whooping interference, and these he took to be another sort of war, one of sabotage, the Germans infiltrating communications, which to his mind, was as bad as dropping bombs. He kneeled before the wireless as if at an altar and fiddled with the knobs while Miriam sat in her chair, gazing out the window.

"How is he? The boy?"

"He lived, but a broken leg has made him near useless on the farm now. No charges laid, but this blasted war that's still hovering's been put to blame."

The war wasn't to blame for everything, Miriam wanted to say. She rubbed her hand up and down the upholstery of her chair, her agitation mounting as the whir and crackle of the wireless rose and fell, thinking of progress and its aftermath. People knocked off bikes, wireless radios that hissed, wars that failed to materialize.

War had become a ghost to them, as chilling as a spectre and just as elusive.

It was the lack of bananas that frightened Miriam for some reason. They hadn't gone yet, but soon would be. That's what Mr Staines, the greengrocer, had told her. "Sure as not," he'd said. It was the government, he'd said, they were pulling back, keeping reserves.

"I've got it, here it is." Edmund lifted his hands from the knob and the voice of the newsreader pulsed through the wireless.

"Prioritizing," is what Mr Staines, had told her, cocking his head as if to suggest something ominous. Earlier that day she'd been to the market after her flight with Frank and had noticed the reduced stock. They'd seen the effect in the shop, but now the weekly market was diminishing, too. Like a thief who pilfered in increments, the war that was not was stealing bits of their lives. Mildred had complained about the lack of cherries when Miriam had seen her at the village fête a few months back. For them the shortages were the most significant sign that the world was turning on an altered axis.

Edmund finally settled back in his chair, confident the wireless would deliver the evening news, while Miriam continued to work the arm of her chair, thinking of her conversation with Mr Staines, who had also told her that the man from the Ministry of Agriculture had gone around to the Hutching farm and told them they would have to turn one of the pastures over to flax. Labourers would be a premium now, with many young men signing up, inflamed by war talk. When Mildred told Miriam that her children cried at the sight of the gas masks, thinking them to be the face of a monster, they'd agreed that things had gone too far.

"Come, love, drink your tea. It will get cold." The wireless was supposed to ease their mind, allow them to feel modern while keeping up with events. Give them a shared ritual outside of work. But Edmund had become fretful lately, and she'd wondered if the uncertainty of war was starting to grind him down. Would having a war make things easier? Funny to think how his mind worked, the need for a clear decision outweighing the actuality of war.

What exactly was on his mind? she wondered. She could ask him. This seemed to occupy her conversations with Audrey these days, this question of desire. What is it you desire, Edmund? He'd come up behind her in the store the other day when they were closing, slipped his hand under her blouse, brushed his lips against her cheek. Is it me you desire, Edmund? He'd mentioned a baby again the other night, not in so many words, just that he should finish the cradle so that they'd be ready next time around. Did he think the fact that it had not yet been finished would affect the outcome of a pregnancy?

"Sit down, Edmund," she said, as he leaned forward, his thumb and finger making a slight adjustment on the wireless. "The music will start soon."

He turned to her, his eyes blinking wildly. "Yes, the music," he said, looking at his watch. "It will start soon."

26 JANUARY 1939

FRANK'S FEEL FOR
MECHANICS

"I was given the gift of a wireless when I was nine. It was more the gift of a talent than a link to the wider world, because the thing was broken, and therefore silent." Frank was placing the spanners he'd used on the airplane back into the cupboard.

"And you fixed it." Peter stood leaning on the workbench, his arms crossed tightly against the chill of the hangar.

"My father's brother gave it to me. It seemed a luxury to have such a portable unit that I could claim for myself. My uncle didn't know it was broken when he offered it, only knew that he wanted me out of his garden room, and so he told me to take it up to the bedroom, to listen to it where he would not be able to hear me.

"It wasn't the voices and music on the airwaves that I was interested in, it was the tubes and wires that transmitted the sound. Up in my room, away from the fitful glare of my uncle, I peeled away the back of it. It was a gem, the vacuum tubes like a cluster of perfectly formed stalagmites. I removed the screws on the casing and pulled out the chassis with no clear idea of what I was doing. I ran my hand over the components, held the chassis in my lap as if I could intuit the workings through touch and proximity. Later I would have the language to make sense of each part—transformer, capacitor, resister—the poetry of mechanics."

"It stays with you still, this language of poetry."

"My talent is in mechanics; I only aspire to poetry."

They packed the airplane away, the cold too much to work in, and covered it with the canvas draping. They would go to lunch, they decided. A pint and a warm fire would do them good. They tromped across the field to the car, with Frank still thinking back to that time at his uncle's place. It was cold then, too. He'd worked on the wireless by the fireplace in his room, the air so draughty he would pull the bed covering around his shoulders. He ran his fingers over the tubes one by one, feeling something like a mystic, the art and science of the machine a mystery that held power he could perceive but not yet fully understand. He wanted to consult his uncle, wondering whether he dared ask if this were a knowledge common to adults.

The knowledge of adults, that, too, he was learning during his time with his uncle. He'd been sent to this northern home to recover from his surgery and allow his mother a rest. That's what his father had told him, but his mother didn't seem tired, more that she was unsure of all the talk around her, her words held back, especially with Frank, who would ask again and again when he would be well because he'd been promised he would be.

His father used words like resilience, robust, vigour—words that confused Frank. His uncle had been in a war, his father told him before Frank left, as if this held some meaning for the boy. When would he return? Frank wanted to know. Two months would soon pass, his father assured him.

But they hadn't. Not at first, when his uncle left him in the hours between breakfast and dinner, telling him to walk the perimeter of the meadow as if that alone would fill a day. The neighbour's son, a boy two years older, helped fill that clawing loneliness. Frank's body splayed among the flowers by the side of the path, his leg aching from the rain that would arrive later in the day, and a voice jarring him from a dream of his mother so that when he opened his eyes, it was his mother's face he saw, his own face collapsing into a smile that moved through his body in an instant, so that he sat up abruptly. The voice again, but not his mother's, which rendered him further startled, and then threatened so that he jumped up to his feet, tipsy from the swift movement of his weak leg. Easy, the voice said, easy, this time with a hand reaching out to steady him.

He drew pictures, the boy did, of birds, foxes, badgers, things he saw in nature, which was stated in a manner that suggested a place with an address. The boy began joining Frank on his walks, and they enjoyed this exploration of their surroundings, of each other. They developed a coded language, ways of seeing, that drew a circle around them and chipped away at the lonely hours Frank spent on his own.

After a few weeks he and his uncle were invited to dinner by the boy's father. Frank's recollection of the evening was of dazzling lights shimmering off any number of surfaces—crystal, silver, mirrored glass—the talk so loud and certain that it floated over him, leaving him feeling that he was hidden from it, and that the boy, too, was hidden, with no one directing the conversation to either. It seemed obvious that they should use their secret language, their private gestures. They did not notice the raised eyebrows of the adults, they only knew the conversation around them marched on throughout the evening. Only later did he realize he'd failed somehow. His uncle fuming in a silence that lasted days, the only clue an utterance about his behaviour, and Frank, heartbroken, retreated to his room knowing he'd seen the last of the boy.

"I remember that the chassis felt alive, and I hugged it gently so as not to break the glass tubes." They had settled into the pub, ordered pints of bitter, a couple of pies. "I looked down on them one by one, examining the clear tubes with the silver mirror-like spot on them, then found one with a white haze inside, one that did not look like the others. I jiggled it until it came loose, and when I pulled it out, I wrapped it in my handkerchief and put it in the drawer with my underwear."

At this Peter laughed.

"Later, when I could sneak away, I spoke to the car mechanic, who explained that the tube had lost its vacuum and would need to be replaced. A week later with the help of the mechanic I bought a new tube and placed it in the vacant spot. I put the chassis back into the case and tightened the screws, then adjusted with the knobs until I was able to hear voices."

"A feel for mechanics." Peter tipped his beer toward Frank's in congratulations of this feat. "To fix a wireless at that young age. Now, that's a talent."

But Frank could not tell him that in fixing the wireless, in listening to those voices, he'd been made to feel lonely all over again.

20 JANUARY 1939

ALL AT SEA

The storm blew in before dawn, ice pellets attacking the caravan so that Audrey in her dreamy fog thought it was finally the war at her door. The sway of her home made her feel as though she were at sea, and she blamed her nausea on the wind and not on the tooth extraction she'd had three days ago. Too ill to eat, too tired to make tea, all she could do was stay in bed and listen to the world outside. She feared for the birds in this onslaught, hearing tree branches snap under the weight of ice.

From her window she saw ice forming in the eddy of the river, the water coursing through the floes like a snake following its prey. The wind through the conifers like a machine gathering strength.

She wished Frank would come to her. She would not say as much to him, but she needed him and this need frightened her. If he would just bring her tea, sit with her a while.

Surely, he would worry, she thought. It had been two days since he'd checked on her.

She imagined the war arriving in the cover of night, taking out her world beyond the caravan. It was capable of doing that she knew, the insidious, heartless nature of it, capable of that and more.

She remembered hearing planes overhead, the relentless drone that came from some point beyond the trees working its way up to a roar as they came overhead. There may have been the sound of a gun, too. Had that been last night? Yesterday? Or was this a memory from long ago? The medication had made her drowsy, her thinking woolly. Her days and nights confused, a coasting in and out of consciousness.

Perhaps she had lived here too long.

In this enfeebled state she felt panic rise within her, so she pulled back the blankets, and sat up in the bed, only to collapse on one elbow from dizziness. Deep breath. Eyes closed. The world stopped moving, so she gingerly placed one foot then the other on the floor, checked for water in the kettle, and turned on the hob.

A branch clattered on the front landing. She needed to get up, get out. She could be crushed under the weight of a fallen tree. She pulled the nightgown over her head and caught sight of herself in the mirror, her skin the colour of cement, the exposure a shock as if she had never seen her own flesh. The musky scent of her body, like that of springtime soil. Ice rain tapped at her window, and a gust sent the caravan back to sea.

She couldn't leave, she knew, not now with the weather holding her captive.

She made her tea and got back in bed to drift off again. When she awoke two hours later, she had no idea where she was.

Eyes held shut, the silence so pure that she felt she'd been transported to an inner sanctum, separate from all she knew. Then the cry of a wood pigeon and, with it, relief that she was indeed home and not relegated to an institution. She reached for the book she'd been reading and opened it up, but the words floated across the page, incomprehensible. In the presence of everything that held her to her bed, the weather, her fear, the pain of her tooth, she was left with a solitude that took her back to herself, restored in her all the reasons to be in the caravan, to be alone. She patted the blankets around her body and propped up a pillow. She peered through the curtains to see blazing sunshine.

The party. Was it just five days ago? The Carringtons' anniversary, and Frank insisting they must go. She protested because she was privy to a history Frank would never know, of young Carrington, the idiot son of decent parents, a brash and entitled man whom Audrey knew only through the servant Elspeth.

She spotted him immediately, his swagger giving him away. He filled the room as though everyone was aware he needed more space than most. She could hardly bear to watch him talk to one guest then the next as if he had something pressing to share. She questioned her own moral compass in that moment. Was she a voyeur, was she accepting that, after all, what was done was done? She'd been curious, watching him, and keeping watch on him throughout the evening, knowing she was invisible to him. She behaved beautifully, had her full kit of charm on so that even Frank was under the impression she was enjoying herself. She sipped her sherry and felt her face burn with pain from the infected tooth, and when he finally came to her, introduced himself, she leaned into him so that he alone would hear her words.

"I'm sorry for your loss."

He flashed back, half smiling, confusion washing over him, his mouth parted as if he might speak, but clearly unable to as his mind whizzed through a past that held too many stories of negligence, though hardly any amounting to loss in his mind. He would never know what she knew of the young woman he impregnated in the library that night, rape not a word he thought applied to him. He would never understand the desperation Elspeth felt when she came to Audrey, wild with worry, shame, horrified at a future that could see her on the streets. He would never understand the level of terror Elspeth felt when the hemorrhaging began, when life spilled out of her as a final punishment to the invasion she'd all but blamed herself for. *I'm sorry for your loss.*

This was her triumph, satisfying beyond the waving of placards, yet she was filled with a despair soon overwhelmed by pain as her tooth worsened, and Frank, rescuing her from the party, insisted they see a doctor immediately.

11 FEBRUARY 1939

THE GERMANS

I n the village the cockerel sounded. The soft, clear light of early morning brought sparkle to the night dew, a warm day promised. It was Saturday, market day, and as Miriam made her way to the village centre, her strides long and impatient, she slipped on a stone that sent her basket rolling ahead of her. She was distracted, anxious to be done with her shopping, to get to Hackley for her morning flight. Losing her footing brought her back to the awakening village, the low whispers of two women across the street, a motor car firing up, a dog barking. The bell on the door of Grange Butchers jangled as a woman exited, glaring at Miriam, who blocked her way, bent over to rub her ankle.

She straightened up, re-pinned a strand of hair, and continued on. She walked more slowly, favouring her bruised ankle, perspiration gathering in the folds of her dress. She stopped again, noting a poster for Air Raid Precaution volunteers, and one advertising milk, praising the effects on charm and beauty. *It's not just luck—it's milk.* From around the corner, she heard the calls of the market traders, the village coming to life as the sun crested the buildings.

"Filthy language, and behaving like wild beasts." The gossip of Mrs Grange, the butcher's wife, and a woman Miriam didn't recognize. They were speaking of an incident from the night before, the Williams brothers drunk and disorderly again, this time striking the police constable "directly on the nose."

Miriam skirted the women and was nearly run down by young Penny Franklin, who was cycling to the market, late as usual to help her mother at the stall.

Miriam limped over to a bench on the edge of the village green. The sun was high enough to give warmth, and Miriam sat back for a moment, watching the bunting from the village fête last September flutter in the breeze. It had been a good fête, Edmund on the winning team of the cricket match, his dahlias garnering second prize at the village hall, and the abundance of pies, cakes, and other delicacies pushed all thoughts of shortages aside. They'd had hope then, a relief that carried them through days of uncertainty.

She spotted Mildred crossing the green, the slow lumber of a woman used to hauling laundry and children. She shouted at them now, lagging behind, playing some sort of game of tag, and Miriam thought back to the play at the village hall, *Robin Hood*, in which Mildred's eldest took part. At the end, in a rousing celebratory stance, she'd shouted "Heil Robin Hood," her arm flung out before her. The audience laughed, then looked side-ways to one another, the girl falling into a fit of giggles. How would she know such a thing? Miriam wondered.

It was the wireless, no doubt, all the villagers glued to it each evening. For Edmund it was the news, for Miriam everything else the new wireless offered. She could hardly wait to turn it on in the morning when service began at 10:15. It was the music she liked most, and she was past caring about what others would think of her listening to it on her own when taking a break from the shop. She suffered through the organ music played at noon and had begun listening to the German language lessons because she'd heard others say it might be useful. But for what, she wondered, not daring to think what an invasion might look like.

Miriam stretched and rotated her ankle, tested her weight on it, and rose to meet Mildred, her source of village news. Last week it was the vicar's son who signed up to the Royal Air Force, and this after the vicar himself had given a sermon only six months ago warning of the image of war, how it had become a dangerous attraction to the youth of today, the medals and uniform luring them in.

This week it was the shortage of oranges.

The two women mourned the oranges and complained about the government decisions. But Miriam didn't really want to talk about this; she wanted to tell Mildred about an airplane crash near Alton she'd read about in the morning paper. The RAF pilot had survived, having jumped at a thousand feet, but the wireless operator and bomber observer were killed in the accident witnessed by a fourteen-year-old boy.

Miriam wanted to know more about the boy and how he might have reacted after such a sighting. It wasn't the spectacle of the event that drew her, it was how one might deal with the tragedy. She imagined the talk at the Coach and Horses, where Mildred's husband was publican. Not much really happened in the village, someone knocked off a bicycle, a drunken spat—the gossip almost a consolation, a sense of normalcy they'd lean into in these days where the morning papers brought only bad news from the continent alongside the advertisements for milk, rejuvenation tonics, and settee sets.

But the air crash brought everything close to her.

"Are you all right?" Mildred asked when Miriam took a handkerchief to her brow.

"Yes, it's my ankle. Turned on a cobble."

"That'll keep you grounded."

Miriam caught sight of Mildred's youngest pointing to the sky, a whir of engines suddenly grabbing their attention.

"The Germans. The Germans," the eight-year-old called out, manic with excitement and fear, his arms flailing as he ran back and forth between mother and siblings. "The Germans." His cry weakened when he saw the squadron still in the distance, unsure now what he should do.

Miriam saw them exposed as prey, there on the great expanse of green and nowhere to hide. She thought of Edmund, wondered if he was still at the shop or if he'd gone home for elevenses. The boy was running scared now, the planes, all five of them bearing down on the village, the noise building so that Miriam felt the vibration in her body.

Her mind on Edmund, their vague plan of sheltering in the shed at the bottom of the garden should the attack come. How could they have thought it would save them from this machinery, how could they be so naive not to match strength with cunning?

Just as the boy dived at this mother's skirts, the planes banked.

"Ours," cried Miriam, her hand to her face. "They're ours."

How could she have been thinking of oranges, listening to some trifling village gossip just moments ago? she wondered, shaken. It could have been the Germans. The image of a spray of bullets tearing up the green or a bomb landing in the square haunted her for the rest of the day.

26 FEBRUARY 1939

DANGER

Nights melded into days, the hours marked with a cup of broth, a cold cloth on his brow, tepid tea that Annie forced on him. The pre-dawn hours were the worst; the long night not easily relenting. His bed sheets damp, the soft rattle of the window told him snow was afoot. Sure enough, within the hour, a thrumming at the window, then, before long, an insistent padded tapping that told him that there was ice, too. He yearned to witness the wintry theatrics, went so far as to lift the covers and place one foot on the floor, but the effort proved too much, the room drifting, and he sunk back into the pillows.

He should not be here. Three days captive in his bedroom, a weakness from fever, from dehydration, and from mental exhaustion as he worried about what it meant to have influenza at a time like this. At a time when he should be training with the Air Transport Auxiliary. He'd received the letter two weeks ago. Report to Maidenhead, Feb 23, 1939.

A summons. An official letter that told him to come. He was wanted.

A drink in the pub to celebrate. Peter insisted. A beer, a whisky, the over-stoked fire that turned their cheeks ruddy. The talk of flights made, near misses, failed engines, bad winds, superb landings. Then plans, to Canada. There were air races in Canada, and Frank imagined a kind of freedom that allowed him to be someone else, someone who could travel that far, fly in those races. Was there a future in this, an enterprise they might make of it? They could think about it. Dream about it.

But for now, cheers! To the ATA. Now, that's worth celebrating. A chance to fly across the country, a different airplane each time. He was going to be paid to train, as they saw it. Lancasters, Spitfires—an opportunity, that's what it was. It was temporary, of course, but still if he did it for a year, he'd have experience, and, yes, he could go to Canada; they could establish an enterprise, he and Peter.

Let's drink to it. More whisky. Another beer.

The influenza made details a fog. Had they agreed to fly in Canada, or merely suggested it?

"It's dangerous what we do."

Did Peter say this, or was it the fever's contortion?

Where was Peter now? The weather abysmal these days, he would surely not be flying. London. That's what he'd said. He would be going to London for a few days, and Frank had wanted more. Why London? But they did not possess each other in the way Frank wanted to be possessed, so the question remained unasked.

Once, on his third solo flight, Frank flew through a thin layer of unbroken cloud, and flying above this white blanket, the rapturous blue sky above, he had this intense sensation that he was entirely alone, so much so that he panicked. He cut the throttle and sliced through the clouds back to the dull grey he'd left not minutes before. That was the one time, his one moment of panic in flight. It was enough, all the danger he wanted.

Frank held on to that word, danger. Wrapped up in damp sheets, his body fighting itself, the cool draught from the window recalibrating his temperature. It was not a brave thing that he would be doing with the ATA. He would not be a fighting man. He would be a flying postman. He would deliver planes where they needed to be. This was the brainchild of Gerard d'Erlanger, who proposed to the government that if war should come to their shores, should the expected German attack take place, communications across the country might be lost, and in such circumstances a pool of amateur pilots in light aircraft would be useful.

Is this what he talked about, Peter, when he spoke of danger?

28 FEBRUARY 1939

STRENGTH AND GOODNESS

Miriam took off early as she tended to, noting the red hue of the horizon, thinking of shepherds who would take warning.

They lived in the sky that month. That February had an intensity brought on by excessive sunshine, solar halos, and the appearance of the aurora borealis on the twenty-fourth. The month was packed with activity, and the sky was afire, and in the mapping, Miriam thought of the sparkle of a solar halo as a normal feature. She had decided to work her way to Birmingham, creating segments of a nearly three-dimensional map with contrasting shades of green, the textures of fields, trees, and the endless ladder of railway tracks that she'd included to help give depth and contour to the land below.

On this morning she would be back long before the weather moved in; sometimes she just needed to go up for an hour to free herself from terra firma and its entanglements. The breeze jostled her, but the air was so clear and pure it felt like her entire body was being aerated, her scalp tingling.

Frank had been ill, so she'd made several trips on her own these past weeks, going farther each time. She'd made a padded seat to protect against the cold wooden one, and a pouch to hold a tea Thermos, a tin of biscuits, a flask of whisky. The cold up there was like nothing else.

It was the paper Frank had given her two days ago that added to the normal frisson she felt when flying. Her ticket to the race. The King's Cup.

The last time a Gipsy Moth had won this competition was 1928, and since then the modern airplane had become streamlined, efficient. They were in a new age of aerodynamics.

But the race was for all comers, so a handicap had been established. This meant that the Gipsy Moth could fly next to the new machines, and the calculation of physics would give it a fighting chance.

She held the vision of Frank in the hangar, leaning against the workbench, his face aglow with the news that they would be in the race, and in that moment, a self-reckoning. She had no idea how she'd got there, entering a race with him when there were so many other pilots around, and she said as much. Why me?

"You could be better than me, and I wouldn't care," he said.

"I don't see the sense in that," she told him. "Why would I be better than you?"

"The point is not that you would, but that I wouldn't care. I trust you."

"I think you are saying that we each have our handicap. Mine being a woman."

Frank had laughed at that, said he understood why his aunt Audrey was so fond of her.

Her relationship with Frank was complicated, Miriam knew. There was the class divide, and of course, he was a man. Were people talking about the time they spent together, their newfound status as flying partners? That day of the crash they had somehow come together, each understanding what needed to be done, each understanding the other's limits, so that together they were able to get Peter free. It was that early test that had set them, proved a lingering bond.

Miriam, who had come to trust Frank, understood that sometimes a person just knew, with a sense so deep that it might just sit in their marrow, of the strength and goodness in another. So she was happy for him in this new venture, and happy to be with him in this monumental race. Anything she'd witnessed, which some might consider a mark against his character, was brushed aside like the tiny bits of dust that she found in her airplane each morning.

She took the plane down toward Winchester to the sea, the morning light on the water like dazzling emeralds. She felt the cold front on an icy breeze that burned her cheeks and reached for a second set of gloves. As she neared Southampton, she peered over the edge and saw a cluster of warships tethered to the dock, waiting. Some days when she flew, she'd see them out at sea. Were they so eager for war that they needed a test run? She wondered what it would be like to be a pilot in the war, the town below enemy territory. Those ships eager to take aim at her. From this distance it was impossible to see the people on the ground, only evidence of their existence. Moving vehicles, smoke from chimneys, and yet inside they'd be having a cup of tea, bathing the baby, knotting a tie. How was it possible to harm them? How was it possible to destroy so much life?

16 MARCH 1939

THE MANCHESTER GUARDIAN

A POLICY IN RUINS

It was a melancholy House of Commons that discussed the end of Czecho-Slovakia last night. The Prime Minister had to face the ruins of his policy, had to confess that the 'spirit of Munich' had been broken, had to call off the visit of the British Ministers to Berlin, and had to declare that we could throw no more money to the state we promised to succour. And although Mr Chamberlain lisped his old formulas about returning to the atmosphere of 'peace and goodwill' the conviction was out of them.

NYLON IN BRITAIN: COURTAULDS AND I.C.I.
TAKING UP NEW SUBSTITUTE FOR SILK

Nylon is one of the most striking of the synthetic fibres recently introduced. It promises to be a strong competitor to natural silk and the American claim is that it has an enormous future in hosiery. It has many other uses and has already been employed for toothbrush bristles. Nylon is an entirely new synthetic protein product, having great strength, toughness, and elasticity. It is made from such basic raw materials as coal, air, and water.

17 MARCH 1939

FALLEN

Czecho-Slovakia had fallen to Germany, and Hitler wanted Gdańsk to surrender. The newspapers did not have good news, and Audrey could not bear to read any more. She had recovered, tooth and infection now just a memory. But another malaise had replaced it; her work was stalled, the winter bringing everything to a halt, and she was in mourning. Not only for Elspeth, but for her own past that she seemed unable to surrender. She ignored the headlines but was drawn to the images: of soldiers in formation, of German lorries lined up to enter Czecho-Slovakia, of troops with anti-aircraft guns in the streets of Prague. In an instant she was there, at war again, twenty-three and behind the wheel of an ambulance, somewhere in the depths of the French countryside.

The night alive with light but none where she needed it.

The road appears and disappears according to incendiary activity—bombs, flashes, explosions. The words have become part of Audrey's vocabulary.

Her foot pressed hard into the metal, hands numb, fingers gripping the steering wheel as she manoeuvres the ambulance. Her eyes hard open, alert to the shapes in the darkness, her heart pumping with such force she feels it pulsing under her skin.

Sparks, shrapnel, embers. The residue she has to watch out for as she tries to get back to safety.

Darkness again and she is driving into an abyss, trying to intuit the road, feeling it as she goes along, trying to let the tires guide her back to the hospital.

She shouldn't have kept moving, she knows, shouldn't have gone that far in, that close to the front. One more mile, one more mile, muttered under her breath as the sky explodes around her.

The moaning again.

This time it forces her to stop. She is not sure if she's still on the road or off it, but she jumps out of the vehicle, senses the compression of air, even though the last blast was too far away to have any impact here, and goes to him. Swings open the back door, the squeal of hinges, the metal still warm from the explosion that sent a wall of fire at them not twenty minutes ago.

"I'm here, I'm here," she says, but thinks he can't hear her, can only listen to the pain that has seared the nerves in so much of his body she wonders how he is still alive.

"I'm here."

She doesn't touch him, she knows better, but she wants him to know she is going to get him out of here.

"You're here."

He's conscious. The smell in the back of the ambulance is one of iodine, metal, singed skin, and she is glad she left the door open, the night air a relief to her at least.

The flashes go on and on across the sky, and she can see that he is looking at his hands as if they are no longer his.

"I took them off," he whispers.

"It's okay. I'm here," she repeats. She sits beside him, leans into him, talking quietly as if there were others who might be listening.

"My goggles. My gloves."

"Yes, I know."

Another bomb. This time she does feel the compression and is knocked sideways into him. He does not move, does not react, and she panics, thinking for a second he is dead, that she has killed him. But he is whispering again.

She is taking short, quick breaths, her body humming as she calculates the distance to the hospital, but he is talking so she moves in closer, her mouth sour with dehydration.

"I had to feel it," he was saying. "My thumb on the button. I had to feel when I was shooting." He was lifting his head to her. "I couldn't see. The goggles. I couldn't see." He was flicking his eyes back and forth, from right to left. "I couldn't see when they came on the side of me."

Peripheral vision. Audrey looks around, suddenly aware of how limited her own vision is here in this darkness, knowing she is an easy target despite the Red Cross signs on the ambulance.

"No peripheral vision. I know," her voice soft, reassuring, despite this being the fourth time she's heard the story since she picked him up.

She knows he can't see her now, knows that she is too close as she crouches low, her mouth against his ear. She is outside his vision, even here, in the small space with his goggles off and nothing to stop him from turning to look at her, but she has decided that his sight has been compromised and that he needs her to be that close to him so that he only knows her by touch, by smell.

"You did the right thing," she says. "That was the only way you could have shot down the German plane."

She feels his hair, soft as though freshly washed, and she thinks about what he'd been like as a man, before he was a soldier, a pilot.

"What's your name?" she asks.

A pause. Did he even know it now?

"John."

"We need to go now, John."

The moan like a pained sigh tells her he isn't ready to move and that he'd like to stay forever listening to her try to placate him while their enemies toss bombs in all directions around them, and she would have liked to tell him some of her adventures since becoming an ambulance driver, this one the most daring, though there were others that came close. She could tell him she'd volunteered out of a sense of duty but would be lying because the only duty she'd had was to herself and the need to pour something into her that had substance, a weight that made her story one worth telling, especially after the familiar one that had been told so many times before. Jilted. Humiliated. No one had any appetite for these tales anymore. She'd signed up on impulse, without a thought to consequences. She could drive, it was her talent. She could drive into her own escape.

The night is too long for these stories. Another bomb goes off and Audrey jumps, throws her feet out the back of the ambulance, and starts the engine, driving like she has a bomber on her tail, like the noise that is all around her is bearing down on her alone, as if it were a matter of life and death.

Audrey opened her eyes, put her hands to her face, the remembered smell of diesel filling the caravan. The smell of his singed skin, too. She shivered and threw the blanket from her lap, pushed the caravan door open so that she could breathe air that did not smell like war. She needed to get out, to get back to work, for war would find her here if it were looking. It would find her anywhere.

25 MARCH 1939

PERSPECTIVES

S he was shading the trees along the River Meon as she flew over, an insect scampering across this forest. There was farmland on either side and a road that ran alongside it. A farm marked by the slate roof of the barn, and the covered hay rick next to it. There was a tractor in the yard, she'd seen it when they'd banked, and a paddock where the horses were kept.

But this was too much detail. For now she'd focus on the pear-shaped forest, the river that curled around fields, disappeared into trees, widened and narrowed. The drawing would have to mirror what she saw in the air to be of any use, and, somehow, she'd have to piece together the sections she was working on so that they all lined up.

It had been two hours since she'd taken off, and her mind, soaked in topological markings, had been given a reprieve from the thoughts that were creeping around the edges.

A week late.

The shock of it almost as unbearable as her reaction. Disappointment.

She could never say that out loud, never say this to Edmund, to Mildred, to Audrey, or to the doctor when the time came. The waves of nausea also pointed a finger, accusing her of something she wanted no part of, and this was met with an overarching sense of shame for allowing it to happen, for denying that it was happening, and for wishing it all away.

That day in the clinic, that woman, Betty, why did she keep thinking of her? It was hostility she felt for her, thinking of her now, a resentment. She didn't know the woman; why would she have such feelings toward her? The clinic forced memories, disappointments, fear, dread, and anger.

Her body was making her crazy, the emotions insidious. Did she think poor Betty a witch who allowed her to be impregnated? The hum and purr of this fleshy machinery she inhabited, now possibly taken over by another life, was just that, a place she inhabited, in which she wielded little control. Twinges, aches, waves of nausea all speaking to her, demanding her attention. What more could she give it, this body? What more?

Her new drawings were good, that's what Frank had told her. She showed him the rough sketches she'd made after her latest flight, the perspective so stunning she had to get it down on paper. The irregularity of the landscape told the story of land usage and ownership that went back to medieval times when the open field system and communal pastures were the norm, where peasants would have a shared plough and team of oxen, and the individual farmers would work strips of land in proportion to their investment in the oxen team. This gave way to enclosures in modern times.

Miriam thought about this collaborative way of working, the lands farmed in two- or three-course rotations, and in sync with other farmers. A farmer had to do what was complementary to what others were doing and when they were doing it, otherwise his crops might be grazed by another's animals. There also needed to be communal pastures for the animals. It was a system of survival, an intrinsic community formed to serve all rather than the few. This equitable system of land use was lost when the wealthy landowners decided to privatize the pastures.

How different the landscape would look if this had not changed, if the pastures had remained open.

Perspective was hard. To see things while in motion, without a steady orientation, required an intense engagement with whatever was before her, a gathering of every significant landmark that would add to the picture.

She had to create seams in the map as well, deciding on the perimeter of each section and ensuring the seam met up with the integrity of the overall image. This is what she worked on when back home. Recreating all that she'd seen from the air.

Perspective and boundaries, she thought, as she banked once more over the River Meon. Would these be her guiding principles from now on?

She would wait a week before going to the doctor. Perhaps it was just the flying that had upset her system. She'd been overdoing it these past months, and so soon after the last pregnancy. Perhaps it was all the changes that had caused the delay, and the nausea might be from the banking, the swift descents that Frank was having her do. She would carry dry bread with her now, just in case. She would take a break from flying. She would go to the rally in Guildford with Audrey. She would try not to think about what might be happening to her.

30 MARCH 1939

TOO MUCH TO ASK

S he was stalling, she knew. Her hand lighting on the objects on the top shelf over her desk: a bird carved from oak given to her by Robert (why did she still keep it?), a photo of her as a baby in her mother's arms, a small crystal vase where she kept posies gathered on her walks, a magnifying glass with a turquoise beaded handle given to her by her father. Each a talisman that offered some sort of protection: the bird to remind her of the importance of freedom, the photo the complexity of love, the vase. confirmation that beauty must be present in her life, and the magnifying glass to tell her that things were not as they appeared.

Yes, she was stalling.

Well, not stalling. Thinking. She pulled her mirror out from the cupboard and began pinning her hair up. There were things going on around her, and she needed clarity on the letter from her brother. And she had not seen Miriam in four days, not since their day in Guildford, the day of the demonstration sidetracked by Miriam's condition. The condition of her pregnancy, and the condition of her mind, that of distress.

Audrey checked the clock. Twelve forty-five. Frank would be expecting her in fifteen minutes, and she was hardly ready. She would have liked to cancel the lunch date; she knew that's what they wanted not because they didn't want her there, just that they wanted to be alone. Propriety. That was what she was bringing to this lunch engagement.

It was to be a celebration, too, of course. Frank was leaving for Maidenhead tomorrow to train for the Air Transport Auxiliary, something that would give him an official role should war break out. He was happy these days, more at ease with himself, his shoulders back, his tone less hesitant. She recognized the signs. Fresh love. She could not decide how worried to be.

Up until a few months ago she and Frank had each ring-fenced their contentment. Now they were becoming heedless in a world that was changing day by day, taking risks they'd not considered. Was this how it was to be from now on?

The fact was that both she and Frank had carved out lives defined by isolation. She understood that they thought this was enough to protect them, like others in the country who thought isolation was a protection from war. Though it was not war they hid from.

She could live her unorthodox life, had sought it, but Frank's life had a different complexity that worried Audrey. She had known for some time that he favoured men, that the attentions of all those young women fluttering around at family parties were wasted on him. He deserved to have Peter over for lunch. He deserved love.

Oh, the time, the time. She must hurry.

She pulled the stopper from her perfume bottle and dabbed it behind her ears, then ran a quick hand over her dress, a tug at her sleeves, an adjustment of her collar before snatching her coat from the hook. She stepped outside and paused to feel the warm air on her face. She stood for a few moments in this manner, on her stoop, where the breeze was a tonic. How she longed to turn and go back into the caravan. She would get out of the dress, put on her bathing costume, slip into the river.

Her body taut as a braided rope these days.

Worry seemed to be an occupation; concern for Frank, concern for Miriam, how could she help her without influencing her, without guiding her to the conclusion she suspected Miriam was after.

Audrey walked down the steps slowly, carefully, placing each footstep as if it were ice she was treading on, and at the bottom she stopped again, her hands bunching into fists. The letter from her brother. Received the day before, quickly read and tucked away in the drawer. She would need to go to London, speak to him. He'd heard that Lord Derwent had opened his family home in Osterley Park three days a week at sixpence for admission to the grounds and another shilling to see the house; her brother was forming similar plans for Wentworth House.

A movement in the grass caught her eye, and she looked over to see a hedgehog waddle into the reeds near the river. She took a few steps closer, careful not to frighten it but eager for a closer look. She traced the quivering grass as the hedgehog made its way toward the water. Audrey took another step.

Snap.

A twig.

She bent down, peering through the grass, and saw that the hedgehog, startled, had curled into a spiky ball.

"I know how you feel," Audrey whispered. "But I am no danger to you. I am just curious. But I will go now so as not to disturb you." She was walking backward, stealthily creeping away from the animal that was still as a rock. "I should like to have your defences," she said, still whispering. "Especially when facing my brother." Muttering as she walked to the river, she dipped her fingers in the water then coiled her hands around her neck, the chill rushing through her body. "How can I tell my dear Frank that his father wants to make a zoo of his home?" She was still talking out loud, no longer whispering as she strode up the hill toward the house. "I could tell my brother about Frank's proclivities, that they might not be good for business. Though, perhaps he'd consider this an added bonus to the spectacle. 'Visit the home of a real homosexual.'" Her voice rose at this, her breath heavy as she hiked up the hill, her arms pumping as she neared the top.

She sat down on the bench that served as a resting spot below the house. Two chestnut horses grazed near the fence, and she spotted the gardener cutting back hazel bushes around the paddock gate. She heard the thrumming of an engine and looked up, her tendency these days, the blank sky making her uneasy until she realized that it was most likely a motor car she was hearing and not an airplane. Not a warplane.

She would have to stop reading the newspapers. The south coast would be an easy target. She began imagining a pilot, a German pilot, one who had crossed the channel and was hunkering down across Kent, then Sussex. What would he be looking for? A military base? A town where destruction would be noticed? A woman on a bench would not be on his radar, obscured by the fields, his attention drawn to the house, the nearby village. Still, in the open, perched on the bench of this hill, she felt herself an easy target, because one thing she knew with certainty was the randomness of war.

Audrey pulled herself up tall on the bench, her back straight, her chest thrust out as she drew three deep breaths. She needed to focus on Frank today, his happiness, his future.

This should not be too much to ask.

10 APRIL 1939

FLY FISHING

*F**ly fishing is essentially a simple operation. Swing the rod back holding the line taut, swing it forward releasing the line. It is the weight of the line that gives it momentum so that the fly can land on the water some distance from the fisherman. The fisherman then gently pulls the line, allowing the fly to twitch as it passes through the water so that it looks like a living thing, attracting the attention of passing fish.*

Once you have a bite, however, you have not yet won. Patience and skill are required to secure the lure; any sudden jerking or releasing of the line will send the fish on his way before the hook is fully in place. The trick is to maintain tension in the line, a gentle tug then loosening as the fish swims toward the net, then circling outward only to return, until with careful guiding by the fisherman's steady hand, he swims into the net.

Edmund had been coming to the river for nearly ten years with a rod inherited from his uncle. He began not as a boy like the other men who frequented the river but as a grown man. He had taught himself by reading a pamphlet someone had left in the store: "Chalk Valley Instructions for Fly Fishing." He liked following instructions. He liked that he could learn things in that manner. He'd learned how to plant a garden, how to fly fish, how to cook Yorkshire pudding, all from pamphlets, manuals, recipes, brochures. The careful methodology was freeing for Edmund. Once he knew the science of a thing, he could concentrate on the art—the combination of colours that favoured his garden, the stickiness of the dough, the magic of tracking a fish.

The British brown trout were lazy, couldn't be bothered to swim for their food. They positioned themselves headlong into the stream and let the water bring the food to them. They were hard buggers to catch. The Canadian rainbow trout were stupid but quick. Any twitch in the water and they were after it. A free lunch.

He'd been outwitted by both.

Edmund had been on the river since first light but had not caught a fish. The abundant dew smearing grass on his Wellingtons, the mist filling in the edges along the treeline, his clothes, even his face, moist from the sodden air. Three hours and two bacon baps later, and still no fish.

He'd been out late the night before. More air raid training. Hitler had invaded Czecho-Slovakia a month ago after promising he wouldn't, and everyone had become skittish.

Even Miriam was in a frenzy, trying to increase her air miles as though it were a test to enter the war.

What was his own measure as an air raid warden? One who doesn't believe that war will arrive . . . He was still convinced there would be no war, so it was easy enough to ask the question. He walked through the village with the air raid band on his arm, his notebook in hand, knocking on doors to talk about the particulars of covering windows, explaining how light could leak through the tiniest sliver. Sometimes he just listened to complaints about the nuisance of it. What test was he enduring? War would not come to them. They were protected by the

English Channel, the vast ring of water around them making an attack difficult, unlikely. Yet he was doing his bit, almost as though he believed in it, almost as though he were a double of himself—one who knew and cared about wartime rules and procedures, the most visible embodiment of duty in their village. The other saw it all as a charade.

He would put a pond in the garden come summer, he thought. Then he could have his own fish. Not to catch, but to watch. He liked watching them, their slow, aimless bodies balancing against the current, and he could imagine himself sitting of an evening, the sun warming him as he gazed at his own fish in their enclosure. He'd get started in the next week or so. He'd seen an instruction pamphlet at the post office for that, too.

Fishing required a steady hand and excess patience. That's one point the manual stressed. Patience. It seemed the most important skill of all.

A bite!

The rainbow trout glistened in the clear, pure water as it swam, darting around with the line held taut. Edmund gripped his reel so that there was the illusion of freedom for the trout, albeit one confined to a twelve-foot range in the river.

Edmund reached for the net that rested on a nearby rock, his eyes unblinking as he held the line, releasing a little then tugging the fish back. The range was narrowing so that the fish could only swim a few feet then turn back, the circle tighter and tighter until Edmund slid the net into the water positioned so that the fish would swim straight into it.

Edmund dragged the trout up onto the grass and reached for his priest, one he'd fashioned himself, the metal head heavy enough to kill the fish instantly.

A pond, he thought. Why hadn't he thought of it before?

He did not expect to be called to combat, but he asked himself what he would do if war came to him. What if he were in his garden having just dug a hole for the new apple tree he was planting, the new pond he'd put in shimmering in the background, and a German soldier strode in demanding food, ammunition, shelter. What if this soldier were armed with just a handgun, the question of whether it was loaded hanging in the air as the man, with his jerky, frantic movements, swept down on Edmund, his demands now a threat, and Edmund wielding a spade that suddenly felt like a weapon. The question of speed and reflexes would come into this thought process. Would his spade reach the German's head before he had a chance to react with a shot? If the soldier did try to shoot, would it be half-cocked, perhaps fly across Edmund's shoulder or off to the side because it was a panic reaction and not done with calculated aim?

But then that is what soldiers are trained for, calculated aim in times of unexpected attack. That is what they must do in every situation in which the threat of enemies is close and real. So, the soldier would surely kill him, Edmund concluded, and the spade that would be so awkwardly swung would only agitate him. If he did manage to injure or kill the soldier, it would be done in self-defence, a reaction, so not considered in the same light as if he were actually planning to kill a man, like he did with the fish he caught, the swing of the priest on the fish's head an intentional action. He could not do that to a man, he knew. This thought reassured him. A moral dilemma solved.

Then a thought. What if this were how soldiers thought? What if no one really intended on killing another man in battle?

16 APRIL 1938

LOVE

She'd been curious, nothing more, when she asked Audrey about the river swim. This is something you do, she'd said when she had come by the caravan early to a meeting for tea the week before, but why? Miriam had come upon her as Audrey emerged from the river, her swimming costume clinging to her as she reached for her dressing gown. But "why" was the question she wouldn't answer, couldn't answer, she told Miriam. Miriam would have to go in herself to understand.

Now here they were, upstream from the caravan, Miriam's arms already tired as they flailed against the mild current. The river was not deep, so she pushed off the ground when her foot found it. She had not yet relaxed into it, her memory of swimming so far in the past, it was like starting anew. The water, brisk against her skin, felt like heat when she'd first stepped in, but now that her heart was pumping, her skin prickled, the hot and cold sensations another layer, a pelt that held her.

"Here—over here," Audrey called to her. She'd drifted to an eddy where a tree had fallen and had taken hold of a branch. "We can rest here for a bit."

Miriam paddled over, splashing Audrey as she neared her, her breath quick and shallow.

"Keep kicking to keep warm," Audrey instructed, holding out a branch to Miriam.

They let their bodies move to the current of the water, and soon Miriam was taking longer, more measured breaths.

"Does Edmund know where you are?"

"That I've gone swimming, you mean. Yes, he knows. He can't swim, so it worries him."

"A worrier. That carries its own weight."

Miriam shifted position, glancing to Audrey because she had something on her mind, something she wanted to ask her but did not know how.

"Was Robert a worrier?"

A flash of surprise, then irritation. "So this is where you want to take the conversation." Audrey filled her lungs as if she were about to dive under but instead took a long deep exhale. "A worrier? No, I would not say that of him. There are other qualities that better describe him.

"He was the most intelligent man I knew. He had a special interest in the war poets, yet could discuss politics of the day as if he were part of the inner circle. That's what drew me to him, what kept me attached long after I should have released myself from him.

"It was his great talent to be something to everyone he met. A chameleon. I only saw this later. One can feel terribly good in these circumstances, having someone shape themselves around you.

"It was the chameleon part of him that I loved, then later came to hate."

Audrey pushed away from the branch and began swimming upstream. "We need to keep warm," she called back to her. When Miriam had caught up, and when they had reached a point where they could nearly stand, they treaded water with faces tilted to the sun.

"He was such fun to be with. He was open to doing anything—a picnic by the river, an impromptu game of charades after dinner, a mad dash down a country road as if he were in a rally. He was unlike anyone I ever knew.

"He was ten years older than I was, which accounts for a lot when you're twenty-one.

"Everyone liked him immediately, but he did not have many friends, people he confided in, argued with. He told me once that he was a loner. I never met his family. They were abroad, he told me.

"I had not been alone with a man before, not spoken to one on my own, away from family. I talked to him as I'd been taught, with a small smile and an interested manner. He asked me who I read, thus disarming me immediately. This was something other than what I'd been used to, so I couldn't say, not knowing if he'd approve of my novel-reading habit.

"In the beginning when he took me to parties, I could hardly breathe for the first hour, to have moved from being a child at such events to an adult seemed a strange leap for me. My life was less open as a child. Growing up I felt the isolation of a country house. Guests, infrequent, came to see my mother and father, and I was often presented and released only to sneak back, listening in doorways, adjoining rooms, pretending to be reading. I was curious about the world but starved of it.

"Perhaps it was going to the party with Robert that made the difference. It somehow gave me an identity that I hadn't considered before. Rubbing up against the kind of people Robert associated with, the glamour, the style, the sense of self-actualization they all portrayed taught me what I lacked, what I hadn't considered, an identity of my own. He introduced me as 'the lovely Miss Wentworth,' which made my cheeks burn. No one had considered me lovely before, let alone presented me as such.

"It was much later that I overheard someone refer to another woman as one of Robert's lovelies.

"When he broke my heart, he did so slowly, unknowingly, with all the charm he had practised over the years. He told me he was the luckiest man alive to have met me. I think even he was surprised by how much I loved him."

Audrey scooped up water in her hands and spilled it over her face. She looked at Miriam. "So, a worrier? No. Robert was a lot of things, but not a worrier."

She jumped then dived under the water, surfacing several feet away.

"Come, time to head downstream," she called after Miriam.

Their bodies drifted like abandoned logs, swirling as the current took them. Miriam's mind on Edmund, on Robert, and the Audrey she hadn't known in those years when her heart was soaring, then breaking. Things had been steadier with Edmund, the love never extravagant or showy, it was one of attention, of tending to, of seeing. This is why her secret felt all the more like a betrayal. Every gesture seemed one of knowing, his care, his noticing when she thought he wasn't looking. Did he know her condition? Did he see the changes in her body? This a thought she could not bear.

They reached the place in the river by the caravan, and they lifted their bodies out of the water once they'd crept toward the bank, but the river seemed to hold them, such was the weight of air. The weight of air, the lure of water. That's what Audrey could not explain when Miriam had asked her about her river swims.

"It turned out that Robert did not approve of novels," Audrey said, handing Miriam her dressing gown.

19 APRIL 1939

EDMUND'S DAILY LIST

Newspaper headlines from *Hampshire Telegraph*:
A Whirlwind Romance: Portsmouth Drama: Said Farewell
and Gassed Herself

The Führer's Birthday: Millions Celebrate Hitler's 50th:
Serenade by Black Guard Band

Temperance Queen Crowned: "My Pledge" Sung by 200

Royal Tour of Canada: Health Precaution: Staff Under
Close Medical Supervision

Bank Clerk Still Missing: £25 Reward: Father Believes
Memory Loss to Blame

Woman Killed in Husband's Car: Negligent Drivers

Theft of Trousers: Two Boys Not to Associate: Others
Discharged

Weather:
Annular solar eclipse, partial cloudiness

Observations: Wildlife in the Garden
A pair of mallards on the pond with twelve ducklings
Two moor hens
Buzzards
Cock pheasants
Angry green woodpecker
Magpies
Robins
Blackbird

Observations: Plants in the Garden
Quince in blossom
Apple blossom
Last vestiges of laurel flowers
Brambles in flower, blackberries to come
Almond blossom
Evergreen oak
Weeping willow out, always the first
Three medlars
Pussy willow
Walnut emerging, always last in leaf, and first to drop
Cherry blossom
Rosehips

22 APRIL 1939

REUNITED

Peter was late. Not actually late because they'd agreed on four o'clock and it was still five minutes away, but in Frank's mind, as he sat festering in the upstairs study, he was late. Frank looked across the great expanse of the lawn that ran alongside the gravelled drive. Beyond the grass, the land dropped a tier, a ledge cut out of a hillside, and here the family crypt was the boundary marker on that side of their property. Pyramid shaped, the crypt had been a curiosity for him and his brother, and now peering down to the cluster of trees that obscured it, he could just make out the tip of it. As boys they would play games that took them to it, always a focus, even then. Hide and seek, races where Frank would be given a one-minute head start due to his crippled foot. Looking now at the sheep that grazed the edges of the great lawn, he wondered how he'd managed. There and back, racing against his brother, who was taller, faster, always sure of himself.

A quick glance to the opening in the trees that marked the drive. No sign of him. Audrey would be here soon, but he could not see her approach as her route was from the back of the house. He wanted to see Peter arrive, wanted to watch his uncle's convertible motor car roar through the trees, to see if he was as anxious as Frank to be here. He looked for signs, a trail of dust, a disturbance of swallows, the rustling of leaves that would announce Peter's arrival. But nothing.

He was nervous, he knew. More than he should be. Frank had not seen him for three weeks as Peter had gone to Scotland with his uncle on family business. But it was just tea. Why did it feel like so much more? He fingered his lapel, wool on one side, silk on the other. The rubbing a habit since boyhood, a gesture that calmed him.

He stepped away, and in that moment he heard something, a deep rumble that drove him back to the window in three long strides.

Peter.

He was not roaring down the drive as Frank had envisioned, but drove as though he had no set appointment, his gaze drifting around the estate, peering back at the summerhouse that sat near the orchard, then ahead to the house. Frank wondered what Peter's impressions were of this house, the only one Frank had known. Ivy spreading up to the second level, rose bushes lining the foundation. It was an early eighteenth-century manor with haphazard additions, the place where his father had retreated with his young family, the country house a return to nature, a symbol of continuity after the sting of the Great War. The long and silent walks around the garden the only intimation that the battlefield still lingered. That and the lavender bushes that he'd had removed because they reminded him too much of the smell of France. He needed to be away from London, he'd told Frank in a rare moment of intimacy. He needed the quiet, the trees, the sound of owls in the copse. That his father had all but given up on Wentworth House these days remained a bemusement to Frank. It was as though he'd needed the intensity of nature as a cure back then, and, once achieved, he'd tossed it aside for a life in London, one that crowded out any memories that might creep in.

Frank watched as Peter backed the car against the lawn as if ready for a quick departure. His blond hair firm against his head even though he'd removed his hat and thrown it into the back seat. Frank stood back against the curtain, watched as Peter jumped from his car, watched him turn in response to a voice that Frank could not hear through the closed window.

Audrey.

He saw her walk to Peter, her face open and generous. Frank knew he should go down to greet them, knew it was ridiculous to stand up here as though he were spying, but he wanted this moment to stretch, to see the two of them in full view, the sun shining on both, the promise of a glorious afternoon ahead. He adored his aunt, never so fully than in times like this when her acceptance was a constant gift.

What was it his father had said to him once? I've a mind to send you to sea to cure you of your addiction to reading. Oh, to be so easily lured from temptation. What had been on his father's mind all those years ago? What had he been so afraid of?

Frank ran downstairs and swung the door open. "Come in," he said. "Come in."

24 APRIL 1939

GYPSY MOTHS

I t was Edmund who told her that female gypsy moths could not fly. They were at the river, a late April day when the heat seemed to sit in their garden, and Miriam longed for a walk in the countryside. They'd packed a lunch, their books, and Edmund took his binoculars; today it was hawks he was looking for.

They'd found an alder tree near the river where, once they'd settled, Miriam had noticed a moth clutching the bark of the tree. A gypsy moth, she'd said, turning to Edmund. It remained still despite their activity—the flapping of the blanket, the light chatter, the clink of bottles that held beer and lemonade as they placed them in the river to keep cool.

"Is it dead?" Miriam asked, looking closer at the wings, cream coloured with brown striations, tucked in close to its body. She hovered a finger over it as if about to touch it then pulled back.

"Just resting," Edmund said as he stretched out on a blanket, and Miriam wondered if he was referring to himself or the moth. Miriam lay down beside him and closed her eyes.

The lull of the river and occasional trill of a blackcap soon sent them off to sleep, and when they awoke, they ate and drank from their supplies. Edmund wandered out to the field in search of a hawk while Miriam lay reading with one eye to the moth that still had not moved. From her outlook she could see more moths farther up the trunk, and when she got up and circled the tree, she saw that there were even more on the other side. There was something joyful in this gathering, a village of female moths. She felt the stillness of them, the intensity of their brief existence, and wondered how long they'd been there, how long they would stay.

When Edmund returned, they dipped their feet in the river, one last attempt to cool down before returning home. The empty bottles rattled in the basket as they walked along the road, until Edmund held out a hand to quiet her when he spotted a kestrel overhead. He stood for several minutes watching it through his binoculars as it hovered over a field waiting to swoop down on its prey.

It had been a good day, one that left them feeling fulfilled in ways they could not express. It was evening by the time they returned, and, tired from the fresh air and change of routine, Edmund pulled his encyclopedic book of animals and insects from the shelf and sat in his armchair.

"They had just laid their eggs, I'd guess," he said when she came in with his tea. "Six hundred to a thousand each."

"So many?"

Miriam peered over his shoulder at the colour plates of the male and female moth as Edmund continued to read from the book. "The male can sense the female pheromones from up to a mile away and mate multiple times while the female produces only one egg mass. The males are relentless in their pursuit of females."

"Well then, philanderers all, are they?"

"The adult moths do not feed," he read on. "They live for about two weeks for the sole purpose of reproducing." He looked up at her. "The females are not able to fly."

"But why? Why would they have wings and no ability to use them?"

"To protect their eggs."

Miriam took the book and sat next to him. "In the larva stage, they spin a silken thread that can be picked up by the wind and swept across the land in a phenomenon called ballooning." She looked up to Edmund. "So they are flying before they are formed. Then once formed, grounded." She looked down at the book, her fingers gliding across the illustrations. She noticed that the female wings were held tight to the body, while the male wings remained spread and flat.

"It's the female gypsy moth the airplane is named after," she said, pointing to it. "See how the wings are held close to her body like that, just as it is with the airplane. We swing the wings back against the body, right to the tail, in order to get the airplane into the hangar. I wonder if this is de Havilland's little joke. To name an airplane after a moth that doesn't fly. I've heard he was a lepidopterist—he would know the difference between a male and female moth."

Miriam sat back in her chair. "They will die soon," she said looking up at Edmund. "Those moths in the tree, all of them will protect their eggs, and then they will die."

The next day Miriam walked back to the tree to see the moths, and the day after that, and then again three days later when the first female had fallen. It lay with its wings twitching in the breeze. The next day four more had fallen, and by the second week at least two dozen lay at the base of the tree.

She could do nothing with this knowledge, these sightings, but still she felt the loss. It was not so much sorrow for their death, as that was as normal as life itself, but it seemed a cruel design to give them wings but not the ability to use them for flight. She collected the moth carcasses and put them in a box with no clear intention, but two days later when she was scheduled to fly with Frank, she took them with her, and just before their descent she released them from the side of the cockpit.

26 APRIL 1939

FRAILTIES

I t was a week after she'd rescued the dead moths that Miriam dreamt of babies.

It was an intensive week of flying, false landings, stalled engines, the airplane flipped over entirely, all part of the basics Frank insisted on. You're a good pilot, he told her, you need to get better, you need to be better than all of us for this race. She was going up two, sometimes three times a day, Frank urging her on to the brink of disaster, insisting it was part of her safety training. Through this her mind itself like a Spitfire, revving, agile, as if she, too, were breaking away from herself. The flying had now become a test, not only one set by Frank.

The first baby she had named Catherine, though she was only four months along in her pregnancy when she miscarried.

There were those who thought it was a step down when she married Edmund because her father was an educated man, but on this she would never agree. Not a word uttered. Instead, rumours of what might have been were brushed aside like spider silk before they'd had a chance to gain purchase. Her father liked to tell her that Albert was the better man, more ambitious, more outward. This, her father's version of truth.

She heard he owned two shops selling cars now.

But Miriam knew there were different ways of measuring a man. The drink lessened some, a temper, others. Arrogance, ignorance, a roving eye, all things to watch out for, but Miriam saw none of this in Albert. At first it was a too quick and uneasy laugh that set her thinking. Too eager to please, a promise swiftly whispered. It could have been the easy life. But on a jasmine-scented day when she went to meet him, she heard voices as she neared the garage, low and conspiratorial from inside the building. Albert and a man whose voice she didn't recognize, then Albert's laughter, a brash cackle she'd learned to ignore. Then, *Watch it*, the other man's voice a sharp rebuke, while in the background the sound of liquid pouring. Silence followed, marking a task undertaken with concentration before the conversation resumed, Albert telling the man he was engaged to be married. A pretty face, he said, but her mother is a right cow and the father a stupid bastard. The words shot through her, pinned her to the side of the building as she listened to him talk of others, imbeciles all, who came to his garage for service, too backward to realize he siphoned petrol from them while fixing their car. A wee bit off each one, he boasted, against the squeal from the lid as he tightened it on a barrel that held his booty.

Miriam walked away that day and kept walking until she fell into Edmund's arms some two years later. She walked across fields, down country lanes, through villages, traipsing to shed herself of the man she now knew was evil—not evil in a criminal manner but in his outlook, in the world he created where everyone was a mark, someone deserving of being taken. Until she found Edmund, who was not outward or ambitious, and whom her father politely tolerated.

She walked away all those years ago and thought she'd escaped, but now Albert was appearing in her dreams, a ghost that presented children as though part of a deal they could strike. These were children she might have had with him, she knew, their faces grotesque versions of him, aged, their skin hoary.

By the third night she had to escape her dreams, so she crawled out of bed, pulled her cardigan from the hook, and went downstairs, out the door, and through the maze of gardens until she reached the public right-of-way to the field. She had no thought of where she was going. The moon ablaze, throwing long shadows on the back of fence posts, illuminating the night so she glimpsed two rabbits dart across the field, saw fists of fog crouching in hollows, silhouettes everywhere.

She sat on a fallen tree, pulled out the pack of cigarettes left behind by one of the pilots at Hackley that she'd pocketed after the last wild ride. She sat watching the glory of the moon, thinking of Edmund sound asleep, unaware of her torment. How could she talk to him of these grotesque babies?

It was different falling in love with Edmund. Where Albert had taken her to dances, long drives to the next village for dinner, Edmund would pack a flask of tea along with sandwiches and suggest a hike across the downs, mushroom gathering, or a picnic, and because she was young and didn't yet know who she was, she was unsure which was the true form of courtship, which one she could trust.

She'd met Edmund in a field not unlike where she now sat. He came up to her, scarf in hand, asking if it was hers. She'd not noticed it gone. The heat of the day had prompted her to undo the scarf, and the wind had gathered it up and sent it sailing into his hands as he made his way to visit a friend. She'd been sketching the landscape, oblivious to everything but the view. He stood over her, holding the scarf as if he were selling it, so that her first thought was that he'd stolen it. Seeing her startled look, he apologized and crouched beside her to see what she was drawing. The swift movement, from his holding the scarf while looming over her to making himself so small that she was looking down at him, brought a sudden intimacy to their meeting.

"You have a talent," he told her. "You don't take care of your belongings," he continued, holding up the scarf, "but you're a dab hand at drawing."

That she had been so intensely assessed, insulted, and complimented in the same sentence, confused her. No one had ever observed her with such singularity, and she was not sure what to do with it. But that was so long ago, his own distractions now clouding his perspective. She inhaled the cigarette deeply and watched the smoke wither before her.

How had she not seen what was happening to her? How had she not seen why these nights were haunting her? Earlier it was the magnolia tree that got to her. She'd been tired and unsettled by a day of flying, Frank pushing her harder, banking, spinning, loops, and rough landings. Then a manoeuvre that left her disoriented, rattled, and everything about her day unravelling. Mistakes made, confidence slipped, then finally the blessed words, return to base.

On the walk home her bones had ached, and the sun streamed through the magnolias, their limbs drawing spidery prints across the path that somehow made her weep. Tears welling for the pain, the frustration of the day, so that the sparkle of the evening, the complete and utter magic of the image was her undoing. Chastising herself, her mood suddenly wary. The tyranny of that magnolia tree. After all this time it could still undermine her.

It had been six years since that spring. Late daffodils and even later blossoms on the trees, and Miriam pregnant. She'd known life to be hopeful then, had not learned it did not run on a straight trajectory. The change in course was abrupt and brutal. The magnolias at the end of the street ablaze with blossoms, only for the glorious spring to collapse under a cold wind that ripped branches off trees, threw slate tiles from rooftops, and her body reacting to the weather, giving up a baby that was still only a mass of cells not four months along. The magnolia, too, suffered, its pink blossoms frayed and curled, turned brown overnight. This she saw as an omen.

Miriam drew figure eights with her cigarette and dropped her head into her hand, releasing tears that spotted her dress. She pulled her body in, knee to chin, arms wrapped around her legs, and replayed the scene that triggered this string of useless memories. A landing, a forced false landing, lower, lower, power reduced, then one wheel making contact and Frank shouting at her to power up. She, knowing she wasn't to touch ground, panicked and pulled the throttle too quickly so the thrust was intense. She knew that it could stall at any time, yet they were flying higher, breaking through the low scattered clouds, her heart suddenly like a locomotive out of control, her hands quivering, her only thought to get to the ground. But they went higher and higher until once again they were in the clouds, her hands shaking so that she could hardly grip the controls. Her hands ached with the force of holding on as they made one last circle around. The landing was uneventful, Frank congratulating her on her skills which told her his experience of the flight was altogether different from hers.

Her frailties, that was what had occupied her since she'd left the airfield. Her weakened body, too damaged to produce even a single baby. Her shattered nerves that had left her panicked as she flew above her home. Her inability to slough any of this off.

30 APRIL 1939

BRAVERY

Hitler's Speech, *Manchester Guardian*

... On March 15, Hitler spoke of little else except 'wild outrages' perpetrated by the Czech people on the Germans, and the 'cries for help'; he declared that he had been compelled to order the German army to invade Bohemia in order to 'disarm the terrorists and the Czech forces.' He claimed to have 'destroyed an instrument that was used against Germany in a war.'

He went on to claim that Czecho-Slovakia had split up herself and that it was therefore natural that Germany should annex Bohemia and Moravia where she had interests a thousand years ago. It is so simple.

Hitler says that he is accused of threatening war, but that he has gained his successes, immense successes, without war. He says to President Roosevelt that he has waged no war, that he abhors war, and that 'I am not aware for what purpose I should wage war at all.' Yet his neighbours arm industriously; some join a coalition that has no reason for its existence except in fear of him. There can be no war unless he himself makes it.

The news, how it haunted Audrey. Mandatory conscription meant that Britain would have over a million men in service by the end of the year; a major military power, they said. Meanwhile, surgeons were practising operating with gas masks to see if they could manage, elaborate plans were being made for London to become a "shadow city", with the evacuation of its populations and businesses to other parts of England. And Spencer Tracy arrived in London for a weekend holiday and was met with a "vulgar display" by those in the crowd who "whooped" in excitement when he arrived on the *Queen Mary* boat-train.

A holiday was what she needed.

Perhaps she could be lured to the spas in Budapest, also known as "The Effervescent City," which according to the papers was "bubbling with health and gaiety." Enough, she thought. Escape is what she wanted, not a holiday.

It was this way after the Great War, this thinking. The need to escape.

Her motorcycle. The war done and gone, and all she'd seen, all she'd done, could not be put into any sequence of words her family would understand.

Blood. Torn lives. The ravages of war.

There was much to talk about, but nothing to say, so she'd bought a motorcycle, another impulsive decision, but what could she do? Panniers packed with a few books and some clean knickers, and she was off to Southwold. Only she thought to stop off and see her family on the way, because she was thrilled to be riding this beautiful beast of a machine, despite the piercing sleet that doused her on that road through the village of Billings and her laughing like a fool while mud splattered across her face. She wasn't thinking beyond the joy of it, the fierce and relentless wind battering her, the constant thundering vibration that held her body to the machine, shaking it into existence; it was possible to get lost in such jubilance.

Southwold beckoned while her family quavered. It was a mistake, she knew, too late. Her mother's hand held at her mouth, her eyes floating in tears that didn't fall. Her father pacing, working up an argument that might bring her back to their way of thinking.

Their way of thinking.

She needed to understand her own way of thinking, so she donned goggles and cap, checked the map, and roared off to Southwold. To the sea, and to her friend Mary, who'd also driven an ambulance in the war, and who insisted that Audrey visit when it was over. The sea will do you good, she'd said.

Four days it took. Stops in Tonbridge, in Tiptree, with a visit to the Wilkin jam factory, two nights in Wickham. Her hands shaking, her knees collapsing under her whenever she stood after a long ride, the steady blast of the engine ringing in her ear long after she'd turned the engine off.

But the ride itself.

Flying through the back roads of the South Downs, the rush of the hills, the pit of her stomach dropping on the way down, the juddering like a constant mantra: "you're alive, you're alive." A stop at a roadside café for a bacon bap, just outside Ardleigh, the proprietor squealing when she'd discovered the driver was a woman. "On the house, love," she'd said, pressing the sandwich in her hand. The farmer who pulled out of his lane too quickly, his own metal beast, a Fordson tractor, forcing Audrey into the hedgerow, picking hawthorn twigs off her suit, not feeling the bruises that would bloom later. Head over handlebars, a miracle she wasn't hurt, but she could take a knocking about, it was the least she could do, because it was the men she thought of. Those men, those reckless pilots. She'd spent the night at the farmer's, his wife had served pie while he fixed the fender the Fordson had twisted. His wife had eyed her as though she were feral at first, the accent marked Audrey, but when she told the woman she'd been to war, spotting medals on the mantelpiece, the mood softened. My brother, the woman had beamed, but her face had dropped as she'd leaned in, explaining that his head wasn't quite right since the war. And Audrey, touching the woman's arm, had told her that was common enough.

The road had flattened out as she entered East Anglia, and that one day, her arms well used to the steering, she had pushed harder, feeling the constant resistance on her body, the thrust of the machine reaching into her heart as if it had a hand in its running as well. A flock of sparrows had erupted around her, sheep had darted from the road, that was when she knew the world to be hers—in that moment, on that A-road shared with cyclists, motor cars, horses, and even some workmen who'd spotted her a cup of tea because the air was damp with the wind off the North Sea. They hadn't believed her about the heated suit and kept shaking their heads in exaggerated disbelief after she showed them how she plugged it in at night, ready for the morning.

That feeling was the closest she got to driving an ambulance, the closest she got to feeling as though her body itself were on fire, a feeling she came close to that one time Frank took her flying. But like then, and like the war, she knew it wouldn't last, she could not sustain this level of exhilaration. When she'd arrived in Southwold, her skin chafed, her bones like iron weights, she had collapsed in bed and slept until the next day.

This memory seemed an escape in itself. Who was this woman she once was who crossed the countryside astride a motorcycle? She hardly recognized herself. How brave she'd been.

She had not seen this version of herself for a very long time. It was a lure, this memory. Tugging at her as if there might be a way to relive it.

But escape was not possible. Not now. She was needed. She would summon a different sort of bravery tomorrow.

1 MAY 1939

THE SCENT OF FLOWERS

T he flowers. Such a bouquet of them. What were they? Honeysuckle? Sweet pea? No, it was lilies. She wanted to see them, but when she opened her eyes, she saw instead a glass cupboard of vials, a scale. Where was she?

There was the scrape and clatter of utensils, too, and a woman's voice. Was it speaking to her?

"Cold," Miriam whispered.

"Here you go, love." A blanket draped over her. "We're done now. Just rest for a bit."

The flowers. Where had they gone? She reached for her face, remembering the inhaler, still feeling the pressure of it against the bridge of her nose, but it had been removed. The smell of flowers gone. Chloroform. Her body floating into a different sort of garden.

They were talking now, the two women, but their low murmurs were out of reach, and her mind drifted, out to the wildflower meadow near Audrey's. There was a forest along the edge, and she knew there to be a path there. The path would lead to the river, and from there she would find Audrey's caravan. She was pleased with how clever she was, finding her way on this new route. Then her perspective shifted and she was over the trees, seeing the path through the forest from above, and she wished she'd brought her pencils so she could sketch it because the world was so much larger from up there. And if you could not see the magic of a robin's egg nest from this vantage, you could see the glory of an irregularly shaped building, and this gave you a different sort of vision of the world, gave you an unusual sort of outlook. She felt this as a warmth that seeped through her, her feet now covered, the light touch of someone tucking her in, and the gentle patting prompted her eyelids open and she saw Audrey.

"Hello," she said, but Audrey didn't hear her, went on adjusting the blanket. This, too, gave her comfort, to have Audrey here, and she wanted to tell her that she was glad that she'd taken her inside.

The procedure.

Eyes open again, this time with Mrs Whittaker, Edith, in view, and the tinge of discomfort in her abdomen was a clear reminder of where she was and why.

"You're doing fine, Miriam." Edith's voice clear now. "You just need to rest a while."

The clutch in her chest. What was it? Pain? Sorrow? Relief? It was over. That's what she knew. Five weeks. That's how long it had taken her to discover that she was pregnant and to become unpregnant.

"Tea and toast. That's what she needs." Edith again.

She closed her eyes, tried to imagine that she was flying, but the presence of the women, the shifting of feet, cupboard doors opening and closing, drawers slid shut as they put the examining room back in order, kept her solidly on the ground.

She needed to get up, get dressed. Edmund would be expecting her.

"Easy, Miriam." Audrey quick at her side. "You'll feel dizzy if you rush it."

"Rush what?"

Audrey and Edith each at her side, helping her up.

"Tea and toast," Edith said, easing her arm around Miriam's back. "It will make you right as rain."

1 MAY 1939

WITHHOLDING

'll have her arrested. His first thought. Then, What has she done?
He clawed the ground, his fingernails scraping the dirt as if tilling the garden was a priority, his fingers aching, and his mind gone mad with the knowledge that she'd betrayed him.

I'll have her arrested. I will.

He kept digging and digging until there was a hole. He knelt before it, staring into it as if he had no idea its purpose, clumps of asters nearby, waiting to be planted.

Did she think he would have stopped her? Yes, of course he would have. He would have told her they could never know for sure which one would take. He would have talked to her about the need to keep going, the need for one more chance.

What has she done? This question over and over, then, who has she become, this woman who would terminate her child. Their child. The child that could have been. All the imaginings: a girl sitting in the garden plucking petals from flowers he'd grown, flowers they'd grown together; a boy who would collect stamps, work a saw, identify birds the way Edmund had done as a boy. They were real to him, these imaginings, and now he real-ized how real the children were to him. Despite all their losses, the hope had been there, that one day they would have a child and this would make their family complete. He thought back to that first time, four months into the marriage and neither aware what the relationship was aside from desire and awkward habits, then Miriam got pregnant. The assumption was there from the start, a healthy baby, one of many, and looking back he saw that there was a feeling of having accomplished something in having so much happen in such a short time. The cradle with hand-hewn maple he'd started back then still unfinished. Sometimes he wondered whether in not completing the cradle there was something in him that knew the baby would not survive.

Who has she become?

It was the flying business and that Audrey Wentworth, they were changing his Miriam, changing her into someone who wanted something other than just their quiet life. Their routine was eroding. On days she was flying she raced out after breakfast and was barely home in time to make tea. Even with her at his side listening to the wireless each night, she was not fully there, drifting to places that had nothing to do with him.

He held his hand before him, the skin torn, battered, feeling as if the core of him had dropped, like an anvil set inside him.

She didn't mean him to find out, but he'd been lying in the bushes tying up his arum lilies, their elegant flowers like falter-ing swans, anchoring them to the fence, to give them a more respectful pose.

Then voices. Miriam had been out for the day, a vague explana-tion of helping the doctor's wife. And he, too, was meant to be out, training for his air raid warden duties, but it had been cancelled at the last minute and so he found himself lying in the garden, trying to give dignity to the arum lilies.

"You must take it easy," he heard, "there might be bleeding."

Bleeding?

He'd propped himself up on one elbow, thinking about whether he ought to see what was wrong, why his Miriam would be bleeding, then he heard Miriam, her voice halting as she thanked the woman he thought to be Audrey Wentworth. Procedure. Rest. Recovery. Wicked words surfacing in explanation. There was gratitude in the murmurings, not regret, and this shook him. He lay back down, his hair in the soil now, and listened to the nightingale as if there were some message in the singing.

His anger rising, listening to low whispers, deceit taken further than he could imagine. He lifted himself, feeling his fury pooling inside, feeling that he might pounce on her, accuse her of what they both knew to be true.

Who had he become?

But the whispering continued, fraying him, making him feel less a man than he ever was, knowing that he would not have her arrested, knowing that he would not accuse her, knowing that this anger would be folded up inside him, unable to be released.

Why? The question that torments. What was stopping him?

This he could hardly face. Did he still have hope? No, it was no longer that. It was fear. Of what they would become, what he would become if this all came out. Would she feel remorse? Regret? That would be unbearable, having her admit she'd made a mistake.

He clutched a rock, his hand gripping it, pushing it into the dirt, working it through the loose soil, his brow gritty with sweat and grime. How could he forget this, how could he erase this? How could they see out their future together with this deception between them? He was pounding the rock now, pounding it into the loose gravel with such force that his nail cracked, his fingers bled, rage like acid running through him.

Then later, spent: she mustn't know I know.

It would be the end of them, he knew. He would have to bury this anger, not let it grow into a wild thing. This was something he knew, this demolishing of loss. He'd been doing it since he was a child, first with his mother, then his father. Back then he had pretended that his pain was an actual physical thing he could remove from his heart. He imagined putting the pain in a wooden crate they kept in the cupboard, so that it didn't belong to him anymore. When he would feel the pain, he would correct himself. That is not my pain, he'd say, that belongs in the crate.

He loved Miriam, and that filtered everything. He had no idea how he could live his life as he'd done till now but he knew he must. They would continue their relations, but he knew now that no child would come of it. They would eat their meals, repair the back gate, paint the windowsills, sit by the wireless each night, plan a holiday at the seaside as they'd intended, and speak nothing of a child. Their lives taken up with the world around them, he in his garden, she with her flying.

He would suggest she inquire about birth control devices, no longer able to trust that she would not deceive him again. She might wonder if he knew of the abortion, wonder if someone in the village had found out and let him know. They would both be withholding.

Lying there listening to the nightingale broke something in him so that he was unable to move, unable to hear the women's voices. Then, it was quiet. Miriam now in the house on her own.

He should go to her, he thought, but still he did not move. He should go to her to make sure she was recuperating. He should go to her and make her a cup of tea. He lay there listening to the nightingale, listening for something that might be a sign for what he ought to do. The sun dipped in the sky, the nightingale sang, and Edmund lay in the bushes. He blinked a lone tear that slipped into his hairline.

The cold ground finally forced him out, and he crawled into the late-day sun filling his garden with that mystical light he loved, long shadows and dark spaces. It was time to put his garden tools away. He dropped the asters into the hole, patted the earth around it, tied the twine around the arum lilies, gathered his secateurs and garden waste, and went to the shed. When he'd put everything in place he turned to go back to the house. A cup of tea, that's what he wanted. And to see Miriam.

5 MAY 1939

FRIENDSHIP

"Why do you care so much?"

Audrey was halfway up the hill, her head full of the words she'd put together on sheets of paper now tucked away in her leather satchel, when she stopped, wondering if she'd secured the latch on the caravan. The wild wind whipped the hair that had escaped her hat as she walked along the path.

She conjured a mental picture of herself back at the caravan, stuffing her papers into her bag, peering into her handbag for her ticket, wallet, handkerchief, closing the overnight bag, checking that the gas burner had been turned off, adjusting her hat, making a note to fix the loose button on her coat.

But securing the latch, in fact, even stepping out of the caravan, was a complete blank. It was as though she'd fallen into a trance, from the moment of putting on her coat up to this point halfway up the hill. The practicalities of it were not an issue. She could ask Michael to check on the caravan after he dropped her off at the station. But the implications, those are what bothered her. What did it mean for her mind to slip into a cave like that?

She'd been distracted. It was something Miriam had said to her, that overtook all other thoughts.

Why do you care so much? It was the campaign they'd been talking about, both in agreement about the principles, but Audrey's passion more pronounced than Miriam's. It was the way she'd said it, as though Audrey didn't have a right, as if she'd overstepped somehow. She knew this was not Miriam's intention, aware that her friend knew one way to ask a question and that was straight out.

But the question had rattled her, made her consider why she continued to go out on lectures, why she pushed the issue of reproductive rights when she could do so less forcibly, with less fervour. This "caring" as Miriam suggested, could this be read as an assertiveness that undermined her purpose?

That day when Miriam came to her, what had she said exactly?

It was a few days after the Alton rally. The train ride had made her ill, Miriam had said. Some lunch would set her straight, but there was something off, the pallor a stark contrast to Miriam's normal complexion, frequently ruddy from flying. Lunch had been a temporary solution. But sherry was needed three days later when Miriam appeared at her door, the gift of damson jam she'd made held out to Audrey.

How they circled around it, the reason for her visit. Words eventually found their way. Glasses poured, windows open, and Miriam painfully battling the urge to reveal why she was there, against the need for secrecy. The abortionist was mentioned early in the conversation. The day they went out to see him, the mess of his garden and the unseen mess of his mind. When they were travelling home Miriam had wondered aloud if this might be a form of punishment, this illness he now had after all the babies he'd gotten rid of over the years. Audrey had told her she had no time for punitive faiths, but Miriam said it was more complicated, the way the world worked, far too complex for religion to take the credit.

This thought lingered long after Audrey had returned to the caravan, this complicated world of which Miriam seemed to have some knowledge.

Was it Miriam who had brought up the abortionist's wife that day? No, it was Audrey who had considered it. Edith had performed the procedure before, Audrey said aloud. Could she do it again? Would she?

This conversation replayed over and again as she continued up the hill, to a waiting Michael who drove her to the station.

The train was late, and Audrey paced the platform, still working through the details of that day, seeking a clarity that was just out of reach. It was obvious to her at the time that Miriam was asking for help, and Audrey moved in quickly as confidante. Yes, an assumption had been made, she admitted now. It was something that Frank had scolded her for in the past—her quick assumptions. But it did seem that Miriam was seeking something from her, something Audrey was actually able to give. When it came to the rights of women, Audrey held the belief that once explained, the tenets would be accepted.

This was Stella Browne's influence. "The right to refuse maternity is an inalienable right. A woman's will is her own," she had told Frank, quoting Stella. "Any reasonable person would see the truth in this."

"Reasonable person," Frank had taunted her, "that's where it all falls apart, the desire to deal only with reasonable people."

But it was fear, not reason, that ruled Miriam that day in the caravan. A second glass of sherry brought colour to her cheeks, brought a hand to her abdomen, and had her eyes darting all around like a butterfly seeking a place to land. And Audrey talked about rights, a woman's need for control over her body, as if she were lecturing a roomful at the village hall, while Miriam shifted in her seat looking like she wanted to escape. Audrey did not relent, continuing to offer solutions as if it were information she needed, and not a knowing hand placed on hers. Audrey may have even cited statistics.

Later Audrey would realize what she'd done. The next day she sent a note asking for Miriam to meet her for a walk. They went out on the downs where Audrey knew Miriam would feel comfortable so that she could talk about the pregnancy, the fear, the shame in having gotten in this situation again, knowing that this time she had nothing left in her to continue.

This was all history now, but it mattered to Audrey, her part in it.

The tea at the station café was tepid. The woman who served it had shoved it across the counter so that some leaked from the spout, her mood one that Audrey understood could not be challenged.

The train was further delayed, and so she was forced to wait in the café. She did not want to go to Manchester; she'd been travelling too much lately. There were things she wanted to do, needed to do.

A swim in the river for one. How long had it been? A week? She felt the stiffening of her body in this time. An aching that was proof enough that her body did better in motion.

How long had it been since she had begun swimming in the River Meon? Six years? Seven? That day so long ago, that had started with a walk around the Iron Age fort and down the slopes of the hill, her legs quivering, buckling under the strain, the heat gathering in her core, sweat seeping through.

The river like a mirage. The sun had made the water invisible, such was the clarity of it. This was a chalk river, the water flowed from the chalk aquifer across flinty gravel beds out to sea and made it clear as glass. At the bend in the river, under cover of a clump of willows, she slipped out of her clothes and walked into the water. Her legs cramped from the cold, and her mind flipped back to her childhood, when she would sneak away from the house to sit on the riverbank, her legs dangling in the frigid water as she read a book, the cool, crisp water drifting over her feet. The swim triggered more memories, of a time when her body felt vital, vibrant, when she could feel blood pulsing through her, like the cogs and hydraulics of an industrial machine.

Her heart was alert as she thrust her body into the water, her breath caught in her lungs, and she felt the familiar cold compression. After few quick, sharp breaths, her face loosened into a smile. Her body floated in front of her as she leaned back. She could see her toes, the pebbles on the riverbed, the tree roots submerged on the other side. This had been the beginning of her ritual.

Now sitting in the café, wanting to be back home while held hostage to the train's schedule, she knew she'd have figured things out with Miriam, she knew she would have been able to see what her friend needed if she'd maintained this routine, if she hadn't been so busy with her lectures. That's what the river gave her. Clarity.

Audrey had invited Miriam to join her, thinking a trip would do her good, but she'd refused, saying Edmund needed help at the shop. But it was the King's Cup, Audrey knew. That's what she was competing with. With the big race coming up, Miriam seemed more in the air than ever, even when she wasn't flying.

If Miriam had joined her, they would have had a chance to talk, this would have been an opportunity to know her better. Audrey understood that so far she'd only really observed Miriam, their conversations following pathways she had set. Audrey wanted Miriam to confide in her, to tell her something of her world, of her past.

It was possible they could reveal something to the other. They had come close, she knew. But there were still things to share, about Edmund, for example, or what it felt like to control a plane, about her own fears for a war. It was hard to talk about these things outright. If Miriam could have come with her on this trip it might have been bearable.

Is this what she wanted? Was it friendship she needed, rather than just to be admired?

The train whistle bellowed, and she took one last sip of her tea. The woman was wiping down the counter as if urging her out the door but Audrey would not be cowed, so she waited until the train pulled into the station before gathering her bags and stepping outside.

6 MAY 1939

THE POND

Edmund had dug a hole in the garden, not for the Anderson shelter as Miriam had wanted but for the pond that he'd been thinking about. He knew it should be in full sun, well away from the shade and drifting leaves from overhanging trees. It should contain still, shallow water not more than eighteen inches deep. He had no intention of sticking a fountain in the middle as some had done. There was something artificial to him in having a jet of water spurting out of what he hoped would be a natural looking pool.

The soil was clay-like, dense and clumpy, so he'd had to break it up with the garden fork, stabbing the ground until it would relent to the spade. The sun was at his back, but the breeze was cool and spoke of rain, a good day for digging, though Edmund was not getting the pleasure he'd hoped from it. The morning newspaper had brought news of conscription for men between the ages of twenty and twenty-two, and this brought on a general unease, a steady drip in the constant flow that was the developing war. The conscription did not affect him, that's true, but it was the unknowing of what was really happening behind these headlines that worried him. Preparations for war did not necessarily mean war. That had been his mantra, until the issue of the Anderson shelter had come up. This still seemed a step too far, one he found he couldn't make.

But Miriam was quick on the case, unable to see how this was the right time to be digging for a pond.

"There's no sense in it, not now," she'd told him.

"We have to carry on, not live our lives to news headlines," he'd argued. But he, too, was more unsettled than he wanted to admit, though he could not back down from his plans for the pond.

The hole was nearly two feet deep now, and six feet around, large enough to accommodate the water plants he had in mind. He stood back to assess it, calculate whether he'd gone deeper than he should have. He would put rocks at the base—that, too, needed calculating. He glanced over to the house, saw Miriam in the window, saw her look up briefly from what she was doing then return to it without a smile or a wave. He felt her presence as a judgment, watching him betray her wishes like this so that for a brief moment he wondered if it was worth it, the tension between them till now so rare a thing, he had no way to read it. She had recovered from her procedure but she seemed more tense these days, which he took to be unsteady nerves in preparation to the race.

He wondered whether the pond he'd dug might be turned into a shelter after all, whether that might settle things between them.

Just then Miriam came through the door with a tray, the tea pot rattling, and she pulled the door closed behind her.

"Elevenses," she announced, putting the tray on the table.

"Oh, yes. Good." He stabbed the spade into the ground and went to her. She fixed the teacups in place, put the plate of biscuits on the table, and poured from the pot. Edmund brushed his hands on his trousers and stood across the table from her, glancing back to see the pond from the house end of the garden, wanting her to admire it, be impressed with the progress, imagine the beauty of it once it had the flowering lilies in place. He sat down opposite her and picked up the teacup. She reached for a biscuit then sat back and looked at the sky.

"It looks like rain," she said.

20 MAY 1939

A HIGHER PURPOSE

"**Y**ou need to be part of this," Frank told her. "Flying a Lancaster one day, a Hurricane the next. Spitfires." His arms raised in excitement.

"I'm flying for the race now, Frank. That's all I can think about."

Miriam had been glad when Frank went to Maidenhead for the Air Transport Auxiliary training, and equally glad when he had returned. She'd been unwell for a time after her procedure as she'd come to call it. Not physically unwell. She'd been lucky in that regard, but unwell in her mind. It was hard for her to say what was wrong exactly, just that she wasn't quite right. She'd flown on her own, continuing with her mapping, and that had been good for her. This darkness and need for release familiar to her. It took her back to those days when she was a teenager, unable to focus, too quickly drawn into distractions, a kind of dim fog that she carried around to the point that her mother would tell her to shake out of it and get on with her work. Her efforts were rather mechanical back then, a slow slog through the day when only a long walk would have been a remedy. This time it was flying—that isolation, the feeling of escape, not from anyone in particular, but to be set apart from the world seemed a just and necessary thing.

When Frank returned, she was forced out of her stupor, his newfound enthusiasm bringing her back. By then Chamberlain had pledged his support of Poland if they were to be invaded, and suddenly the war was back on everyone's mind.

"We'll win the race, then you'll join the ATA. It will give you the training to pilot bigger airplanes."

"How do you know I want to fly bigger airplanes?" Miriam asked. "How do you know that's what I want?"

Frank exuberance was somewhat jarring, the constant talk of the planes he would fly. The ATA was not yet up and running, but this preparation had hooked him, told him he had a higher purpose, and this troubled her, that war would have the power to do this. This was the reason she was curt with him when he suggested she could join the ATA, too. There was talk of opening up a women's pool, and he thought her as good a pilot as anyone he'd seen. It seemed obvious to him that she join.

But she was trying to pull herself out of her thick and gloomy state, keeping her sights on the King's Race, keeping her mapping going, flying farther and farther each time. She didn't want to think of more change.

Everything was surging forward. Audrey needed her help, and there was talk of a trip to London. Stella Browne had invited Audrey to speak at one of her events, and Audrey had told Miriam she must accompany her, for strength and good luck if nothing else. Edmund needed her, too, but not in the way he once had. He was constantly escaping into his garden, putting in more flowers despite the Ministry of Agriculture's advice to grow more vegetables. He had started building a pond of all things and could see no sense in installing an Anderson shelter. It was as though his air raid training was merely an obligation in the same way that playing for the village cricket team was during the annual fête, not something real and necessary. Though they kept up with the news, for Edmund, the talk of war was all a lot of posturing by political leaders. This urging from Frank to join the ATA was drawing war closer, adding more pressure to her relationship with Edmund.

"Let's keep our eye on the race, Frank."

It was Peter who had suggested Frank join the ATA, and it was for him he wanted to succeed. Miriam had not seen much of Peter lately, bound up in the work for his uncle, but she'd seen Frank's urgent need to make gains, to impress him. She wished he didn't feel the need to try so hard.

25 MAY 1939

EDMUND MAKES A
SUGGESTION

A pamphlet on the table. That's how he broached the subject. Edmund was still at the shop, Miriam just back from a meeting with Audrey, her throat parched, her eyelids like sandpaper. She needed tea, nourishment. She pulled off her shoes. Heard the kettle murmur to a boil. She pulled the lid off the tin of biscuits and took two in her hand, the other reaching for the pamphlet, marked "Feminine Hygiene and Intimacy Products," and began reading: *Rubber protectors—washable and can be used any number of times; the French Letter—with a velvety finish, each one tested to 10 lbs air pressure per square inch; contraceptive Foaming Tablets—reliable, harmless, non-greasy, non-irritant, when in contact with the natural humidity of the vagina are released in the form of foam; Check Pessary—made of finest quality of para rubber, with silken cord so that it is very simple to use in accordance with female organs; Whirling Spray—gives a very powerful flushing action and thoroughly cleanses the entire vaginal canal, can also be used as a travelling enema, as there is a*

separate rectal piece which can alternatively be used for other trou-
bles of nose, throat, ears, etc.

She imagined Edmund scanning the adverts in the newspapers; what did he know of such things? He'd had to send away
for the pamphlet. He would have done that while sitting beside
her of an evening, or at the shop, working in the post office,
when she was in the next room.

The kettle whistled, and the latch on the front door clicked
open, a symmetry that jolted Miriam from her seat. Edmund
called out to her, rushing as if he were late, then caught sight of
the pamphlet and stopped, loosened his tie, and sat down.

Silence. The pamphlet like a corpse they were stepping
around. She was kept busy making the tea, while he sat as if
needing to adjust to the space he had just entered.

"Unexpected post," Miriam said, sitting down.

"It's time, love." He looked down to peel a sliver from his
nail. "It's not our fate to have children."

That was it then. What's said out loud must be true.

She rested a hand on her chest, felt it rise and fall to her
breath, and felt a kind of hollowness in her stomach that she
knew to be grief.

The lost children, she grieved. And hope, too. She wondered
how to grieve for a future. Constant anticipation had been a
hard companion.

Rise and fall, rise and fall, as if her hand were working bel-
lows. Breathe in, breathe out. Edmund looking at her like he
wanted an answer, as if she could give one.

It had been two months since her abortion, their marital
relations only recently resurrected, and she wondered at the timing of this discussion. Her head quite literally in the clouds these
days, an urgency to get her flying hours up.

She glanced at the pamphlet on the table. She saw how
the benefits of each option were laid out, as though they were

planning to buy a new garden implement. She imagined them going through them one by one, deciding on advantages and disadvantages. How would they choose what to use when they barely had the words to talk about it?

This is how it would be from now on, intimacy that required words and planning. They would have to fiddle with these devices; how much humiliation would they have to bear? How much of themselves, previously hidden, would they be forced to reveal?

Miriam saw that this was a defining moment in their relationship. How they were now would be how they were forever.

They'd had an early start; love was there, a home, some prosperity. They still had all of it, but they had not gained in the way that was expected; their gains were internal, a settling in, a slow-burn in their relationship. The ability to withstand pain was one measure of progress, that's what Miriam had been telling herself for some time now. There had been great love in her marriage to Edmund, especially in the early days, a luminous period where everything sparkled, where they carved out rituals that would have them together: toast and tea in the morning, lunch together at the back of the shop, a walk through the village, an evening reading before they had the wireless. But they had been worn down by their struggles, a slow devastating leak that had drained their marriage of that vitality she now felt only with flying.

Looking at him, his face in the shadows, his head bent to button the cardigan he'd put on, she saw that this was hard for him, too. But she did not want to talk to Edmund about birth control methods, there was something else she needed, something more from him than this gesture, which seemed laden with defeat.

"That's it? Is there nothing more to say?"

She saw his cheek twitch as he stepped away from the table. He walked to the sink where he washed his hands.

"What then? What more is there?"

"Well, we could talk about the sadness of it all. The grief."

"Grief?" He swung around, his face haunted as if expecting more news to break them.

"We have lost so much, Edmund. Can we not just acknowledge that before we talk of this?" She gestured to the pamphlet on the table.

He came to her, lay his hand on hers, pushed the hair from her eyes, and looked at her as he hadn't for some time. But Miriam felt that he was looking through her, that some part of him had taken in all that she'd said while another remained deep inside, a protective shell she was not sure she could ever get past to fully know him.

"I've had enough," he said.

Miriam flashed him a look, thinking he was speaking of her. "Enough?"

"Of waiting for things to get better. We have each other."

Miriam stood and went to him. This was the truest thing Edmund could have said to her. She knew now that whatever they'd had, they would have again. They were free to look to the future; they could finally look ahead.

2 JUNE 1939

THE PAST THAT IS
ALWAYS PRESENT

"**W**hy do you care so much?"

That question again.

They were at the Brown's Hotel, in the lobby with a glass of champagne each.

"This was where the first telephone call was made in London," Audrey said as she took a sip. "Alexander Graham Bell himself called the owner of the hotel."

Audrey had thought Miriam needed to get away. She'd told her she needed Miriam's help as a ruse to have her join her for the lecture she would later give.

But somehow it became Audrey who needed to get away, who needed to confide in someone. The war pressing at them, and all the truths of their lives were bubbling to the surface.

Why do you care so much?

"I was not the daughter my parents had hoped for," Audrey said. "First of all, I was not a son for my father, and I was too curious, too vocal for my mother. *It's not right to have so many opinions*, my mother would warn. But what was I to do with these thoughts? I would speak aloud in my room, knowing that no one could hear me, and it was a release, a kind of purging of the thoughts that swirled in my head like bees trying to escape. I was angry back then, always battling against those around me, both in the way I challenged and provoked and the way my body existed in the world, as if my arms and legs could not be controlled, leaving a trail of bumps and clatters as I made my way through rooms. I could not see their way of thinking, their way of living, the way they scolded the servants, were obsessed with the small matter of whether my hat was properly worn. *Slapdash.* That's what my mother would have called my appearance if she had not intervened. I was her work, and hard it was."

"Slapdash is hardly a word I'd use on you," Miriam said. She had held the champagne glass with the pads of her fingers of both hands on the bowl for her first sip, then watched how Audrey held it in one, at the stem.

"My mother saw hope in Robert, and it seemed for the first time our thoughts were in alignment. There was nothing to discuss, but she stayed in the shadows, in case I missed my cue. To say that she was horrified when she learned of the pregnancy, and then later of the abandonment, is a gross understatement. That day I remember well. Her face like alabaster, I thought she would faint."

"And Robert? Where did he go?"

"To France, then Germany. Funny, I wondered if I'd see him once I left for the war. But there were only trails that quickly went cold. Not that I was looking."

"And your mother?"

"She was well trained in dealing with what she regarded as my calamitous life, so I was sent to France in the care of my older cousin Margaret, where several months later my son was born and given to a local family."

"Your son."

"For just a few moments."

"Oh." Miriam placed her glass on the table. "I'm sorry."

The lobby was emptying out now, the soft swish of the swinging door an occasional reminder of where they were.

"Your son, did you ever hear about him after that?"

"What none of them knew, in fact, never came to know, was that in that terrible time of the birth, when they were in the process of giving my baby away, I had the presence of mind to look at the papers where the names of the parents were written, as well as the village where they lived. It took me years to go back and look for them. The war was over, and I told myself this was a holiday, since I didn't quite know what I would do when I got there. Oh, I had fantasies of sneaking up and snatching him away, my French was good enough to communicate that I was his mother, that I would take care of him. But really it was my curiosity that had taken me there, not the deep yearning that loss brings. I wanted to see this child to see if there was anything of me in him, anything of Robert. The village was two hours from Paris by train, and the heat that July was oppressive. I watched the French countryside go by, and my handkerchief was damp from dabbing my face, a thunderstorm threatening the entire way. I ran to the hotel next to the station, barely missing the cloudburst that sent a wave of water through the streets. Mud, grit, and water washing the cobblestones as I sat with my tea waiting to go out.

"The barmaid was an older woman, so I thought to ask directions to the house of the family whose name I'd written on a slip of paper. Her puzzled look made me print the name again for clarity.

"Ils sont morts."

Miriam's hand shot to her chest. "Oh, Audrey."

"Because I was unable to speak, she repeated it, this time more slowly, thinking I hadn't understood. 'Et le garçon?' I asked her, to which she nodded. A tragedy. A year earlier, a fire in the chimney of the house next door dropped cinders on their roof. They died in their sleep.

"The woman offered to take me to their graves, though perplexed why this English woman was so interested in this family. But I was unable to move, and so she fed me, gave me absinthe, arranged to have my bag taken to the station for the next train. Her kindness remains with me still."

Miriam reached out toward Audrey, placed her hand on her arm. "I'm sorry."

"It was as though all the stories of my life ended that day, all the tributaries of people, experiences, my whole history, it all flowed away. When the war started I signed up as an ambulance driver. Having left myself behind, I needed to rush headlong into the tragedy of others."

Once Audrey had started to tell Miriam about her past it was as though she needed to hear the details of it herself so she could understand the enormity of it—those events that began with what she thought was love.

"Why do I care?" Audrey said. "I have no idea."

5 JUNE 1939

EDMUND CONSIDERS HIS NEIGHBOUR

Edmund stood and slapped the dirt from his hands, the sound of it calling attention to Mr Stokes, who gave his usual nod, this time adding, "Good evening."

"Rain in the forecast. Need to get the soil turned over." Edmund knew to start with the weather.

"Yes, of course," he responded, his pipe in one hand, a clutch of papers in the other.

The azaleas were like a constant sunset at the back of the garden. The blaze of petals kept the backyard alight with colour for most of the day, fighting a war for attention with the bank of rhododendrons along the west wall of the fence. The evening sun cast an amber glow in the garden. It was Edmund's idyll and escape. He kept a flask of whisky in his garden shed and had taken to keeping notes on his neighbour. At first it was a way of tracking the times when he came out to his garden so Edmund could adjust his own schedule to avoid any chatter. But he'd grown used to having the man out in his garden, and, aside from the initial nod, they seemed to have tacitly agreed that no conversation was necessary. This was both a relief and a curiosity to Edmund.

Edmund worked at deadheading, weeding, rearranging the potted plants, and soon had the odd feeling of being ignored. He worked with one eye to the fence but couldn't focus on his own garden. He was back and forth to the shed collecting tools, securing a sip of whisky, and he found himself glancing over to Mr Stokes, wondering what he was up to. That garden paled dramatically to Edmund's, and there was little to do beside tend to the geraniums lined up around the fence and mow the lawn once a week. Mr Stokes liked to smoke his pipe, of course, but he also seemed preoccupied in some vague manner, the papers or drawings held in his hand like a baton or rolled out in front of him like a scroll. Because Edmund had caught a glimpse of the drawings, he was convinced that his neighbour played some important role in the war effort. And this suspicion grew to an obsession so that he would try to catch a look at them when he could.

There was a need to be very careful these days, he told himself. They'd told him that in his training. Be vigilant. Your neighbour could be collecting information for the enemy. For the enemy? They weren't even at war, just doing a dance around it, keeping everyone hopping, from one week to the next. And really Edmund didn't want to report him, it was just a curiosity.

There was something else on Edmund's mind as he worked on putting the annuals in the plant pots. The Anderson shelter. He had talked to Miriam about it last night, as a kind of peace offering.

"Of course we should put one in. You know that."

He couldn't bear to think about tearing up his garden to put in an oversized tin can—for that's what it seemed to him, that they would shelter in a tin can. They had distributed them in London, and Miriam still thought that they should get one. He felt that she was overreacting, listening too much to the pilots out at the airfield. He'd been shocked when she raised her voice at him, telling him to forget his precious garden for once. It was the word "his" that struck him, his not theirs, for although he did most of the work and spent most of his time there, he had always thought of the garden as theirs. His decisions would often have her in mind—I'll get some honeysuckle because I know it's Miriam's favourite; I'll plant the arum lilies so she can see them from the kitchen window. Now he couldn't separate the his-their issue from that about whether they ought to get one of the shelters.

"If I may . . ." Edmund took two steps closer to the fence. Mr Stokes looked up, a flash of confusion across his face before allowing it to brighten.

"These Anderson shelters. I'm wondering whether you're considering it, getting one, I mean."

Mr Stokes looked off to his own garden, puzzling through a response.

"I hadn't, no. Too far from London, I think. The Germans, if they come," his tone deepening, "won't be interested in a small village like ours."

"That's what I thought." Edmund was quick with his reply, feeling validated in the stance he'd held the night before, and only a little guilty at consulting Mr Stokes without Miriam present. "And anyway, we'll have early warning if they come from the coast, the Chain Home and all."

"You seem rather interested in the Chain Home." Mr Stokes took a few steps back to the fence. "Someone else asked me about them the other day."

Edmund hadn't meant to mention the drawings at the air warden meeting last week. He'd only been curious, and he didn't dare share his suspicions with Miriam. Edmund knew Andrew Miller to be a discreet man, not bothering to make a fuss when he learned of the soldiers breaking curfew at the local pub. But he was in charge of the local Air Raid Precaution unit, so Edmund thought to approach him.

He'd only just mentioned it, and now he wondered if Miller had confronted Mr Stokes. He suddenly felt awkward at being exposed, of having his suspicions overplayed.

"That's good news for us," he snapped, turning back to his garden. "Fair warning."

The evening sun was drifting through the mackerel sky, that harbinger of rain, so they were in and out of light, which seemed to mirror their conversation. Edmund adjusted the secateurs, the back of his hand brushing a thorn as he clipped the rose bush. He kept glancing at his neighbour to see if he would say anything more, whether the conversation was over.

It was going on six, and he still wanted to finish turning the soil in the border and do a light trimming of the herbaceous plants, the lavender and hydrangeas if possible.

"Yes, I suppose if they come from the south there will be fair warning."

The light was going down and the chill was now upon him, so he began to pack up his garden tools.

8 JUNE 1939

IRRELEVANCE

"**W**ar will make us irrelevant."

Stella's ill health had made her despondent. Audrey had gone to see her in London, saw how depressed she was. She'd had to give up her flat to move in with her sister, her financial situation so diminished.

"At least the flat has a decent warm water supply," she'd said to Audrey. "Though my sister refuses to install a telephone. How can I do campaign work when I am so cut off?"

Audrey had begun to take Stella's place at lectures, pressing on with the campaign, hardly able to keep up. Letters to MPs and the newspapers between lectures; exhausted, she began to wonder if she had the true stuff required of an agitator.

"I'm not ready for irrelevance," she told Stella. Theirs, she believed, was not so much a struggle between man and woman, but between those who were gripped by the past and those with forward-looking minds. She held on to this idea of progression. It allowed her to preserve the belief that war could not happen again in Europe. "There are still some rational people in Europe that don't want this war to happen."

Rational people? Frank had warned her against this kind of thinking.

She'd been in the river the day before, usually a place that was like a steady hand at her shoulder, but this time when she swam up past the willow tree, she saw that a large branch had fallen into the water. Still attached to the tree, tendons stretched like a lifeline to the fallen branch. The destruction jolted her as if she herself had been struck. The savage tearing away of bark and sinew, leaving the tree raw, exposed, left her with a great sense of unease, and she'd stayed in the river for some time gripping the branch as if trying to save it somehow. The rook, too, seemed distressed, flittering about, unable to settle on one tree or another. The tree had been a marker for her, the point in the river to rest before continuing on or turning back. To see it torn like that spoke of a kind of disintegration.

Disintegration. How could she think of such a thing? She was overreacting, taking everything too keenly, seeing disaster where there was nothing to see. There was something else that was troubling her, the true reason she'd gone to the river.

Another trip to London a week ago, this time to see her brother to try to determine how serious he was about opening Wentworth House to the public. The usual hustle of the city so familiar to her was marked by the escalating signs of pending war, trenches dug in city parks, the preparation of shelters, a sense of disquiet in the streets.

The meeting with her brother was its own kind of disaster. She knew he dismissed her work as a passing fad; he made her feel like some relentless bluebottle spoiling the gin and tonic he took on the terrace. She would find something else, eventually. That was his view, and until then she must be endured. He'd come to the restaurant in a bluster, which she later understood to be connected to an earlier meeting. He had, it turned out, financial concerns, so the timing of their meeting was inopportune.

She, too, had come to the meeting in a bit of a state. She'd taken an early train to London with a plan to meet Stella, but that had fallen through when Audrey had received a note saying Stella was too ill to meet with her. She had retreated to a tea shop near the train station, and, with her mind already full of arguments she would make to her brother, she wasn't fully aware of the immediate world around her. So when she swung open the door to the tea shop, she barged in without noticing the couple coming toward her.

"Peter," she said, after apologies were blurted out. "Peter, what are you doing here?" Peter, shocked, alarmed, flustered, unable to come out with anything so that it was the woman behind who stepped forward. "I'm Helena." And this seemed to prompt Peter. "Yes, yes, Helena, and this is Audrey Wentworth." But there needed to be more of the dangling introduction that left them outside the tea shop, standing on the pavement as if waiting for a bus.

"I'm Peter's wife," Helena offered, and just then a bus did come by, and Audrey stepped back as though she meant to catch it.

"Oh. How nice to meet you." Audrey recovering, unable to look at Peter, suddenly feeling in her chest the pain she now saw would come to Frank.

"She arrived two days ago."

"From Canada."

As if she were a parcel that had come in the post.

Peter's look of alarm did not leave him, his face sober, earnest, as if constantly searching for some word or phrase that he was meant to utter.

Disintegration.

Audrey had come home from London needing to reclaim something of herself and so immediately went to the river. She would not solve the problem of her brother's insularity, his arrogance; she would not solve the problem of Frank's broken heart. She could do little for them, but she needed to replenish something of herself. She swam the river like an otter, up and down until her arms could only dangle. None of this was fair, yet she'd been tested on fairness before.

"I've been communicating with a colleague in America," Stella told her, holding a note for her to read. "Will you post this for me?" Audrey nodding, taking it from her. *I so want to urge all our friends outside Europe to keep on with the good work of general and social reform, all the harder. We here are probably doomed—in this generation anyway. But let us at least feel we've lighted a torch!*

"Copies of all our ALRA literature should be forwarded for record purposes to sympathizers in North America, Australia, and New Zealand," Stella said, easing into her chair. "We need to have some record of our achievement, that we did have progress."

20 JUNE 1939

THE PRACTICE RUN

They were in the clouds by eight, only the clouds were more like feathers, fine strands that maimed the sky, a threat of what might come. They would do it in two legs, starting at Heston, then on to Desford Aerodrome, near Leicester, Norwich, Nottingham, then to Brough and Sherburn, Castle Bromwich to Manchester. They had scheduled a day of rest that was really a chance to meet up with Audrey, who was booked to do a speech. They had joked about this being the true race, Miriam by air, Audrey by rail.

The timing was critical. This from Frank, who was intent on measuring everything—air speed, wind speed, barometric pressure. This seemed to occupy him to the point that he was not so much anxious about the race but driven to the results. They had talked about winning and what it would mean to him. I'm flying to take the cup, Frank had told Miriam, and from this she understood that he had something to prove. To himself? she wondered. Or to Peter.

They had not talked about what would happen if they lost.

Miriam had forgotten the reason she'd agreed to the race, forgotten who she was in the time before flying. She'd been in the air so much it had become her natural habitat. The vantage point was one from which she was able to see the world in a way that made sense to her, to create the maps, her way of capturing the landscape that at ground level seemed off-kilter to her.

By Norwich the rain had come, and they decided to land and take refuge in the hangar, the deluge on the metal roof of the building as if the gods were trying to rip it off. If this were the actual race, they would have to press on, but now they had the luxury to wait it out.

"How's our time?" she asked Frank over a cup of tea one of the local pilots had brought them.

"Six minutes behind."

It was just an estimate, she knew, they would not be landing in the actual race as they'd done here, but Frank wanted to keep track of each segment, and this would be a setback in his mind. Miriam was tracking the journey, too, but in pictures. The images that she would later draw, doing a rough sketch to remind her, then later filling it in.

By Nottingham they'd gained two minutes, another three by Sherburn, and by Castle Bromwich they were ahead by six minutes. They landed in Manchester a full eight minutes ahead of the winner of last year's race.

"Champagne's on me," Frank said, jubilant, eyes wide, face flushed.

Miriam grabbed the drawings she'd been sitting on, her own mood one of urgency to get to the hotel and complete them while still fresh.

"We still have the return journey," Miriam said, and the brief look of concern made her regret the remark. Why could she not let him have this? Why did she need to remind him that the moment of success was just that, a moment? What was wrong with celebrating this?

For her the flying had become her own measure of achievement. If I can't have a child, then who am I, she'd said to Edmund, when he'd asked if she would continue flying after the race. She had learned this skill, perfected it, and had given in to Frank's suggestion to join the ATA. Thinking beyond the race, she'd created a flipbook of instructions just as they had done at the ATA, outlining the peculiarities of each cockpit, each engine, each airplane. The maps were part of this, too, creating the tools she would need to operate in this world she had chosen. The race was not so much about winning as about the recognition of being unquestionably good at something she loved. If they won this race, and now she could see this as a possibility, it would legitimize all the efforts she had put into it. She would no longer be the shopkeeper's wife who could not have children, she could be Miriam, the woman who excelled at flying. Edmund would be proud, in his way. He was a believer in hard work and earned accomplishments. He'd been confused by it all lately, bewildered by her commitment, her dedication to something that he might have seen as a passing fad, might have hoped was a passing fad. He would balk at her joining the ATA, but he would understand it. Duty meant something to him.

"Champagne, yes, we need champagne. But first we need to see Audrey."

20 JUNE 1939

AGITATION

Bunting draped along the side walls of the hall, a banner spread her name across the stage. Rows of wooden chairs held over two hundred women who had come out to hear her speak. These were disciples of Stella Browne who had read about Audrey in the local newspaper, how the two of them had met, how they were working on the abortion legislation together, how Audrey was the embodiment of Stella's work and would speak for her until she recovered. Would they accept her? Audrey wondered. Did she want them to? She was not sure she wanted disciples.

An encounter at lunch had shaken her. She could do this, she knew, but only if she thought of it as a swim upriver. This was her territory, and it must be held despite resistance.

She stood in the wings, watching the room fill, she saw how hats and scarves were unfurled, a protective layer removed, identities concealed when they entered the building to be revealed once inside. Who are these women? Audrey wondered from the shadow of the stage. Were they seeking help for themselves, or were they driven by the urge to make changes? There was a look of pinched desperation on some.

"I couldn't feed the last one," she heard one woman say, one hand on her belly revealing that she was almost to term. Her look, so haunted, forced Audrey to think about the possibility the child had starved to death. But this was not the story that would invite change. Women's health was tied to the economic health of the country. This was their angle when speaking to members of Parliament. This was an argument they understood. There was no way to reach these men of power if the conversation was about the well-being of women.

"Ladies," she began. "War may be coming, but our own battles have been raging for some time." For the next hour she assured the audience that someone was listening, action was being taken.

"Women have been driven to make their own concoctions, to experiment with procedures that left them infected, or worse. I hear stories of children as young as five or six pressed into work to help feed the family. We need to hear your stories. Write them down, or tell them to someone who will for you. This is not for you to endure alone. We will take your stories to Parliament."

Then Audrey changed tack and asked them to imagine a freedom where they could choose to have a child or not, one where all women had control over their bodies, could determine whether they wished to get pregnant in the first place, and, if they did, could choose whether to follow through.

"This is not a utopian ideal," she told them "There is a possibility of women enjoying the intimacy of a relationship without this great fear. It is within our reach."

Her breathing had become a kind of pant as she reached her concluding remarks. "This is our battle. And it is a battle. For control over our bodies, for relief from economic despair. This is the language of men, the only language they understand, so we must use it as we push for change."

Chairs screeched back, the women erupting in applause, the energy surging, and the room suddenly felt hot, electric. Audrey felt a flash of heat in her body, so that when she saw Miriam approaching the stage, she asked for a handkerchief, some fresh air.

"Your finest speech," Miriam told her, as she led her to the side door.

"We'll send that one to the MPs," one of the organizers called out to her.

"Thank you," said another.

Later, the champagne at the hotel restaurant was barely chilled, but they drank it like greedy children.

"A solid speech," Frank told his aunt, but she remained unsteadied by the day's events.

"Thank you. And you, tell me of your journey."

"We hit rain in Norwich, but otherwise a perfect flight," Frank said. "Wasn't it, Miriam?"

Miriam had gone back to the hotel in the hour before Audrey's speech and filled in the sketch she had made of the route they would take in eight weeks. It was an odd sort of map, a hopscotching across the country in a way that would only make sense to them in the race. Now at dinner she pulled it out, showing Audrey where they'd been, showing her the various perspectives, but all Audrey could see was the great talent in Miriam's work, and that, too, was celebrated.

It was a day of exuberance, of achievement, and the celebration of any suitable thing. They drank too much champagne, ate dinner in a restaurant, the finest Miriam had been in by a long shot, and then each retreated to their room. A day they would not forget.

20 JUNE 1939

AN ENCOUNTER

I t was 1:36 p.m. when Robert walked into the tea shop. She remembered this because she'd looked up to the clock next to the door to check how much time she had left before her speech.

He saw her immediately, of course; he was looking for her, had sought her out just as he'd done over a war ago when she was too young to know anything.

Did he pause as he entered, the momentary stillness drawing her attention to him? She recognized him instantly. Almost. He was older now, a man who still moved like one much younger, those first few steps that were strides really, always moving forward, moving on.

A waiter brought her tea and a sandwich, and she thanked him, eyes still locked on Robert. When the rattle of a cup and saucer jolted her from him, it was fleeting, like a watchful hunter careful not to lose its prey.

But she was the one who felt like prey. Just as she'd always been.

Only she didn't recognize it as that back then, wouldn't have used that word. To her it was love. At that age, so pure, uncomplicated.

"Audrey?"

"Robert."

"They said I'd find you here."

"Who? Who told you I'd be here?"

He was standing at her table, she could see a grease stain on the front of his jacket and somehow that reminded her that she'd heard he'd married, many years after his time with her. A good marriage, not great, was the rumour. They were talking money, class, status. She'd heard his wife died a few years later.

"The man from the theatre. He said you'd come here before your speech."

Henry, the caretaker. The only one who knew where she was.

"I saw the posters. I recognized you."

"The posters, yes. The movement is gaining strength. We're hoping for a change in legislation."

She was about to say that women needed control over their bodies but stopped herself. To lecture him on that seemed an impossible joke.

She felt her hand shake a little as she reached for her teacup. She didn't know what to do with him, standing there like a waiter impatient for an order. She did not want a scene here in the tea shop, a public apology, an expression of regret—what did he want of her?

"It's lucky I saw the poster. I'd just come out of the bank, and normally I don't notice such things, but then I caught the image of your face, and I thought, That's Audrey. You have hardly changed. I knew immediately that I must see you. I live in London now, only in town for a few days. So you see, very lucky indeed."

"Indeed."

He pulled the chair out. "May I?"

"Of course."

He ordered some tea, and Audrey felt as if she'd stepped into a time loop. The chronology of her life scrambled, the impossibility of sitting across from Robert again after so much time had passed, triggered a sequence of memories—the days when she felt she was walking through a fog with the slow, painful realization that he had abandoned her, then the swift and sure knowledge that she was pregnant.

She had lived an entire life since then.

There was a time when she yearned for this moment, a casual encounter where she would sit across from him again. But that, too, was conflicted. One version, a slim fantasy of reconciliation, of misunderstood messages, something put right. Another, the opportunity to tell him how he'd destroyed her.

What would her life have been like with him? she wondered again. They might have married, settled in London. Would they have had children? It was hard to imagine a man like Robert as a father. Her life without her caravan, her river, her lectures? This time the question had a jarring objectivity, his presence like a sudden and miraculous cure for an ache long suffered. He accepted his tea without a word to the waiter and poured himself a cup as if the two of them had arranged a date, as if this were a routine they had been practising for years.

He wanted nothing of her, she realized, had come to her as if they were old friends, happy to be reunited. He was not curious about her lecture, he was not curious about her. As it was all those years ago, there was an innate sense of entitlement with Robert, of being cherished, prized.

Could she tell him about the child? Would that be a story he would understand, even find sympathy with or regret after all these years? Robert's lovelies. That's what kept her from revealing his unknown legacy. He would always find a place to alight, she knew. But he never fully landed. Any feeling for her could easily be replaced with another.

Audrey stood, jolting the table as she did so.

"I must prepare for my lecture," she said. He'd spilled some tea on the saucer and was looking bewildered, unsure whether to call a waiter or focus on Audrey's departure.

21 JUNE 1939

OBSERVATIONS

Three days is what she told him. Three days and she'd be back. A practice run. The King's Cup Race. London to Manchester. One day there, one day of rest, then one day back. This was day two, and already he felt the loss of daily routines— breakfast and the morning papers, a cup of tea at elevenses, a hot meal, and the news on the wireless at six.

"How's the pond?" The bell above the door jangled at that moment, and Edmund had to lean toward his neighbour to say that it was fine, just fine, the lilies starting now.

The pub crowding, the usual Wednesday night scrum, Edmund supposed. Observing the merriment, he could almost see the appeal of it, this weekly gathering. The food satisfied as well, steak and kidney pie. A lot of meal with no effort. He'd been enjoying himself until Mr Stokes came along, Nigel, it turned out, and because the pub was crowded and because Nigel had spotted him and said hello upon entering, the seat at the bench next to him seemed a natural place to sit. But Edmund was used to talking to Miriam, and this conversation carried out with them sitting beside each other made it feel as though they were watching a cricket match together.

"My wife's away."

"Oh?"

Edmund was not sure how much to tell him. It was not a secret that Miriam would be taking part in the King's Cup Race in August, but somehow he couldn't talk to his neighbour about it.

"Manchester."

"I used to work in Manchester."

"Oh?"

"Three months."

They returned to their drinks, watching the crowd, Edmund wiping the sweat from his glass, then drying his hand on his trousers.

"What exactly do you do, Nigel?" Edmund had grown courage through his half pint.

"I build bridges."

"Bridges. Not towers?"

"Towers?"

Edmund sat back in his seat, aware that now it was he who was under suspicion.

"It's just the drawings. I saw towers."

"You've seen drawings. What is this?"

"It's nothing, Nigel. It's just when we were in the garden, I saw drawings of towers."

"Ah the blueprints." It was his turn to drink from his glass. "It's hard to know who to trust these days. I thought for a moment you'd been in my house by the way you were talking, thought you might have sneaked in and seen my drawings. One can't be too careful."

"No. Exactly. One can't be too careful."

Edmund had imagined an identity for Nigel. Watching him night after night across the fence, noticing his neighbour's reserve, or perhaps indifference, had made Edmund curious, had let his mind wander. Miriam had scolded him for it, caught him edging toward the fence, spending too long out there, secateurs in hand, snapping at the air long after he'd clipped the rose bush.

"You're as good as spying on him," she'd said.

"It's what they taught us in training at the Air Raid Precautions. Vigilance." This is what he'd told her, his excuse.

"Vigilance doesn't mean spying," she'd said. And she was right. He felt foolish to be here at the pub on a Wednesday night, a mood of gaiety, companionship, quizzing his neighbour on his work, not with a casual interest but with an accusation of some kind.

Beside the door an Air Raid Precaution poster advertised for recruits.

"Have they been around?" Nigel asked, gesturing to the sign.

"I'm one of them."

"Them?"

"A warden."

Edmund felt Nigel shift next to him, knew without looking that his neighbour was eyeing him, seeing him as something other than the quiet shopkeeper who kept a garden. Now all Edmund's questions would be suspect, all comments of the war taken as coming from some sort of authority. It was he who would be observed now, he who would be suspect.

"Been around twice to mine." Nigel's voice suddenly clipped.

"Oh?"

"Warned about a chink of light coming through at the bottom of the window. I asked him if he thought the Germans would be flying overhead or arriving on their hands and knees. He was the keen sort. Likes his authority a bit too much I'd say."

Edmund knew the man Nigel was talking about, knew that he was indeed keen. Edmund wanted to tell his neighbour that he himself was not like that, that he was only trying to help, not get people in trouble. He'd barely issued a warning yet, and in hearing Nigel speak of this warden, felt his sense of inadequacy blooming.

"How is the pond?" Nigel asked, obviously forgetting he'd already inquired. "Any frogs yet?"

"The frogs have come," Edmund told him. "I hope their croaking won't disturb you."

13 AUGUST 1939

A CELEBRATION

A party! With bunting and cake and champagne. They would celebrate her birthday, Audrey decided.

She'd been in Cambridge; airplanes had flown overhead with only a cursory upwards acknowledgement as onlookers cheered for the home team in the boat race. Everyone seemed giddy, a surging energy that had drawn Audrey in as she strolled the riverbank following her meeting with the Women's Reproductive Rights Committee.

The green by the river was filled with blankets, picnic baskets sprawled open near lounging bodies, glasses tilted on the uneven surface, teacups clinking against saucers. The boats approached like water striders skimming across the surface, and the onlookers, one by one, started to stand to cheer them on. It was this that inspired her to have her own celebration.

Audrey had decided to have a party because there was a general mood, so prevalent these days, of *one more before it comes*. She'd invited Miriam and her husband, Frank was welcome to invite Peter, she could not say no to that. Peter had become invisible since his sighting in London, a relief to her, truth be told. How would she face him? What would he say that could make her accept what she saw as a betrayal?

"Miriam told me you lived in a caravan," Edmund said. "I hardly believed her."

Miriam looked at Audrey, a flash of worry across her face, thinking he might have insulted her in some way. Edmund was not usually so forward.

Frank had arranged for chairs and a table to be brought from the house, and they'd sat by the river, glancing at the gathering clouds, wondering if rain would spoil their day.

"Why a caravan, if you don't mind my asking?" Edmund pressed, ignoring Miriam's look.

"I was with Frank. We were late for a luncheon," Audrey said, placing the glasses on the table.

"We were never ones to arrive early at family functions, so were rushing as usual, and on this day I felt slightly ill, a head-ache coming on. Dark clouds followed us on a road we'd never travelled before, one that narrowed dangerously and where trees reached across from one side to another. We came to an opening, and there it was, sprouting from the landscape. From a distance we didn't know what it was, but I told Frank to slow down, then ordered him to stop when I saw it clearly. A caravan."

"I kept telling her that we would be late," Frank said. "The wrath of my father is something I generally try to avoid."

"I found the gate to the fence, ignoring Frank's pleas to re-turn, and traipsed through knowing this was not a public way. The caravan came alive as I got closer, the colours and designs, it was like a giant music box against the forest.

"I knew the caravan would be my home," Audrey continued. "Frank was beside himself, but I called out to see if anyone was inside. There was no reply, as I knew there wouldn't be, for at that moment, the moment I stood at the steps and reached up to the door, my hand tracing the design, I knew it was already mine. I walked all around it and came back and tried the handle."

"I kept telling her, don't go in," Frank said, "it's trespassing."

"I told Frank he would do well to do a bit more trespassing himself." Audrey leaned over to pat him on the arm before continuing.

"There was a sign, handwritten, made on a piece of card, tacked under the window. *For Sale*. Frank kept telling me to get back into the car, the luncheon surely spoiled. I pulled the sign off and saw that the address was near where we stood. Come, I told him. We need to speak to the owner. I bought it that day."

"Our next celebration will be the race," Miriam cut in, worried that Edmund would start asking about the particulars of Audrey's living arrangement. "One week to go."

"What do you make of the chances of winning then, Frank?" Edmund, normal reserve pushed aside, becoming more voluble out of nervousness.

"A good chance—a very good chance," Frank clipped, glancing up the pathway as if watching for Peter. He seemed agitated, fussing with his jacket. "Our calculated time is now twelve minutes better than the last winner."

"There's so much activity in the air these days," Audrey said. "One wonders how they will manage to squeeze in a war, should it come." She passed a slice of cake to Edmund, who offered it to Miriam.

Miriam flashed him a brief smile, searching his face to make sure he was all right. She'd been to visit Audrey so many times, it seemed natural to sit by the river, discussing plans, and yet with Edmund here it all felt different. Audrey would notice the way he held himself, spine stiff, appearing to judge when really it was he who felt judged.

"They'll find space to fit in war," Frank replied. "If that's what they decide to do in the end."

"The villagers have already decided," Edmund piped in again. "They've been stockpiling for weeks. I can't keep Lyle's syrup on the shelf."

"As long as they are talking, there is a chance to avert war." Audrey was standing over them offering more water for tea. "I know wishing it will not make it so. But I believe that discussing it is a kind of progress. Surely you don't talk your way *into* a war."

Audrey began telling them about the recent trip to Cambridge, how she'd stopped to watch the boat race, which, despite all that was going on, seemed the most natural thing to do, a bit of excitement on an afternoon. When the RAF planes flew past, she'd noticed an older man sitting back from the river on a bench. He was not really watching the race, just watching all that was going on around him, and she'd happened to catch his eye as they passed, a swarm whose drone she could feel in her body, and she knew at once he'd been in the last war. He was completely and utterly still, one hand gripping the bench arm, his eyes full of fear while all around them young people merely glanced upward, the distraction fleeting, seen as a spectacle rather than a threat.

"I just knew that he'd been a soldier. I knew it was all too much for him."

Just then the magpie that Audrey had not seen for some days flew into their clearing and landed on the caravan.

"Maudie, where have you been?" Audrey scolded. To the others she said, "He takes care of me when I'm here on my own."

"Mind he doesn't take off with a teaspoon," Edmund said. "Though, I admit, I've never seen a magpie actually steal anything."

"My father hated magpies," said Miriam. "He said they brought bad luck. 'I salute you, Mr Magpie,' he would say whenever one came around in order to negate its dark forces."

"Well then, I salute you, Mr Magpie," said Edmund.

They opened the champagne, and their mood loosened somewhat. Miriam brought the sketches from the trip to show the others.

Soon Edmund spotted Peter coming over the rise at the top of the hill, and Audrey rose to greet him, meeting him halfway, their murmurs unheard by the others as they walked together to the table.

"I've just come from the airfield," he said, his eyes focussed on the drawings laid out on the table. "The King's Cup Race has been cancelled."

1 SEPTEMBER 1939

EDMUND IN HIS GARDEN

The dawn chorus pulled Edmund from bed. He had set himself the task of pruning the raspberry and blackcurrant bushes. They should have been done by now, and with a storm forecast he knew he'd need to cut back all the old branches to allow fresh young shoots to grow. He'd failed to do the pruning a few years ago, and the bushes weren't strong enough to produce fruit the next year. A lesson learned.

He'd left Miriam in bed, crept from her warmth with the stealth of a thief, not wanting to wake her, but hoping she would join him for breakfast. He was still tired from the night before, wondered why he'd let Miriam talk him into such a long walk, but she seemed quite desperate, unable to settle into the news, barely listening to details of ongoing negotiations. There was still hope after all. They'd set off to the field outside the village; with the cancelled race and Miriam in a constant state of bewildered loss, he could not say no to a walk.

He was happy in his garden, barely noticing the passing of time until he felt the heat on his forehead. He poured himself a cup of tea from the Thermos he had filled and made plans to build an espalier for the roses.

It seemed to him that Miriam was happier now. Well, perhaps not happy, but content, despite the disappointment of the race. He'd been surprised by the force of her feelings for it, even more surprised at Frank's reaction, which seemed altogether inappropriate. Audrey tried to cover it up, of course, but Edmund had seen his face. He might as well have been told they were at war with Germany. The poor woman's birthday celebration had fallen apart at that point, and when Peter had told them he'd joined the RAF, Frank surprised them all by insisting on another bottle of champagne. He'd got himself quite drunk after that, could hardly stand up. It was good of Peter to see Frank home. But still the whole evening jarred him, though Audrey hadn't seemed to mind. He'd never met such a calm woman. Miriam had told him she'd driven an ambulance in the last war, and he could believe it. They'd all had too much champagne. Miriam on the way home insisting she would join the Air Transport Auxiliary if war came. What was she talking about? She'd be needed at the shop, the post office an essential service, especially if he were to be called up.

Edmund pricked his finger on a raspberry thorn and the trickle of blood got mixed with the grease from the bands he put around the branches to capture invading insects, the wound stinging a bit until he could wipe his hands. He was tired, exhausted really—the long hours in the store and his evenings in the garden were catching up with him. He wasn't sleeping well either. The news a drip-feed of things out of his control and so far away. He could do something here that saw results, prune and plant with a simple counteraction of growth and harvest.

He leaned against the fence, wondered why he hadn't seen anything of Miriam yet, then smelled the smoke from his neighbour's pipe.

"Nigel," he called out to him, getting to his feet.

"Edmund."

"I was thinking my wife and I would go down to the pub again, you're welcome to join us."

"Yes, of course. But you have heard, haven't you? Hitler's gone into Poland."

3 SEPTEMBER 1939

AUDREY IN LONDON

The war, two days old. Not the war officially, but the invasion everyone was talking about. Audrey trapped in London, in a hotel room that felt like she was living in a cupboard. The train pulled into the station two days ago with the news that Poland had been invaded. Shouts on the platform "Hitler's taken Danzig" like a tidal wave that pushed them all back to their seats, eyes searching to others as they tried to figure out what this meant. They'd known for months this would come, and yet had not known. The not knowing had been encased in hope, a blind eye, a faint denial of what was really going on.

What was going on? Audrey wondered. She had not planned to be here, in this public place, on a train of all things, when war came. She wanted to be home, reading the newspaper with Frank or talking to Miriam, someone to help divert the fear that kept darting into her thoughts, pushing, demanding attention.

The speech had been poorly attended, of course, the fervour she'd experienced in Manchester burst as if it were its own form of barrage balloon.

The barrage balloons. Frank had told her of flying over them. A spectacle, he'd called them, and she couldn't tell if he were in favour or not. She'd heard there would be two thousand of them up now. She'd seen a few earlier, leaning into her window, saw them bunched up against the clouds that hung over the city like cotton batting.

Two hours till her return train, and she dared not leave her room. Unable to since she'd arrived several hours after her speech had ended the night before, the city in darkness so black she could barely see in front of her. With cars running with just sidelights and no way to find a taxi, she walked for miles feeling as though she'd already signed up for service, that all the work she'd been doing for the rights of women was now like so many minor irritants that amounted to nothing.

She'd finally hailed a taxi, but the driver, too, was lost, so they drove around Piccadilly and back again before finally getting to the hotel after midnight. Then she stayed in bed till well past breakfast, listening to the storm that raged outside, rain washing the streets of London as though a cleansing were needed, as though an acknowledgement of all the stress they'd been mired in all these months, the storm just part of the greater drama that was unfolding.

Her suitcase was at the door, ready for the porter, who would take it to the taxi she ordered for 11:30. Her notes sprawled across the bed for the lecture that she would give in Tonbridge next week, but she had no heart for her work at the moment. A knock at the door pulled her from her malaise, and she scrambled to put things into her satchel though her watch read 11:08.

"Sorry to bother, ma'am," the porter at her door making no attempt for her case. "I thought you'd like to know. War's been declared. Chamberlain's been on the wireless. No choice, it seems. We're at it now."

Audrey had no chance to respond. The prickles in her head went unnoticed, for at that moment the air raid siren sounded.

The porter, also shaken, grabbed her arm, then let go and motioned for her to go ahead.

"There's a shelter." He ran behind with her suitcase, not skirting his duties even under duress. The shelter was the hotel wine cellar, and as the guests gathered, a kind of awkwardness thickened the air as if this were a party and not a matter of survival. A few of the women perched on cases of wine, and the maître' d'hotel actually jested they were in the best shelter in London as he waved his corkscrew in the air. But this was all too new to them and their uneasy titters faded quickly as they listened for bombs, explosions, having taken the prophesies of devastation and disease that would follow the first air raid to heart. They pictured St Paul's in ruins, a cavity in the ground where the Houses of Parliament stood. The quiet offered no relief at all.

After an hour they returned to the surface, and Audrey dashed off to the train station, eager to catch the next train, her eyes peeled to the glass as she looked for signs of attack.

"Not a sausage," the taxi driver told her. "Just stirring us up they were."

"Indeed," Audrey replied, but she was hardly listening, for she was barely there. Staring at the streets of London, her mind in the river halfway up to the point where the branch had fallen in. She'd learned to dive deep under it so that she could come out on the other side. It was a game she played, a challenge she set herself, how quickly she could dive without worrying about her lungs bursting, her bathing costume getting caught in the twigs. Farther and farther each time, even the rook, who followed her along, seemed impressed, resting on the branch as if waiting for her to surface.

4 SEPTEMBER 1939

THE MANCHESTER GUARDIAN

A FEELING OF DETERMINATION AND RELIEF
Saving World from Pestilence of Nazi Tyranny
Peace in our Hearts —Mr Churchill

In this solemn hour it is a consolation to recall and
to dwell upon our repeated efforts for peace. All
have been ill-starred, but all have been faithful and
sincere. This is of the highest moral value—and
not only moral value but practical value—at the
present time, because the wholehearted concur-
rence of scores of millions of men and women,
whose cooperation is indispensable and whose
comradeship and brotherhood are indispensable,
is the only foundation upon which the trial and
tribulation of modern war can be endured and sur-
mounted. This moral conviction alone affords that
ever-fresh resilience which renews the strength
and energy of people in long, doubtful and dark

days. Outside, the storms of war might blow and the lands may be lashed with the fury of its gales, but in our own hearts this Sunday morning there is peace. Our hands may be active, but our consciences are at rest.

We must not underrate the gravity of the task which lies before us or the temerity of the ordeal, to which we shall not be found unequal. We must expect many disappointments, and many unpleasant surprises, but we may be sure that the task which we have freely accepted is one not beyond the compass and the strength of the British Empire and the French Republic.

8 SEPTEMBER 1939

FRANK PACKS HIS BAG

Frank's bag was sitting in his room, ready for him to join the war. He was waiting for instructions from ATA headquarters in White Waltham, waiting to be told what to do, where to go. Waiting. It seemed that was what they were all doing, waiting for the war to start in earnest. So far it was the most mysterious war. Mysterious because no one knew what was happening. A scarcity of news on the wireless, no cheering crowds, no drafts leaving Victoria, no indication if they were to send an army abroad.

Frank sat in the library drinking his tea, thinking of the war, knowing he would lose his home, at least temporarily. He saw a double-decker bus filled with children driving through the village two days ago. Where would they take them, these lost and timid children? The countryside? Would that be safe? He imagined hordes of them taking over Wentworth House, a small band of matrons to keep them in order. And where would he be? Hiding in his room?

An air raid in Dagenham over the Ford Motor Works, the first true sign of war. Rumours of a plane brought down in flames. Traffic queues, too, as they'd been told to pull over to the side of the road should an alarm sound. Everyone angry that they hadn't done anything yet, hadn't wreaked havoc on Berlin as expected. The only thing was tons of leaflets dropped on north Germany. Cartoonists were having a field day depicting Hitler on his knees, begging them to rain famine, bombs, even gas on Germany, but not the truth. Perhaps the new mode of warfare was persuasion.

The theatres were closed, his old schoolmate Stephen Cochrane, a director, suddenly out of a job after ten years, now driving a delivery van. The television station closed, so, too, the cinema. The entire country appeared to have come to a halt.

He, too, had come to a halt. Rescued by his aunt upon her return from London. What had she said to rouse him from his bed? *Don't be like your father.* What did she mean by that? Any comparison a shock, but it did get him out of bed, did get him dressed and down for tea and to the chiding of his aunt. "This war will come," she'd told him. "It will come in ways you will not expect."

And then she talked about love.

"Our lives will now be marked by extremes," she told him. "Everything that you experience—pain, fear, triumph, even love will be felt with such intensity you'll think it will break you. If you become broken by it, then you'll know your heart is still beating. None of this will feel comfortable, and none of it is sustainable, but for the time we must live in the extremes because the alternative is to live in the shallows, and that is not a place we can survive."

Peter. Where is he now?

He'd been gone almost two weeks, those last few days a blur Frank had been trying to piece together since the night of Audrey's birthday. The sparkling afternoon by the river, dissolved when Peter arrived. Frank's pulse quickening as he watched Peter walk down the hill to join them. He'd come. This thought like an affirmation of love in Frank's mind. Then the news. Crushed. Miriam looking haunted, lost. The champagne had made them happy so Frank wanted more of it, as if it might erase this news, the splendid awkwardness of this moment. Then Peter at his arm as they trudged up the hill. He'd felt cogent, questioning Peter on his decision to join the RAF as if they were discussing it over tea (there would be no choice in the end, Peter had argued), and yet dreamlike, as if all the words they spoke disappeared into the night air the moment they were uttered, leaving only impressions of Peter next to him, his arm guiding him back to the house.

In the hallway, the day's light bringing long shadows, and it felt like a moment of departure, as if they were at a platform, but this one private—no departure could have offered the freedom they had in this moment. There was a vague attempt at making plans, for when it was over—we could go away, New Zealand, Canada, the Hebrides—but standing in the fading light, their faces drifting closer, the smell of booze, cologne, the fresh summer air a tonic that drew them closer until Frank's lips brushed against Peter's cheek, an embrace that fell into a kiss. Frank reliving that moment in the days since, polishing it like sea-washed glass, so that he could carry it with him, the weight like that of his heart.

The kiss, he remembers.

He imagined what might have happened if Michael hadn't come back at that moment, and he fantasized the possibilities hinted at, those that took him to some point in the future, when this chaos that had just begun was over and done with.

But that was looking too far ahead when he could only see the now of his tea, and his bag that sat waiting in the corner.

1 NOVEMBER 1939

MIRIAM IN THE WAR

Miriam stood at the back door of the shop smoking a cigarette. It was an indulgence, this cigarette, just as everything seemed to be these days. The twopenny bars of chocolate were to be made smaller and restricted to standard lines—milk or plain, with or without nuts. The price of sausage was up, as was bread, and Lyle's Golden Syrup was now unobtainable.

She should go home and have her tea, but she was a bit heady with the smoke, feeling as though she'd had a glass of sherry, the evening air sharp with the faint smell of bonfires and chrysanthemums. She let this mood take her where she wanted to be, up in the cobalt blue, staring down at the horizon that was ablaze at just this moment, a match for the actual fires that had started up across the village when the frost moved in a few nights ago. Edmund had caught a few revellers lighting a bonfire in their garden, their excuse an early celebration of Guy Fawkes Day. "They don't have a clue," Edmund had said to her later. "A bonfire! Why not call Hitler himself and give him our co-ordinates?"

Edmund, his role as warden taken so seriously, but she knew it was all for show, for she understood that he was worried about being called up, and between his duties as postmaster and warden, he was doing his best to make himself indispensable.

"I'm a coward," he'd said to her after they'd gone to the pub a few weeks ago. He'd had a few pints and talked to Nigel about what he'd done as a warden, not mentioning names of course, but there had been infractions, he'd had to issue warnings. Not fines, but now that war was on there would be no excuses. "I'm a coward," he'd said, later. "When it comes to it, will I be able to fine Mrs Webster when she tells me she's doing her best for the fifth time?"

She knew he lay awake at night worried that he would fail.

They all had to be extra careful. This is what he'd told Nigel at the pub, and later when she questioned Edmund about why he'd been so insistent with Nigel, he told her their neighbour could be a spy for the government, sent out to villages like theirs to seek those who were working against them. They'd argued about this, Miriam telling him he was getting paranoid, his job as warden causing him to lose judgment.

Three days later, when they found a note from Nigel telling them he'd been transferred in his job and was moving to Sheffield, neither knew what to think.

"I signed up to the Air Transport Auxiliary," she told him on the way home that night. Frank had told her they would start taking women in January. She was not trying to frighten him, it's just that everything had changed, and though she still loved Edmund, she had become someone other than the person he'd married. She had stepped out of herself, out of her role in the relationship, and she knew that he had to test himself for them to continue in some way, so that he could fit alongside her. He'd kept the pond, not willing to give it up for the Anderson shelter. That she gave him for all that he didn't object, at least outwardly, to her time away from the shop, the time she spent flying. It was as though he understood that sometimes the sense of duty must be to oneself.

Edmund's gaze, usually darting like a fly around her, locked on hers, and she could see that he was truly frightened, not of having to go to war himself, but of what her joining would mean.

"Ah, Edmund, I'll be all right," she told him. "It's not like I'm signing up to war."

"What are you signing up to then?" he'd asked.

A question she couldn't answer, and by this time they were home and she was making them a cup of tea, just as she'd done every night since they were married. But strange things were happening all over the place. Edmund's cousin who worked for the London council had called in on his way to visiting family last week and spoke of people leaving London in droves. He'd been going all around the neighbourhood collecting council rates and said there were a number of well-to-do people who had just up and left. A back door left open, breakfast things unwashed, and a half-smoked cigarette dipped in tea, fruit going mouldy in a bowl.

Everything strange.

The cigarette singed her fingers, so she took a quick drag and dropped it, crushing it under her foot, but she didn't move from her spot. This time of night, with the shop closed and the evening ahead of her, was her stolen time. A few moments to be still and not in service to others. Tomorrow she'd see Audrey, just back from Cambridge. They'd sit in the caravan and tell each other how awful things were getting, and then they would settle into talking about their own lives. Miriam knew that her flying was a kind of selfishness, but she also thought that everyone was selfish in some way, otherwise how would anyone see through to their desires.

She was worried about Audrey. The crowds for her lectures were diminishing; the war that wasn't visible turned men's and women's attentions elsewhere, their efforts going in different directions. Duty. That was the only passion that mattered these days, and it did seem a form of passion as she watched men sign up, or grow crops, stockpile, conserve, preserve, look for ways to do without, and the women alongside them coming to grips with rationing, tending to kitchen gardens, mending clothes. They knew so little of what was to come, as little as nothing. This was something that made them greater than they were as individuals.

Time had slowed, and these days held Miriam in a kind of bored agitation. The shop a place to hold out as she waited for the war to truly get started. The skies were all but closed off now as they became military territory. Everything became purposeful. Everything was about preparation. Everything was still about the waiting.

9 SEPTEMBER 1941

EPILOGUE

The moon rose so swiftly in the sky, it was as if it were trying to escape the clouds. The light, a ghostly layer, gave substance to the land below: there a church spire, there a river, there a shadow that must surely be a forest. It also left Miriam exposed, as if the moon had her alone in its beam. It was a gift and a curse, this light, though no Germans had been reported in the area.

She should be there now, but rain at Whitchurch in Bristol had held her up, and when it broke, she gambled the race against daylight because she'd heard that Frank would be at the Hawarden pool near Chester. This was a rare occasion to meet up with him at one of the ferry pools, despite the two of them criss-crossing the country thirteen days a fortnight, banking more hours than RAF pilots as ferry pilots for the Air Transport Auxiliary. This was day twelve for Miriam. Tomorrow she would take the overnight train back home, back to Edmund.

She checked her map and banked just enough to see the northern rail line below her. The night was cool, not yet cold, and she was glad for her sheepskin boots. She took a drink of tea from her flask, felt the warmth move through her, sensed exhaustion seeping in.

Edmund. He'd be listening to the Marconiphone, to news of the two hundred RAF planes that mounted an attack on Berlin while the German army placed Leningrad in a state of siege. He'd be focussed on another broadcast feature, though, that of "Potato Pete," a new campaign by the British food ministry to urge citizens to eat lots of unrationed potatoes. It was a good move for him to switch his wartime duties. His personality was ill-suited to work as air raid warden—too much scolding. He was a natural as an agricultural officer, willing resilience and abundance in the wartime gardens and allotments. He was more himself in this role. He'd said as much to her. "I know who I am now," he'd told her.

But what exactly did it mean to be more yourself? That's what she wanted to ask him. What was the difference? Could he not try new things? Could he not be anyone else? This is what hours alone in the cockpit did. It made her think about her life, and Edmund's, and the lives of others who were now part of her world. Conversations replayed, actions examined, in this way she whiled away the hours between pools. Audrey had said that to be part of the war effort people would see something of themselves that they had not previously seen. A journey into unknown territory, not just of the physical, but the psychological, emotional. This had frightened Miriam at first, especially in those first few months of war, when it was more of just waiting. How much could she take when it came? The question worked over like a worn pebble in her hand. It frightened her more when she saw Audrey retreat in those early months, barely leaving her caravan. Every day in the river, and most days not a soul to talk to. Miriam checked on her as best she could, but days would go by and when she'd return it was as though time had stopped for Audrey. It was as though she were already grieving her losses before they'd even started. Then, one day in April, not long after Miriam signed up to the ATA, Audrey was at her door. "I'm ready," she said, and it took Miriam some time to figure out that in those months she'd been shoring up her strength to face this war, as she knew from the last one what was needed.

A cloud slowly shuttered the moon, and Miriam was flying blind again, her direction held steady with aid of the gyroscope compass. The Spitfire was a dream to fly, faster at two hundred miles per hour than most of the planes she'd flown in the past year. Frank had been right in pushing her in his training sessions. The ATA test was one of will as much as skill: that day she'd climbed into the Tiger Moth, and flown to two thousand feet, turning, first one way, then another, at first gently, then in a steep bank, and finally a forced landing when the examiner cut the engine.

The map between Bristol and Chester was one she'd drawn in her head, and then on paper, and it was a route she'd flown many times. Still, flying blind with no radio required her attention, so thoughts of Edmund, of their reunion in two days, and the birthday celebration they'd planned were put aside. Soon she would be on the ground, soon she would see Frank. They would find a nearby pub, where he would tell her again what he knew of Peter's death—shot down near the Channel Islands, the plane and body recovered. He could not bring himself to go to the funeral, he'd told her when they met a month ago, just four months after Peter's death. There was no question of his going. She'd known of their special friendship; others would have, too.

There was no time for mourning, that, too, a lesson in war. The ATA had saved Frank's life just as it had given shape to hers. Everything more precious now, everything made normal.

And it was normal, their life. Normal in the way that the fundamentals were still in place—the need to eat, to work, to love. But now one had little time to reflect or anticipate. It was a constant of living in present time. Everything was in the moment, just as Audrey had told her it would be.

She would see Audrey this time, an invitation to tea in the caravan arranged in their last letters. She still felt the loss of campaigning, Miriam knew. What now, this cause of hers? Back to war—she was using her skill as a driver, bussing children from one location to another to escape danger. This was something she could do, she'd told Miriam. An acknowledgement that her experience of campaigning, of fighting for the rights of women, would serve no purpose now. Their lives diminished and swelled to fit the purpose. Each of them had become more intimate, more intense in their relationships. They understood the many ways love took shape.

A lightness in her body as she began the descent, the faint light of the airfield her guide as she reduced air speed and watched the numbers decrease on the altimeter.

Upon landing she took the delivery chit to the operations room with nothing to report. No one had been killed. No aircraft had been damaged. There had been no sightings of the enemy even though the entire route had been within range of the Luftwaffe, and bombing raids were still routine a year after the Battle of Britain. She removed her leather helmet and goggles, undid the top button of her Sidcot suit, and looked around to the group of men gathered in the room.

"Frank, there you are," she called out to him.

ACKNOWLEDGEMENTS

I owe a great debt of gratitude to my editor, Susan Rénouf, for her care and enthusiastic support of the book, and to all those at ECW Press for their work on it.

I'm immensely grateful to Kathleen Winter, who ushered me through the writing of this novel with her encouragement, and her rich and profound feedback. I would also like to thank Helen Humphreys, my perennial mentor who helped shape the final draft and continues to inspire my work.

Terry Mulloy took on his assigned role as research assistant for this project with his usual eagerness and dedication, sharing his own knowledge of gardening and sourcing the book *With Mr Middleton in Your Garden* by C.H. Middleton, a renowned gardener, broadcaster, and writer in Britain during the 1930s. This book remains a treasured gift from Terry. I will miss our conversations, his advice, and his everlasting love and support.

Huge thanks to Caroline Ball for her close reading and fact-checking on the manuscript, and to Val Ball for her role as consultant on life in England during the time.

Thanks to Sheila Cameron, Stacey Cameron, Marsha Cameron, Ann Mulloy, Margie Matlack, Pegi McKay, Susan Fish, Kristen Mathies, Erin Bow, Nan Forler, Kim Knowles, Anna Trinca, and Julie Friesen for their support in the writing of this book. I would also like to thank Susan Scott for her boundless wisdom and her feedback on an early draft.

Thanks to Emily Bednarz for her work on my website and Sarah Marsh for the poster of female pilots from the 1930s that sat next to my desk, providing inspiration throughout the process.

I would also like to thank Nick Roche for the virtual tour of his garden in springtime, supplying me with pictures and names of flora and fauna.

In the early days of research for the book I visited the Air Transport Museum and Archive in Maidenhead, a gem of a place that offered the necessary details that brought those intrepid flyers to life, particularly the Ferry Pilots Notes, a pocket-sized flipbook of instructions for each aircraft. During this visit I tried and failed to land a plane successfully on the flight simulator, further strengthening my respect for those pilots.

A day of fly fishing at Meon Springs with Andy Wiggins turned into a lesson about chalk rivers and the art of fly fishing and inspired a section of the book on the subject. I am grateful to Andy for his gift of storytelling and for his wealth of knowledge that he shared that day.

I would like to thank Julian Bell, curator at the Weald & Downland Living Museum in West Sussex, England, for providing me with background information on Esther Maud Udal, an eccentric whose living arrangements inspired those of Audrey, as she herself lived in a Victorian Reading caravan for several decades on the grounds of a farm near Rye. Bell also provided information on the equally fascinating Buffy Everington, whose own experience during war provided further inspiration for Audrey. While out driving with her husband, Buffy spotted Miss Udal's caravan, and after knocking at the door and explaining that she'd like to buy it, was told by the now elderly woman that she could have it, as she would soon be moving to a care home, but only on the condition that she keep all the contents intact with her personal memorabilia. The caravan remained in the Everington family for years, a backyard playhouse and curiosity. I would also like to thank Guy Viney at the Weald and Downland Living Museum for the personal tour of the reading caravan that now remains onsite at the museum.

In my research for the book I discovered the work of Stella Browne, a Canadian-born activist in the field of reproductive rights who lived in England and who, during the 1930s, played a major role in advocating for the right to abortion, giving lectures and becoming a founding member of the Abortion Law Reform Association. Her biography *The Life and Times of Stella Browne* by Lesley A. Hall provided insight into her work and her highly progressive ideology, as she advocated for a woman's right to enjoy a sexual life without the burden of pregnancy.

The spark for this book began many years ago when I read *Spitfire Women of World War II* by Giles Whittell, a comprehensive exploration of the life and work of the women who became part of the Air Transport Auxiliary, flying a range of planes across England with no radio or navigational equipment. Their bravery was unfathomable, their story remarkable in itself. It wasn't until attending the Women's March of 2017 when I saw posters demanding reproductive rights for women that I was able to see how I could write about these pilots through the lens of early feminism and activism on birth control.

With the exception of Stella Browne, the characters in the book are entirely fictional, as are the main locations. Although I aimed for accuracy when referring to historical events, I took some liberty with the dates with regards to the genesis of the Air Transport Auxiliary—officially formed in September 1939—moving the start date forward by some months to fit the structure of the novel.

I am immensely grateful for the funding received from the Waterloo Regional Arts Fund and from the Canada Council for the Arts that supported the writing of the novel.

Finally, thanks to Darren, and to Esme. Your exceptional support and encouragement fuelled the writing of this book. I couldn't have done it without you.

This book is also available as a Global Certified Accessible™ (GCA) ebook. ECW Press's ebooks are screen reader friendly and are built to meet the needs of those who are unable to read standard print due to blindness, low vision, dyslexia, or a physical disability.

At ECW Press, we want you to enjoy our books in whatever format you like. If you've bought a print copy just send an email to ebook@ecwpress.com and include:

- the book title
- the name of the store where you purchased it
- a screenshot or picture of your order/receipt number and your name
- your preference of file type: PDF (for desktop reading), ePub (for a phone/tablet, Kobo, or Nook), mobi (for Kindle)

A real person will respond to your email with your ebook attached. Please note this offer is only for copies bought for personal use and does not apply to school or library copies.

Thank you for supporting an independently owned Canadian publisher with your purchase!

This book is made of paper from well-managed FSC® - certified forests, recycled materials, and other controlled sources.